THE FIFTEEN WONDERS OF DANIEL GREEN

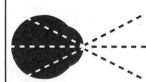

THE FIFTEEN WONDERS
OF DANIEL GREEN

ERICA BOYCE

THORNDIKE PRESS
A part of Gale, a Cengage Company

Farmington Hills, Mich • San Francisco • New York • Waterville, Maine
Meriden, Conn • Mason, Ohio • Chicago

LIBRARY OF CONGRESS CIP DATA ON FILE.
CATALOGUING IN PUBLICATION FOR THIS BOOK
IS AVAILABLE FROM THE LIBRARY OF CONGRESS

ISBN-13: 978-1-4328-6364-7 (hardcover alk. paper)

Published in 2019 by arrangement with Sourcebooks, Inc.

Printed in the United States of America
1 2 3 4 5 6 7 23 22 21 20 19

For my parents, who told me I could,
and for Chris, who told me I should.

CHAPTER ONE:
DANIEL

Most people don't bother to think about crop circles until one shows up in their neighborhood.

And even those people assume the formation was built in one night, all perfect and symmetrical, the only mystery being who or what put it there. They don't know about the weeks of planning, the drafting and redrafting late at night. They don't know about me.

In the trunk of my car back at the Shannons' farm, there are four pressers — wooden boards with a rope strung through the two ends like a swing. I wiggle my hand into my pocket to touch the plans folded up there, stuffed between Claire's old bracelet and the newspaper clipping from the first project we worked on together: "Stranger than Fiction: Formation Proof of Life on Other Planets?" I pull out the plans and flick them open, glance over them. I nod to myself, once. Perfect.

I've done a lot of these by now, but never one like this. This one is exactly right for my last circle. Steep incline from the field to the road, so the circle can be seen by passersby. Plenty of brush along the edges where I can hide if necessary. Small town, word traveling fast. And once it's done, I'll find a place near Claire, maybe go to night school and work in a sunny coffee shop. Fifteen circles in seven years isn't going to break any records necessarily, but it's not bad. It's enough.

This circle started the same as any other: someone found Lionel's email, either through word of mouth or in some dark corner of the internet. Lionel, as the leader of our group of circlers, assigned the new project to me, and after exchanging a few emails, I called the client and heard a low voice on the other end asking if I was the real deal. A lot of guys use me to get their faces on local news shows. Twice, I even helped with some very weird revenge schemes. But this one was different. I knew it right from the moment he said, "Well, to tell you the truth, my town is in trouble."

Now, every farmer I'd ever met up until then hated to admit to trouble, especially to an outsider. It's hard enough for them even to ask for a new farmhand. Circlers usually find cover jobs working on a nearby farm to build trust in the town while they scheme over their plans at night, sometimes staying for months post-reveal to avoid suspicion. And every time I show up at a farmer's door offering sturdy muscles and not much else, I'm met with a lot of sizing up and crossed arms, even though they were the ones who posted the help-wanted ads to begin with.

So I knew I had to meet this guy who told me right off the bat what he needed from me.

By the time I drove past the crunchy farmers markets in southern Vermont and into this stretch of dead fields and collapsed barn roofs, my legs were rubbery from pressing the gas pedal.

"You must be Daniel Green," a woman called through the screen. "Please, come in." Her bony hands waved me into her house. "Sam? Sam, Daniel is here!"

Before I could take in the house and all its rough wood, there was a man, gray and skinny, with his arms unavoidably around me. It took me a few seconds to realize that it must be Sam Barts in the slightly droopy flesh.

"Sam. It's, uh, nice to meet you."

"Oh, Daniel, you have no idea." He

pushed me into an armchair so cushioned, I worried I'd never find my way out again. I sat up to perch on its edge.

"Here, have some apple cider. It was pressed just down the road." There was a cool glass in my hand, and Sam's wife had come and gone again before I could say anything.

I took a sip, the sweetness clinging to my throat, and rearranged a doily on the table next to me to set the cider on it. "So. What is it exactly that you want in that field?"

"All business, I see. I like it." He cleared his throat, crossed his hands over his belly, and half disappeared into the couch across from me. "Well, like I said on the phone, Munsen is in trouble. None of the young folks want to stick around anymore, and us old-timers are having a hard time keeping up with all the day-to-day stuff that goes into this work. We get some kids coming through to work as farmhands for a season or a year, but they're gone in a flash soon as their time's up. Pretty soon, this whole town is gonna die off, unless we can do something to draw kids into this profession. Something's got to give. Now, my daughter sent me this article from . . . what was it, the *Boston Globe*?"

"It was the *New York Times*." His wife was

leaning in a doorway nearby. Buckling laminate flooring and a smudged white refrigerator filled the space behind her.

"Oh, that's right. Well, anyway, this article, it talked about the dying family farm and what communities across the country are doing to support new farmers — charity programs and all that." He flapped his hand, dismissive. "But none of that will do us any good unless we can get folks coming up to Vermont in the first place to think about starting their lives here." His eyes drifted away. His wife started to twist a dish towel like she was trying to wrench it into pieces.

"Um, so," I said, "the crop circle."

"Yes. Well." He slipped to the edge of his seat so our knees hovered near each other. "It's like this. Kids nowadays love to hunt down the newest, weirdest thing they can find on the internet. So what I'm thinking is that maybe you could shape that field out there into something like a great, big 'MUNSEN FOREVER,' you know, something that will spread online and make people come see our little town. You think you could do that?" His hands fell from where they'd been framing his masterpiece in the air in front of his face. His wife stopped twisting her towel.

His vision was a long shot. People don't

11

generally travel more than twenty minutes to see these things. And I'd have to work on his design ideas, make it something more mysterious and less obvious. But I couldn't resist the pull of his field. It was a circler's dream.

"I'd be happy to," I said.

In the two weeks since then, I've been working my cover job on the Shannons' farm nearby while waiting for a bright night like this. The Shannons posted a listing for some help back in the spring — probably from the town library, since their only computer has a dial-up connection so slow you could milk all their cows before a page loads. I got in touch with them as soon as Lionel gave me Sam's name. So in a few hours, at 5:00 a.m., I'll be sitting at the Shannons' round kitchen table eating cornflakes. Connie Shannon will sit with me, shooting the shit until I finish eating and she heads off to Rutland to buy groceries.

But for now, I'm standing here in the middle of Sam's cornfield, the tops of the stalks towering over me. I walk through the field, getting a feel for its bends and hills. My feet sink into the dirt. Ears of corn thunk against my arms. An eighteen-wheeler rattles past on the nearby road, probably carrying fertilizer or Coke. I glance back at the house. Its paint is peeling, big strips of it dipping into the edge of the weedy garden. In a few hours, Sam will be stirring, and I'll be leaving. I breathe in, the air thick with the scent of cow manure, and take one last look at the stars. No matter where I go, they're there with me, shining so brightly, I swear that if I stared at them long enough — to the point of dizziness, I mean — I could taste them, sharp and spicy.

I give myself a second to imagine the explanations that Munsen will settle on. Some towns have true believers who yell from the roadside that they've always known there's life on other planets. Their neighbors laugh it off at first, but when the field owners look into the news camera, just like we've coached them, and insist that they have no idea what happened, everyone falls silent and wonders: What if?

Other times, the general consensus is that they're man-made, and the only question is who made them. After all, a few rogue circlers have done interviews on YouTube with their voices distorted and their faces concealed, so it's possible to find proof that our group exists if you know where to look. The group's fine with that, since we do need someone to spread the word.

What matters is your name, your identity. No one can know you're a part of the circlers. Because without a name and someone specific to blame, the man-made idea could be written off as another crackpot theory, something dreamed up by the accuser after another late night in front of the computer. And then, that one question — *but who?* — is enough to bring people together, giddy with the mystery, a beaten-down farm town suddenly alive again. And, okay, it's a rush to hear those whispers and know that the guy no one looks twice at is the one behind it all.

But if you're caught, if anyone finds out who exactly the circler was, the whole story becomes just a blip on the news channels about some practical joker who's not from around here. You could never make another circle again. You're out of the circlers automatically — unceremoniously dumped. Any new town you go to will probably find you out with just one Google. And then your new circles will be selfish, just displays for you and your ten minutes of fame. Transparent egos like that are not welcome in the circlers.

Then there's the contest. Anyone who makes fifteen circles without getting caught — that's me, after this one — can become a leader and start their own regional branch alongside Lionel's national crew. Rumor is that the leaders meet annually in London, where there's a meet-and-greet with the godfathers of circle making, twinkly eyed old guys who started it all.

To be honest, I don't really care about the contest. Meeting agendas and airplanes both make me twitch. But Claire wanted to win it, badly. She'd never been to London, and on certain nights, she'd get all loopy about it, talking in this terrible fake Cockney accent. Insisting that we'd get there. And then I started to want it, too, just for her sake. I still haven't let go of that, I guess.

I find a spot a few yards back from the road. This will be the beginning. I grab a can of spray paint from my pocket, where it's been dragging down the waistband of my jeans. We don't usually use spray paint on these jobs, instead relying on someone else to spot the next stalk that needs pressing. But I started using it a while back so that I could work on my own, and now I've found it makes the circles truer than I could ever do with a spotter.

The stream of paint flares from my fingers midway down the stalk in front of me. Far enough down that it can't be seen by passing cars but close enough to the tassel that

I can see it when I peer from the roadside. The hiss of the paint sends lightning down my spine. In a few weeks, this field will become something miraculous. People will come from all over to see it, and they'll stand by the side of the road with their mouths hanging open. They'll shake their heads, and then they'll laugh like they haven't in years, childlike, enchanted.

Chapter Two:
Molly

He's dying, my husband. It's the first thing I think every morning, when the sound of his movement wakes me up. All I can do is bury my face in his pillow and breathe and breathe and breathe his air.

Today, I decide instead to visit the store-front that wasn't, that could not be. I climb into the truck and stare out at the fields for a moment. The farm is beautiful at this hour, before the fog has lifted and you start remembering all the ways it has betrayed you. Sam has left a string of footprints on his path toward the fields, dark in the dew-silvered grass. He pauses to give me a wave, and I blow him a kiss, my lips popping against my palm, though I doubt he can see the motion through the windshield. I put the truck into reverse and pull away.

There was a time when I would've joined him and trudged to the barn to help him with the milking. Sam had to sell all eighty-two cows the first time he became too ill to go out every morning and evening to tend to them. The day he sold them, he was silent all afternoon, sitting leaned over the computer, and I rerouted my chores to avoid him. He came into the kitchen at dinnertime, clutching a pile of papers. "Did you know," he said, "that the United States loses 37.6 billion dollars' worth of productivity every year to soil erosion?"

Before I had a chance to say no, I didn't know, he announced that he was spending our money from the cows on a covercropping system that would allow him to plant rye in among the corn and soybeans. The roots of the rye, he explained, would grip the soil, preventing it from washing away down the creek at the back of our property. The system was expensive and labor-intensive, this much I knew, but before I told him so, I looked at his puffy eyes and thought better of it.

This morning, I barely manage to maneuver the truck into a parking space before my fingers are fumbling at the glove box. The cigarettes are tucked into a ziplock bag, hidden between the truck's registration and its last inspection report, the red carton winking wickedly at me. I breathe in the smoke and imagine it burning my lungs and throat clean, starting anew. I've left the window cranked down so I can crane my neck out when I blow. When Sam asks, I'll insist it's a brushfire he's smelling, or residual smoke from some neighbor who just insisted on giving me a hug. I'll know from the furrow flicked into his brow that he sees right through this small secret of mine, but he won't say anything.

There are other secrets. I'll tell him I'm flying out to visit Maggie and will go see our son instead. And then there's this: every week or two, I sit here, in a city twenty minutes away, staring at this dusty, empty shop window with the *For Lease* sign curling at the edges. I picture the bakery I could build here, with a door painted bright blue and the gleaming glass case holding loaves of bread dusted with flour. I would have Sam paint me a sign on one of the boards from our barn and hang it above the lintel.

None of that matters now, not anymore.

A car horn beeps beside me, two jaunty taps, and there's our neighbor, Marlene Cadbury, smiling through her window at me. "What a lovely surprise!" I can almost hear her saying as she rolls down her window. I fling the cigarette to the pavement and flap my fingers at her — so sorry, really must be going. It's time to drive back home.

■ ■ ■ ■

Sam is in the kitchen, rummaging through the cupboard next to the oven for the ancient box of Cocoa Pebbles buried behind the canned tomatoes. Every time I try to throw it out, he plucks it out of the garbage can and slides it right back into place. I poke him in the small of his back and say, "The grapefruit's in the fridge, same as always."

"Oh, come on. Why do you ruin my fun like that every morning?" He squeezes my finger and retrieves the unappetizing bruised fruit from the fridge. I pluck a lumpy bag of granola from the cupboard, special-ordered online every month for its antioxidants, and hand it to him. He pours the granola into his favorite bowl; once upon a time, it had our college insignia printed on it, before decades of washing wore the colors away. He'd bought it for me for our first Valentine's Day together. "For those Cheerios you're always eating," he'd said as I unwrapped it.

"The fields're doing all right," Sam says before I can ask. "Corn feed's a little rangy from the cutworms, but it's almost time to harvest anyway. I'm thinking Nessa might be right about that permaculture thing. Maybe if I start growing something more edible, we can eat something better than this for breakfast."

Vanessa always comes back from California aglow with ideas, making it impossible for her father to listen to any voice of reason. The last time she came home, the two of them hatched a plan to burn out the weeds instead of using chemicals — flame weeding, they called it. I watched them from the window, towing a propane tank that sprayed a line of feral fire behind the tractor. A few minutes in, a bush at the edge of the field caught and went up in a blaze. Nessa spun, spraying it out with an extinguisher, while Sam's hands flapped overhead. Back inside, they glanced slyly at each other when I told them that they would not, under any circumstances, be trying that again.

"Yes, growing something edible would work great, if we could find anyone around here who wanted to pay for the thistle and wild mint that seem to do so well here," I say.

Sam is already shaking his head. "I know, I know. But maybe one of these days, we can give up corn for good and plant some fruits and veggies. Wouldn't that be nice?"

He's scraped his bowl clean by now, and he drops it in the sink before pulling me into a brisk hug. I close my eyes and feel his chin pressing into my forehead as he speaks. "Whatcha got planned for the day?"

I pull away. "Oh, I don't know. I thought I might get started on a new batch of bread, get some laundry and sewing done." Same as always, same as ever. "What about you?"

"Well . . ." He leans back and hooks his thumbs into his fraying front pockets. "I've got to go see about those fungicides, maybe get some more rye seed. Hey, I was thinking." He scratches the gray stubble on his cheek. "If we're gonna try to get going on this veggie thing, it might be good to start with the garden out front, you know? You think you could start clearing out some of the dead stuff in Nessa's patch?"

I can do almost all the things a proper farmer's wife should: I cook, I clean, I sew, I even play hostess every once in a great while. I have never been able to grow anything myself, though. Our front lawn was all tall grass and weeds before Nessa attacked it when she turned thirteen, and to tall grass and weeds it has returned since she left. Sam looks sheepish. "All right, all right." I sigh, but I pat his elbow.

I start to rinse out his bowl as the door

claps shut behind him, and I watch him walk past the window. Instead of continuing toward the barn to stare at the empty stalls, his midmorning routine, he slips down a corn row to his right. The water runs over my hands, gradually growing warmer as he peers at every stalk he passes. He must be thinking of that boy who came by a few weeks ago, the one he chattered about for weeks beforehand. It was ridiculous, really, what Sam was planning to do, but he has a way of sweeping you into his enthusiasm, making you lean forward into your elbows on the table to hear more, to sit closer to the brightness of his ideas. Oh, my Sam.

I was sitting next to him, his fingers curled tightly around my own, when they found the first tumor after the melanoma. It was supposed to be a routine follow-up X-ray. The doctor stood before the screen and pointed at a spot glowing bluer than the rest in the folded balloon of his colon. All I could think was that this was wrong, seeing inside my husband this way, that this was private, that I should not have to layer this new picture of him over all the ones I've taken in the past forty years. I heard the word *tumor* and looked at Sam. Him? No. No. Sam was setting his jaw, he was nodding. Yes. Him.

We've been back in front of that light box five times in the past two years: two remissions, three recurrences. Every time, he nods the same way, so serious. Every time, I refuse. I cannot think about what my days will be without him.

Our last appointment was one of the bad ones. When they're good, he sweeps me up and swings me around, whooping and singing. I can't help but laugh and cradle his face in my hands, even though I know it will never last. This time, instead, he trudged up to our room, shut the door behind him, and stayed there for an hour, emerging with his cheeks all splotched and his mouth set small. And I waited until he'd fallen asleep that night to cry.

The chemo had worked before, though. And it must be working now. It has to. That's what Dr. Cooper said: he had "no reason to believe" it wouldn't work again.

I look down at my hands, suddenly flushed in the scalding water. I turn the faucet off. If Sam is really serious about this garden — and I know he is — I'll have to buy some fertilizer tomorrow, while it's cheaper just before the harvest season. For now, while the sun draws the chill from the air, I will make this dough.

CHAPTER THREE:
DANIEL

The summer I turned seventeen, I went to farm camp. My grandpa had just died, and I needed to get away from the eggshell silence of the upstairs guest room where he used to sleep. I wanted to learn firsthand about the dairy farm that had used up all his better years. My mom sucked in her lips when I told her my plans, but my dad just asked me to bring home some colorful bugs from Delaware for him to study. So I went.

The camp was fun for the most part, once I got some calluses and learned to wear a hat. There was this one guy, Hal, who slept in the bunk above mine. His parents probably sent him there to separate him from the patch of pot plants growing under their porch. He used to rattle our bunk every night from his mattress, moaning and pretending to jack off. It never got old for him somehow. But one night, when the sounds of everyone else's sleep whooshed through the cabin, he stuck his head over the edge of his bed into my face.

"Yo, Danny!" The whites of his eyes glowed. "I heard a rumor there's a crop circle being built tonight in that shithole field down the road. You in or out?"

Any other person, and I probably would've said no. My muscles still screamed every night, pulsing angrily in my shoulders and legs. But this was Hal, and I knew that if I didn't go, he would brag the rest of the week about what I'd missed. Totally insufferable. I stuffed my feet into my sneakers and followed him into the night. On the way there, he filled me in on all the details I hadn't cared enough to ask about. He'd gone out for a walk after lights-out the other night and was smoking a joint on the edge of a field nearby when he saw some kid prowling through the wheat. Hal being Hal, he demanded the kid tell him what he was up to — never mind the cloud of pot smoke wafting above Hal's own head. "He didn't last long," Hal smirked. "I swear I could see the dude sweat, even in the dark. All I had to do was ask a few questions, and he told me everything."

They were already almost done when we got there, two men and a woman, dressed in black and slipping through the neck-high wheat. I still remember how they managed not to shake a single stem of wheat apart from the ones they were crushing.

They were making a simple circle. "Practice for that pussy new guy I saw the other night, I bet," Hal whispered. The "new guy" he pointed at, the skinniest, stood at the center of the circle, his hands stuffed in the pocket of his sweatshirt. He shifted on his spot, moving so that he was always facing the other two. The woman was walking along the edge of the circle, making sure it was even and bending over to snap off stems where it wasn't. The other man was doing the real crushing. He had a board with a piece of rope coming off each end, and he would rest one end closest to the center of the circle on the ground and step slowly on the other end until the board flattened, flush to the earth. He gripped the ropes the whole time, the wheat crumbling beneath him.

When they finished, three white grins flashed, and they padded across the circle toward us. It was beautiful; it really was. The moonlight broke over its surface so it looked like a wheel, spinning if you moved your head. It seemed to almost shimmer from the depths of the wheat around it.

"Pretty awesome, huh?" The woman was beside me.

I couldn't speak. I stared at the wheat. Hal tried to impress her — or maybe intimidate her — with his story about cornering the new guy, but it was me she squinted at, the wrinkles around her eyes scrunched. "We usually make sure we don't have any bystanders," she said over Hal's babble, "but you campers get a special pass. We know you're here to learn and won't tell any townies. Lionel has a soft spot for you kids." Her hand slid toward mine and put a slip of paper in my palm. And then she was gone, hustling with the two other men toward a van parked down the road.

"What'd she give ya, her number?" Hal's sour breath filled my nose.

I stuffed the paper into my pocket, wiped his spittle off my ear, shrugged. He shoved my shoulder, and we turned back to the camp in the dawn light. Hal wouldn't stop talking about some poor girl he'd dated the summer before. When I knew he wasn't paying attention to me anymore, I slipped the paper halfway out of my pocket with one hand. It was just a white strip with a date, time, and address typed across it. And that was it.

My parents still don't know. They think I'm farming, plain and simple. Which is weird enough for them — that their kid reverted to the old family business instead of going off to college like he was supposed to. I call them once a month, and my dad always does the talking, asking about crops and pests. My mom stays quiet mostly. I've gone back to visit a few times, and she spends the whole time almost avoiding me, scooting around me in the kitchen, going on random errands in the middle of the day.

It's my second night of circle work here in Munsen, and I'm just about done marking the first section. My arm's burning a little bit from spending so long above my head, reaching with the paint can. At night, the paint will pulse against the cornstalks, cutting across the rows of the crop. But it's glow-in-the-dark, so during the day, it'll just look like a slightly different shade of the green fields. And like most farms I work on, Sam's road is so remote, there probably won't be anyone driving by to see it shining at night.

I glance down the road that stretches into town and step toward the worn, yellow median line. I put my hands on my hips. For a minute, I'm just another restless farmer, checking on things.

The general store in Munsen was a lot like

all the others. Grimy floors, pegboards hung with fishing tackle, abandoned DVDs on shelves in a corner. I hunted through the aisles for work gloves, past lemonade mix and extension cords, before finding them, lonely and yellow.

There was already a potbellied man at the checkout, pushing his cap up his forehead. "Yeah," he said as the cashier reached back toward the cigarette case, "my wife keeps trying to get me to quit, but not this year. I need them this year."

"Drought's been pretty bad, huh?" The kid slapped two packs on the counter and crossed his arms, settling his hips back against the shelf behind him. I knew that position — he was getting ready for a long one.

"Yep. I can't even get a pile of corn big enough for the pigs to roll in." The man roared one big, meaty laugh.

The kid smiled. "Each year, it gets worse and worse. My brother's working down at the Derrys' farm again, and he says the cutworms are bad, too. Brought home an ear to show us, and it was half eaten away, rotten-looking, you know?"

The man shook his head, ran one hand down the front of his T-shirt. "Yep. They're awful, those cutworms. And did you hear

Sam Barts talking at the town meeting? He wants us to stop using pesticide-coated seed and switch over to some sort of untreated alternative. Meaning, what, we'd have to spray atrazine all over instead? Poor old man, on his way out." They stood there for a while, grunting together at the truth.

I thought back to Sam's words and wondered how long he thought these guys would stick around before they joined the exodus. Sweat beaded under my collar, and I ran a finger over the back of my neck to collect it.

The potbellied man turned and noticed me. "Oh, sorry, buddy, didn't see you there. You new in town?"

"Yup. My name's Daniel."

"Pleasure, Daniel. I'm Norman. You the one I've heard about, the one they hired over at the Shannons'?"

"Yep, that's me."

He seemed to approve. "Well, it's good to meet you. And hey, when you're around town, watch out for an old geezer named Sam Barts. Make sure he doesn't sell you on any pyramid schemes." He laughed again and offered one hand. I shook it, almost feeling like I shouldn't, out of loyalty to Sam.

He waved at the kid and headed for the

door. I paid for the gloves and followed him, returning to the Shannons.

The stream of spray paint starts to sputter just as I'm marking the last stalk of the night. I jam the can in my pocket and turn around. Every few feet, a stripe of paint is glowing, bobbing in the breeze. Waiting.

A set of curtains shift in one window of the house. Sam's standing there, his face barely visible in the slowly graying predawn. He doesn't see me at first, just stares out at his land. I raise my hand in one of those easy waves I've learned since leaving home. His face broadens a bit when he sees me, and he grins, wriggling one white hand. I turn to go. I'll be back on the next good night.

CHAPTER FOUR:
MOLLY

The town crawls by outside the windows of my truck. The neighbor's bull is testing his limits again, nosing over the swirled barbed wire into the street. And there's Joanna, out clipping sheets and underwear to her clothes-drying tree. She waves at me with such vigor that a few clothespins fall from her mouth. She's still new here. Soon, she'll learn to wave like everyone else, one hand paused briefly in midair.

I turn my head a little to avoid the rows of benignly beige plastic huts perched on the hill behind Jimmy Cadbury's barn. Jimmy raises veal, has done so for years, and it used to kill me every time I went past his farm, picturing the calves shut up in those huts for all their short lives. Once, I started crying when Sam drove me past, and he caught up my hand, still smooth as a pearl then, and said, "I know. I sure as hell wouldn't raise my calves like that. But they've got three kids in college, and there's just no other way for them to repay their mortgage." He kissed my knuckles and returned my hand so I could wipe my cheeks dry as he whistled.

After parking the truck, I step into the feed store, the air-conditioning raising every hair on my forearms. I wander through the aisles and brush my fingers over a display board hung with nylon ropes, sidestepping the lawn mower posed in the middle of the store. In the gardening row, I'm lost. Was it mulch or fertilizer Sam always said tomatoes need more of? I can never remember.

"Molly? What are you doing here?" It's Allison Remy, her broad frame straddling the aisle.

"Allison, hi! I can't believe I didn't see you there earlier."

"Oh, I know. I'm kind of hard to miss with this hair." She fluffs up her curly red ponytail. I can't count the number of times I've heard her say this before.

"Well, I was just buying some fertilizer — Sam wants me to work on the garden again. You know how much I love that chore." I bite the edge of my tongue, alarmed at the acid in my tone.

She doesn't even blink. "Tell me about it. Every day, it's something new, isn't it? And, you know, lately, I've been even crazier than usual." She raises her arm and wiggles the basket she's carrying; it clanks with mysterious plumbing parts.

"Oh, of course. Your move." I fuss with the hem of my shirt. Last year, Allison and her husband, Ben, realized that the going rate for corn wouldn't cover both the mortgage payments on their farm and the hospital bills for Allison's ailing mother. They've just moved to a brand-new trailer home at a dip in the road on the edge of town. I should have asked her earlier how the move was going, perhaps offered to help somehow.

Before I can say anything more, she says, "Yeah, our new place is just fine, you know, all things considered. I was actually thinking about getting some gardening supplies myself, see if I can't do something about that awful weed bed we've got in our new backyard." She fingers the handle of a spade hanging near her shoulder. Allison used to grow gorgeous, heavy-headed lilies and daffodils on their old front lawn. Every time I drove past their house, she'd be kneeling in her garden, elbow-deep in piles of weeds and mulch, her hair flashing in the sun.

"That sounds wonderful. Maybe you could give me a hand with my garden. Lord knows, I don't have half your talent."

"I would love to." She lays one freckled hand on her chest, below her collarbone. "Really, I would love that."

I turn back to the shelves. "Speaking of, do you remember what it is that's best for tomatoes?" I say it calmly, as if I would be able to think of it on my own if I just stood there and concentrated long enough.

"Mulch," she says. "Definitely mulch." Without so much as a pause, she adds, "By the way, I haven't seen Charlie up here in a while."

There's a question in her voice that I'd rather not answer. I grip the handle of my cart until my knuckles bleach. Charlie's name has echoed through my thoughts every day since he blasted out our front door. "Yes, he's doing great out west. He's so busy with his new practice that he doesn't have much time to come out to visit." I chuckle weakly.

Allison hums knowingly, sympathy moist in her eyes. Her two daughters, over at UNH and UVM on scholarships, come home to visit every weekend, with their hair ironed straight and their nails painted pink. "Well, good for him, working so hard. I'd better get back to Ben before he gets worried." She laughs, high and clear, and trundles over to the checkout counter.

Alone again with the gardening supplies, I stare at the bright cans of pesticides and weed killers until their greens and yellows blur together and all I can see is Charlie's face, lean and handsome and rough.

He left ten years ago, when he sat us down at the kitchen table just after Christmas and told us he wanted to be a doctor — had in fact already sent in applications to NYU and Columbia. For half a moment, I felt a hiccup of relief. The last we'd heard, Charlie was majoring in agronomy and planning on moving back to Munsen after graduation. Sam had been setting aside bigger and bigger swaths of our fields for him, brainstorming new crops Charlie could grow there every night over dinner.

It turned out, though, that that had never been Charlie's plan. He hadn't been honest with us for four years. Longer than that. He'd held so much back from us. My chest ached to think how he must have imagined us.

Sam's face flushed red. "You're *what*?"

Charlie bit his lip and broke our gaze, staring down at the tabletop. "You heard me, Dad. I'm going to med school."

I reached for Sam's hand, but he shook me off. I found I couldn't try again. I leaned away from him as he shook and spat.

"Bullshit you're going to med school. Do you have any idea how hard your mother and I worked to get you here? How much we've given you to get you where you are today? And now you're just going to leave that all behind? All of this, just abandon it? To go to *medical school*?" He spoke it like a curse, this dream that most parents would cherish.

Charlie's eyes widened, then narrowed. I wanted to say something, anything, to balance out his father's rage, but nothing would come. Some part of me had always known that Charlie shouldn't end up here, and I'd only nodded whenever Sam came in to tell me about his latest plans for him. Still, I'd hoped Charlie would at least tell us he'd been thinking about it before making a final decision. Yes, that's where I would start: the hope. "Charlie, honey, I think what Dad's trying to say is that we wish you would —"

"Do you have any idea how much medical school costs? Do you have any *clue* how much your mom and I are struggling just to get by?" Sam's voice crept back into a roar.

I gaped at him. Never in our lives had he mentioned any doubt that we would survive, that the sun would rise and take away the frost every autumn morning. And now Charlie, across from us, was shoving his lips between his teeth, about to cry.

"Sam, listen. It sounds like this is something he really wants, right, Charlie? So maybe —"

"Not now." Sam's voice was ice and steel. I flinched.

I scraped my chair away from the table, walked over to Charlie, and laid one hand on his shoulder. "You need to calm down," I said to Sam.

"Calm down? *Calm down?* You tell me how, for Christ's sake, we're supposed to afford medical school? And why exactly is our life here not good enough for you? Tell me that, Charlie. You tell me that. You think you're better than us?"

Charlie's shoulder rose and sank under my hand. "I'm getting a scholarship. So you can chill out about that. Remember all those good grades I worked for? Turns out they actually got me somewhere — somewhere outside this town. Vermont may be great for you guys, but it's not for me, and you know it. No."

Sam shook his head.

I knew Sam wasn't finished. I knew that what he had left in him wasn't something that should ever be said.

"Both of you, that's enough," I broke in, but it was as if I were shouting out the window at a passing airplane.

They glared at each other, their hands gripping the edge of the table in exactly the same way.

"I guess you're not who I thought you were," Sam said.

Charlie laughed, and it was mean and fake. "You mean someone who was going to get himself a little wife and settle down and take over this godforsaken dead end? No, you're right. That's not who I am."

Sam's mouth crumpled. The only time I'd ever seen him faint was at his mother's funeral. He'd stood there beside the freshly dug grave and grasped my hand as his face blanched. He looked worse now. "Well then," he said, settling his hands in his lap. "I guess you can forget about ever coming back."

Charlie's shoulder wrenched out from under my palm, the door slammed behind him, and suddenly, the only thing left of him was the sound of his car's engine in the driveway.

The two of us still in the kitchen stared at each other. Sam's jaw was set with determination, an explanation ready.

I raised my hand to stop him and closed

my eyes. "No. If he leaves right now, I will never forgive you," I said. And I left the room.

After that, I used to call Charlie every Friday afternoon, when Sam was meeting with his friends to talk yields and inputs. The bitter coals in my stomach would glow hot after every call, and I could barely look at Sam when he returned home. Then one day, right after we first heard about Sam's tumor, Charlie's voice on the phone was cold and clinical, rattling off survival rates and progressions. I reminded him that this was his father, not just a patient, but I didn't know who I was talking to.

Now we only speak when I fly out to California every once in a while. He is a wary stranger, averting his eyes as he deposits me into his clean, spare guest room. At night, I search the closet and the nightstand, greedy for receipts, ticket stubs, personal details of any sort. There is never anything. My boy is long gone.

In the feed store, I pick up a bag of mulch and drift over, hollow-headed, to the registers. I arrive home, though I remember nothing of the drive. The bag of flour I left out on the counter reminds me that I had other plans earlier, another family wanting another loaf, and I move through the kitchen, shoveling flour, water, and yeast into a big metal bowl.

It started as an obligation, the bread. Years ago, at a church meeting to discuss aid for a newly widowed parishioner, the women around me offered casseroles, childcare, hand-sewn quilts — as if any of that could bring a husband back. Then they turned to me, their hands folded neatly in front of them, a firing squad of unsolicited cheer. I swallowed and said, "I could make a loaf of bread to go with the Waldorf salad, I suppose," though it had been ages since my mother taught me how. I could still feel her poking my arm when my attention wandered. The offer seemed to satisfy the group, though, and the secretary beamed triumphantly as she recorded it on her notepad.

As it turned out, I was actually rather good at it, scooping deep-brown loaves out of the oven over and over again. It became what I could offer, "Molly's bread," automatically added to the list for every family tragedy in town. I learned to love it, too, the meditative process of turning simple ingredients into perfect, round boules.

Today, I need it more than ever. Slowly, slowly, as I stir all the ingredients together and scrape the dough out onto the counter,

I begin to come back. I push my hands through the pale mass, pressing it and pulling it and stretching it, the thumping of my palms against the counter drowning out the *CharlieCharlieCharlie* in my ears. In a few minutes, the muscles in my arms will start to ache, and the dough will cling less and less to my fingers. I will be able to strip off the sticky gloves of flour and water that are collecting on my palms and return to the kneading anew, with clean hands that will stay clean even while I keep coaxing the glossy, tacky pile. I close my eyes and picture the moment when I can pinch off a bit of dough and stretch it until the sun glows through it. Then it will be ready to rise.

"Another loaf in the works?" Sam's voice booms across the kitchen and against my back.

My eyes startle open. "I got the mulch and fertilizer for the garden. Would you mind moving them over to the shed?" I start picking dough out from between my fingers.

"I'll get right on it." He peers out the door at the truck. "You know, maybe we could use some corn husks as mulch instead of the packaged stuff. I mean, it's not like we're gonna use them for anything else, right?"

"Sure, why not." I used to make corn-husk dolls with the children after every harvest. Nessa would tackle the husks like it was her job, busily bending and stuffing the fibers. Sam would tease her, telling her to leave some for the other children, while Charlie would stage battles and races with the finished dolls.

"You all right?" Sam stands in front of me, his hands moving toward my shoulders.

"Of course. I was just remembering the old days, playing with the kids after the harvest."

His hands tap my arms, then fall back to his sides. He reaches out to press one thumb into the bread dough. "That's gonna be a good one, I bet. Good thing the army of do-gooders recruited you, General." He salutes me with one stiffened hand, and I stifle a laugh into my shoulder.

I give the dough a few more presses, Sam's thumbprint disappearing into the fleshy lump, before dropping it back into the bowl and draping it with a kitchen towel to rise. Sam will be hungry, so I start to make lunch, sawing off slices from the end of last week's loaf and piling them with slabs of cheese, squirts of mustard, and cold chicken from last night. I'm just pouring the cider when Sam returns from moving the bags. He rubs his chapped hands to-gether and brings the plates over to the table, placing the sandwich made with the heel of the bread in front of my chair — the crust has always been my favorite part. He's already shoving stray pieces of chicken in his mouth when I bring the glasses over, but he smiles through the food when I run one hand over his shoulder blades.

I sit down across from him. The hair on his arms has gone gray, and much of his head is shiny and hairless now, but his biceps are still muscled. His round belly has shrunk quite a bit in the past couple of years. I can't think about why he's lost that weight, about the walnut of disease packed in there. You wouldn't think, looking at him, that our medicine cabinet is stacked with bottles of pills, that it rattles mercilessly every night when he opens and closes it. Sometimes, when he's fallen asleep and I lie awake, my mind hounded by worry, I trace my fingertips gently over the freckles on his back, ones I memorized long ago. So much of my past is wrapped up in him. If I rub his skin hard enough, would those years and memories peel off like onion skins? Would he be pinker, brighter, newer? Would my skin look fresher, too?

He looks up and winks, not at all startled

45

to find me studying him. I smile back and make myself eat.

CHAPTER FIVE: DANIEL

Sometimes, I think the size of a farming town should be measured not by the number of horses or stoplights but by the number of old men sitting outside the general store. Munsen's a pretty small town, so it has three, with pants pulled up over their bellies and big owl eyes behind their glasses. I've passed them three times today, each time mirroring their four-fingered half waves.

This morning, Connie Shannon shooed me out the door before I'd even had breakfast. "You've worked hard these past few days. Earl's on a trip to buy feed, so why don't you take the day off, and I'll clean this place up," she said. This happens a lot at the farms where I work, and I'm never sure if the days off are for my benefit or the wife's, but Connie was waving around a bottle of Windex as she spoke, so I assumed she meant business and planned an escape route.

I could've jumped in my car and driven the hour to Burlington, maybe grabbed a slice of pizza and a beer and tried to see a movie. But towns like that make me uneasy, alone with all the college kids. I also could've found a corner somewhere and called home, but my mom always sounds so thrown off when I call outside our monthly schedule. Or I could've called Ken, the only friend from high school I still keep in touch with. But over the years, our calls have become less and less frequent, and while they always start cheerfully enough, they end in an exhale of "All right, man. I've gotta get back to studying and/or the party and/or making dinner. Talk later, okay?" We mostly just text now, a message every few weeks that doesn't really say anything at all.

So instead, after calling Lionel for our usual check-in on the circle, I decide to wander around town for the day. Church, paint peeling; post office, square and brick; nursery school sign on someone's front yard. It's a late summer day, and the sun is still strong enough to make me sweat a little as I walk down and across the town's main drag, over and over.

I've done this during every job for years,

pacing the neighborhood until I know it like a local. It gets me a few weird looks from shop owners and kids in playgrounds, but it also means I never have to ask directions, and sometimes, if I'm lucky, they forget I'm an outsider. This was really important in the beginning, when I was still scrawny and video-game pale, looking like someone who'd only read about farming. "The most important part is fitting in," Claire used to say, eyeing my polo shirt and cargo pants. "Otherwise, they'll know exactly where to look when weird shit goes down."

Does it work? It's hard to say. There are always at least a few people who look at me sideways after the big reveal, teenagers usually. But for the most part, you'd be surprised by how many people want to believe, to put aside their day-to-day and think that there's something else out there, some big conspiracy. I always stick around for several months after the work's done — again, to avoid suspicion — and every time, there's this sort of buzzing all over town, a "what if" in the air.

After my third pass through the town center, I find myself wandering farther until I reach the driveway to Sam's house and pick my way through the ruts in the gravel. Sam is riding a once-green tractor through the fields, but somehow, he sees me and lifts up one arm, then points to his house.

I wave back and remember what Norman said in the general store. Sam's a little crazy, it's true — big ideas and a bit of a God complex. Then again, everyone who's ever asked me to build a circle is at least a little crazy. And mostly harmless. I head toward the house.

In the kitchen, Sam's wife's got her hands buried in a churning mass of dough that almost looks alive when I step into the kitchen. When I say hi, she nearly screams.

"Oh!" she exclaims. "I'm sorry. I didn't see you there. I'm baking bread for our neighbors, and sometimes I get caught up in it." There's a streak of flour on her cheek, white over freckles. "Here, take a seat." She pulls a chair away from the small table in the corner. "Sam is out working, but I'm sure he'll be back soon. Have you eaten?"

I start to tell her not to worry, that she can go back to her dough and let the silence sit. But my stomach rumbles at the mention of food, and her smile looks relieved.

"I think we still have some chicken left from last night," she says into the fridge, "although I hope you like white meat. No matter how hard I try, Sam will only eat the dark." Her smile says she doesn't try that hard.

"Chicken breast would be perfect, thank you."

She starts to fix me a plate. I know better than to offer to help, and soon she is sliding a mountain of neatly carved meat in front of me. I chew in silence as she turns back to her dough. With the rhythmic thwack of her kneading as my backbeat, I pull out my plans for Sam's circle.

I'm staring at the curve on the design's upper edge, picturing it traced in the field, when the thwacking suddenly stops. Molly looks up at the ceiling, sighs, and drapes a dish towel over the dough. "Daniel," she says, "there's something I need to talk to you about." She sinks into a chair, tucks her hands under her thighs. "Sam has cancer."

I stay still, wait for more. It's not all that uncommon, being hired by sick farmers — people tired of sterile waiting rooms, looking for something fantastic. "I'm very sorry to hear that," I say, but she shakes her head.

"This is his third recurrence." I grimace. "Skin first. We didn't worry too much about that one. Half the farmers in town have had it, with all that time out in the sun. Then colon. Then prostate, and now stomach." I wonder if she knows she's tracing a path on her own body as she speaks. "All this time, the doctors insist on still calling it skin cancer. They say we're lucky that it's never gone to his lungs or his brain, as if it's a well-trained dog. Stomach cancer, though." Her inhale is shaky. "They say only one in four survive."

I feel like I should touch her shoulder. I think that's what my mom would do. "That's —" I start to say, then stop.

She turns her head, like she's just now noticing me. "That's okay, honey. There's nothing you could say to make it better. Believe me, plenty have tried." On any other face, her expression would look like a smirk. On her, it's just sadness. "I wanted you to know, in case you hear it around town or . . . something." She waves her hand and sweeps it over the table, cleaning crumbs that aren't there. "Also" — her fingers land in front of her, a moth — "you should know why he wants to do this in the first place. The thought of leaving this town where it is . . ."

"Yeah. He's not alone, actually." This much I know. "A lot of my clients are seriously sick. No one needs magic more than they do."

"I suppose that makes sense," she says from somewhere far away. "Well, anyway. You get back to your lunch now. I'll go see if I can find that husband of mine." She pushes herself out of her chair and walks out the door.

I stare down at my plate, swallow, try to imagine back an appetite.

No matter how many cows I've fed or rows I've plowed, it always feels like I'm pretending to farm, like somewhere, a real farmer is shaking his head at me. But I know I'm good at making circles, even though Claire is the only one who's actually seen me do it. I can tell.

Tonight, I'm feeling pretty great about how it's all coming along. I'm about a quarter of the way done with marking the cornstalks, and I've made a few changes to the design already. This might just be the best one yet, my own masterpiece, and I'm humming a Led Zeppelin song as I shuffle back to Sam's porch for my empty paint cans.

I lean on the porch rail and am taking in the sweet, warm air when a voice comes from behind me.

"So, I'm guessing you're Daniel? Or should I be calling the cops?"

I've never really understood that phrase "heart in my throat" until now. I spin around so fast, my hip thunks the railing, and I'm finding it hard to swallow when I see her under the yellowy porch light. A cloud of dark-blond hair. Freckles. Eyes that, even in the dimness, there's no mistaking for anything but green. And a mouth full of crooked teeth, laughing at me.

"Hi," she says. "I'm Nessa."

CHAPTER SIX:
NESSA

Judging from the look on his face, this guy might need a new pair of pants. I'm bent double with laughing, though I know Mom would shake her head if she saw me.

"Um, hi." He struggles to recover. "My name's Daniel, but . . . uh . . . you already knew that." He grips the back of his neck with one hand, bracing himself.

"Don't worry. You should've seen my parents when I walked in at dinner time." My dad had shouted, bits of hamburger bun flying out of his mouth as he swooped me around the room. It was my mom, though, that I watched as I dragged my bag up the stairs to my room. Her smile was like a coat of paint on one of these run-down barns, no bones behind it.

I walk over to the railing where Daniel has settled. "They didn't know you were coming, then?" he says. "Sam didn't mention . . ."

"Nah. I didn't really know myself until a few weeks ago." Until I made my weekly call home and Dad told me Mom couldn't come to the phone. He said something vague about her church friends, but I knew about the doctor's appointment they'd scheduled for that morning. There'd been plenty of doctor's appointments before, of course, and every time there was good news, my mom had been there on the phone, reporting breezily on test results while my dad muttered in the background about boring me with the details. The fact that she wasn't there that time meant they'd heard something bad. And I had to check on them, in person, to see what it was.

"So, spray paint, huh?" I jut my chin toward the can in his hands. "I hate to break it to you, but the neighbors will spot that vandalism within a day. We're pretty nosy around here."

"Oh no, this stuff is glow-in-the-dark." He spins around the can so I can read the label. "It doesn't really look like anything in the day. I used to use white — the only non-glow-in-the-dark color that shows up at night, you know? But then I started to realize all it'd take was one farm worker who didn't know about the project seeing the marks in the field, and . . ."

"Your cover would be blown. Got it." I step closer to him to pick up a can, and the floorboards creak as he shifts away.

"So, uh, you flew in from Georgia? Sam mentioned you were working on a farm there."

"I was last summer, yeah. It was a pretty cool place, basically a closed system where they fed the spent plants to the pigs, then used their waste as compost." The man who owned the place, gnarled and tanned, had narrowed his eyes at me when I first showed up on his doorstep. He finally let me in the door when I explained that I grew up on a farm, and I was looking to learn and strong for a girl. Strong, period. "But now, I've moved on."

It comes in a flash, like always — the farmhand in Georgia who fell from an unsteady ladder, his femur broken clean through the skin. It was all my fault. I needed to get away, far away. I swallow it back down and pick a flake of paint off the railing. "I've been out in California foraging for mushrooms and stuff like that for about a year now."

"Wow." He raises his eyebrows. Moth wings shuffle, panicked, against the bulb of the porch light above us.

"I know. Annoyingly anti–desk job." I twirl

one curl of hair around my finger until I can feel the sharp tug at my scalp.

Daniel only moves one shoulder up and down, a wry twitch. "I mean, I can't really talk."

I release the curl. "Hey, yeah, that's right, Mr. Alien. I can't even imagine how you got into all this." I wave out to the field. "That's gotta be a long story."

"Yes and no," he says. "I learned about it in high school. Until then, I'd always assumed I'd go to college when I graduated, but something just felt right about it." His eyes light up as he says it, like he's never had a chance to say it before.

"Your family must've been thrilled." I can still picture the exact fault lines where my mom's face collapsed when I told her I was going into farming.

"Mmm."

I stare out into the field, my feet dancing nervously beneath me, shushing back and forth across the floorboards in the quiet. "Show me how this works, exactly." I jump off the porch and land on the patch of dirt worn bald and slick from a thousand jumps before. Daniel follows me down the stairs and into the thick of the cornfield.

"First, I draw out the plans with the client." He pulls a disintegrating sheet of notebook paper out of his pocket and waves it in the air, sending a little bubble of night breeze toward my face. The cornstalks rustle around us. "The first couple nights, I pace the field, figuring out how to translate their idea into something in real life. Then, I start to tag." He points at a slash of paint across three cornstalks in front of us. "Starting in the middle, then moving out in a spiral."

"Do you always do the same shape?" I picture the things I've seen on TV, circles sprung with mystery.

He laughs once, which he quickly turns into a cough. "Like a signature design? No, that would mess with the secret. Don't you know that there are thousands and thousands of alien tribes out there? For the same one to mark Earth twice with its symbol would just be too much of a coincidence."

"Oh, right, of course. How could I forget?" The silence stretches between us for a couple of heartbeats, itchy. I reach out and rub a leaf between my fingers. Its surface squeaks under my skin.

"I'll be done tagging in a week or two." He leans back into his heels a little. "Then, I start to press it down, all in one night. There's this tool." He moves his knobby fingers in front of him, mapping it out in the air. "It's like a swing, sort of. The kind that you see hanging from a tree in old movies, a piece of wood with rope attached to either end. And you put one end down against the base of the cornstalk and step down on the other end until the base snaps and you've got a few stalks down."

"It's pretty cool that you can do that whole thing by yourself." I can't even imagine how many nights it would take me, checking so many times to be sure it was right and counting every mark.

"Yeah." His hands drop down to his sides. "I used to do it with someone else, this girl I learned it from in the very beginning. In a lot of ways, it's much easier with someone else. But it's harder in some ways, too." He falls quiet, and I decide not to ask him exactly what he's talking about. Not tonight, anyway.

"Well," I say instead, "that sounds awesome. I can't wait to watch it all unfold." He doesn't respond, just rolls the paint can back and forth between his hands, the ball inside clinking against the sides of the can. "It's been a long day with the travel and everything. I think I'm going to head to bed. See you later?"

"Sure. Good night, Nessa."

When I get back to the porch and look over my shoulder, he's still standing there, tucked into the cornstalks, staring out into the depths of the field. The rolling paint can almost sounds like the bell around a cow's neck as it plods back home.

The next morning, my dad whistles tune-lessly in the kitchen below me. I close my eyes against the dawn and try to remember every time he's done that. When I was a teenager and hated him a little for waking me up, and I'd take the stairs down two at a time and pour myself a thermos of coffee to take out to the fields, silently daring him to tell me I was too young to be drinking that and that I should go back to bed (he never said either). When I was a kid and he was a monument, forever, a giant who knew everything and let me clomp around in his work boots while he laughed and laughed. When I came home from college to visit and he was suddenly just a person, when it hurt to watch him wave to me through my rearview mirror.

"Nessa? Your dad's going to head out to the fields any minute if you want to join him, sweets." It's Mom, standing in the doorway in her old holey sweater.

"Yup. I'm up." I roll out of bed and walk down into the kitchen. I stand in the door-way and watch Dad for a minute. He's skinnier than he once was, it's true, but his movements are still sure and sturdy. He turns from the coffeemaker and pushes a tall mug across the countertop toward me. I take a sip and let the bitterness roll across my tongue. "Man, nobody brews a cup as strong as you."

"It's his trade secret." My mom bumps one bony hip against mine on her way past, reaching for the mug he's pouring her.

"So, what are we tackling today?" I ask.

"Prepping the combine, then dealing with the irrigation system. You know, all our greatest hits." I know he's probably already scripted his midmorning monologue about highway robbery prices and ancient machinery. "You up to it?"

Of course I am, have been since the day I noticed the fringe of grime under his fingernails and knew what it meant. I drain my coffee and drop the mug into the dingy water in the sink. "Let's do it."

Six hours later, the world has fallen away inside the barn. The smell of hay wafts up as I shift on my knees around the combine's gear box, laid out on the ground. The cows used to live right where I'm kneeling, but my parents sold them, every last one. Even Oreo, the black-and-white Holstein that

Charlie and I named when we were kids, who was far too old to produce any milk and kept only for sentimental purposes. Even she was gone.

My work gloves are dark with grease, and my shoulders ache, but I need to replace that bearing. I've missed this farm work since I moved to California. Hunting for mushrooms just doesn't have the same tang to it, the same burn and satisfaction.

Just when I think I've gotten the right angle on the bearing, my dad taps my shoulder. "Lunchtime, Nessa."

I push my sweat-grimy hair out of my eyes, peel off my gloves, and step out into the daylight, squinting.

"You go ahead in. I'm just gonna finish up one more thing," Dad calls as he walks into the barn.

I roll my eyes and smile; those words have meant Dad eats half an hour later than us at almost every meal. Though now that it's just the two of them, maybe Mom waits for him to eat her lunch.

There's only one plate on the kitchen table, hummus and carrots and whole-grain bread she must've driven two towns over to find. "I can make my own lunch now, Mom. You really don't have to do this."

"I know," she calls, folding laundry on the

coffee table in the living room. "I don't mind it."

I sigh, run my hands quickly under the sink, and sit down.

"How's it going out there today?" she says.

"Fine, I guess." I scoop the mealy hummus into my mouth and crunch on the carrot, its vessel.

There's a pause, the dull thump of a pair of jeans hitting the tabletop. "Really, Nessa. What made you come home? We weren't expecting you until Thanksgiving." She steps over to the kitchen doorway, her thin arms wrapping themselves across her chest.

She knows why. She must know why. She'll never bring it up on her own, though, so I may as well ask. "How did Dad's latest appointment go?"

She's startled for a second, her face flying open before settling back into its worried wrinkles. "Oh. It was all right, I suppose. They say no news is good news, don't they?"

I stop chewing and wipe my hands on my lap. "Mom. That's what you said last time, remember? Then it turned out he had prostate cancer. You guys didn't tell me until he was halfway through his chemo." I'm getting too loud, I can feel it, even as my throat closes and my vision blurs.

"Sweets." She reaches for me, dropping

her hand back down at her side before it touches me. "You know Dad just doesn't want you to worry —"

"Worry about what?" The screen door opens, and there he is, taking off his baseball cap and running his thumb over the divot in the wall where the door handle hits. The hat hides his eyes for a second, and I wipe mine dry.

"About the farm, Dad. You know, the usual."

"Yes, you know how she always comes in with some big ideas from her modern farms," Mom finishes smoothly, squeezing my shoulder and stepping back to her laundry.

"Come on now, Nessa. I've been farming since before you were born, and I'll keep farming for as long as it takes for this place to become an overnight success." He winks, one of his old jokes, then grabs his ham sandwich from where my mom left it on the counter and sits down next to me. "Although now that you mention it, I've been meaning to ask if you've read about any new techniques lately."

I tear a crust off the bread on my plate, stuff it in my mouth, and start talking through it. "Well, have you ever heard of polyculture?"

CHAPTER SEVEN: MOLLY

Nessa is back, and just like that, the house is alive again. She has that effect on places, on people. Half the town is in love with her and smiles fondly when she tumbles in the door, picking things up off shelves and asking questions.

At the grocery store when she was sixteen and ambling beside my shopping cart, I overheard a couple of out-of-town boys mumble something rude about her body. It coursed through my veins like fire, and I wanted to stab my finger at their hollow chests until they shrank back to where they came from. I bit my tongue, my shoulders hunching under the weight of all those things I was holding back.

Nessa spun around on one flip-flopped heel, dipped into a curtsy, and said, "Oh, thank you so much for your opinions, boys. You are gentlemen and scholars, and I'm truly blessed that you took the time to critique me. Shall I send you my homework so you can grade that, too?" They froze, mouths half-open and faces glowing red under their suntans. When she stepped toward them, simpering, they turned tail and scurried down the aisle. She walked back to the cart, muttering, "Assholes," and I was too busy swallowing my laughter to tell her not to swear.

Then there were the other times. The times I heard her crying through the closed door and over the sink running. The times I watched her fade off to somewhere else right in front of me, eyebrows pushing together and tongue chewed. The other moms would complain loudly and proudly about their teenagers, battles fought and mostly lost over makeup, video games, and college applications. I always knew there was something different about my Nessa, something lacing her fingers together under the dinner table and whispering over her shoulder at night. It split me in two, and there was nothing I could do.

Sam never saw it. He was head over heels for the daughter in faded jeans following him around the farm, asking him the questions he'd always wanted to be asked about frost forecasts and tractor engines. He told me I was overthinking it and that Nessa was fine, just fine.

And now? It's hard to say. I've watched her closely since her return home, waiting always for her to tell me something went terribly wrong in California, that she cannot cope anymore, that she needs us. With every held breath that's met only with her chatter, I begin to hope that I'm wrong. Even so, the raw raking of your daughter's sobs is not something you'll soon forget.

"That new kid working over on the Shannons' farm is a little weird, don't you think?" I nearly gasp in line at the post office before catching myself.

"You know, I was just wondering about him. Real quiet. Yesterday, I swear I saw him walking down our street five times. Molly, what do you know about him? I thought I caught him talking to Sam after church."

"Oh, well." I spin around to see Betsy and Sharon, their arms full of boxes destined for the Home Shopping Network's returns department. "He's just another in the long line of intern types." I fold and unfold the signature confirmation receipt from our mailbox, running my finger over the crease.

"Lord knows, we've got plenty of those." Betsy nods wisely. "Just the other day, Howard got an email from some college student out in New York City, wanted to get back to his roots." She rolls her eyes. "Well, I looked him up, and turns out he's a music major with college professor parents, no farming experience or background to speak of. Needless to say, he won't be doing any work on our farm."

"What I wouldn't give to see Howard try to teach some scrawny city kid how to farm! Can you imagine?" The two bend over their packages, faces red with twin laughter, and I try to join in.

Jerry, the postman, grunts when I hand him the slip. He hands me an envelope, and I duck out of the building, smiling thinly at Betsy and Sharon. I don't look at the return address until I'm in the truck. It's the community development organization I'd written to last month to ask about a small business loan. I throw the envelope onto the floor of the passenger's seat and reach for the cigarettes in the glove box.

Daniel has been noticed, it seems. The truth is, whenever he's around, my jaw clenches and my shoulders square, fighting the undertow of his still, calm silence. Sam came up with his grand plan after his previous diagnosis, the prostate. We sat in the doctor's office and listened as the percentages they rattled off got lower and lower, then drove home mutely, the local soft rock station prattling on in the background.

As he turned the wheel to head down our driveway, it burst out of him like a held balloon. "A buddy of mine out in Nebraska sent me this video he found hidden way down in the internet. About kids that make crop circles?"

I blinked. Sam is like that, always pulling ideas from thin air — or, more recently, from online — but there was an edge to this one, razor-fine and desperate. "Really?"

"Yeah. And you know, I was thinking. Wouldn't that be a great way to get people to come here, to Munsen? I mean, imagine if they all thought they were getting a message from some greater power asking them — no, telling them — to get to farming here. Well, they might actually do it, before it's too . . ."

He stared off at the house. I patted his hand. "I'll make you a sandwich for lunch."

He didn't bring it up again until the week before his last appointment, but even so, I could tell his last successful remission had not stoppered this particular dream in his head.

"Hey, Molls, come check this out," he'd said, calling me over to his computer after dinner one night. "I followed a couple links from that video and found an email address some person online claimed belonged to one of those crop circle guys. The emailer put me in touch with this boy."

He pointed at the screen, and there, not unlike a personals ad, was his email's subject line: "Vt Farmer Seeks Msg from the Future." And underneath it, the response: "Sure, I can help you. Coming east from Minnesota in a couple weeks. Message me for details.–Daniel"

"I knew he would bite. I messaged him already, and he's going to call me tonight. Isn't that spectacular?"

"Sure. Sure it is." My eyes wandered to the green fields out our window, the corn feathered over with tassels. The question came out unbidden. "How much will he charge for all that?"

He placed his hand on my back. "That's the best part. These kids work for free! They ask you to give them the name of a farm in your town looking to hire another set of hands so they can have a day job, and then they work on your circle in the night. Just like moonlighting, eh?" He nudged my hip with his shoulder, and I gave him half the chuckle he was looking for.

He sighed and pulled me into his lap. I

could feel every rib, every bone in his legs. I laid my head back on his shoulder.

"What am I going to do without you?"

His exhale was sharp in my ear. "Don't even talk like that. I feel great. The doctors won't find anything in me. They can't. I just know it." He tightened his arms around my waist, willing it into truth.

And now that strange boy appears in our house and works carefully in our fields while I stare at the ceiling and hope for sleep. And he knows, because I somehow couldn't stop myself from telling him, because I suddenly couldn't stand the silence. And soon enough, it will seep out through the town, over bottles of cheap beer or in line at the store, whenever he hopes whispered gossip will help him belong. And they'll come, again. They'll come with sad eyes and cold casseroles topped with crushed potato chips in glass dishes that I'll have to return. They'll come to say how much they'd hoped the prostate was the last time. They'll come to lay their callused hands on my arm, to force swift smiles when Sam comes into the room. They'll come to me just as I've come to them a thousand times before, and there's nothing I can do.

CHAPTER EIGHT:
DANIEL

The next time I go to Sam's field, she's there again. The porch light is fighting a losing battle against the surrounding night. She's sitting in a rocking chair beneath it, one leg up and the other pushing against the floor. The chair creaks as she rocks. She holds a paperback in her hands, and she's tugging on that curl again, the one behind her right ear.

"Isn't it a little late for you to be out here reading?"

If she's surprised to see me, she does a great job of hiding it. "What is it, 1:00 a.m.? Perfect time for a little *Anne of Green Gables.*" She waves her book in the air. A girl in red pigtails grins up from the cover. "It was my favorite when I was a kid," she says and hands it to me. "I like to read a little bit from my old copy every time I come home. Did you ever read it?"

I shake my head, using one finger to keep

her place while I run another over the fraying edges of the pages. "No. Can't say that I did."

"That figures. I've yet to meet a guy who's read any L. M. Montgomery." She chews her lip for a beat before scrambling to her feet. "What are we doing tonight, boss?"

I almost choke. "You want to help?"

"Sure, why not? Unless that violates some sort of crop circle code." She smiles lopsidedly.

"No, of course not." I follow her as she bounds down the stairs and out to the field like an overgrown puppy. To be honest, we're not supposed to let other people in on the circles. The more people who know your identity, the more likely it is your cover will be blown. But she caught me off guard the night we met, so now she knows all about it anyway. And it's no use being a stickler for the rules with her. She'll probably just watch me from the window if I send her back to the house.

I'm hoping against hope that she doesn't bring up Claire again when she says, "You must get a kick out of laughing at the dumb hicks who believe in aliens."

I stop short. "No." I shake my head hard. She raises her eyebrows. I may have said it too loudly.

"At first, it just seemed like a cool way to see the country. Move from farm to farm, make these weird things with my own hands. But then." I pause and point up to the empty black road that passes their farm. "You should see it when they come. First, a truck will slow down and some guy will get out, shade his eyes, maybe grab a photo with his phone. Then the truck will peel off, he'll go gather up a few friends, neighbors. And they'll come and leave and get more, until the whole road is lined with cars and everyone in the town is standing there, kids in the front, women and men in the back, all one shape, no book clubs or bowling teams. All of them together, just looking. For that one hour or so, the entire town is there, suspending their disbelief."

I look up. Nessa's staring at me, her head tilted a little to the side. Finally, she just says, "And that's when you jump out and say, 'ta-da.' "

This time, I know she's joking. "I'm in the back of the crowd, usually. Once or twice, I was that first guy in the truck, but people started to look at me sideways when I was the one who found it."

She pokes her tongue into her cheek. "Huh." We stand there for a moment, staring out at the cornstalks swaying in the breeze. "And then the corn harvest for that year is kind of fucked, I guess."

"Most farmers claim they can still harvest everything once it's been broken, no problem."

She nods and reaches for that curl, then seems to change her mind. "What can I do to help?"

"Go check out what it looks like from the road?"

She runs up the steep little hill and stands there with her hands on her hips, scanning the field. Claire used to stand like that and whoop softly, blow me a kiss if it looked good, shake her head a little if it was wrong, her white-blond ponytail swinging.

"Everything looks great, I think," Nessa says after she's loped back down to me. "What's it supposed to look like?"

I show her the plans in the weak glow stretching from the porch light. The paper crackles as she holds it up to her face. I wonder if she knows that everyone in town is talking about her return. They say her name like she's famous, embarrassed by the amount of affection in their voices. They wonder why she's home outside the holidays, argue with each other over where she's working nowadays. Even Mrs. Shannon asked me this morning if I'd met her yet, with the same studied casualness as all the other town matchmakers I've met. I mumbled something noncommittal into a spoonful of cereal.

Even in the dark, though, I could understand the obsession. She's magnetic. Eyes wide enough to confuse you and understand you at the same time. Face sandy with freckles. You wouldn't necessarily think twice about any one of her features, but put them together, and you couldn't look away.

I pull a spray paint can from the plastic bag at my feet and rattle it back and forth. She's still holding the plans. "It's not exactly the best I've done," I say, reaching for them.

She shakes her head twice, firmly. "No, it's great. I'm just dying to see how everyone in town reacts is all. Should we get to marking?" She holds out one hand, open-palmed.

I pass the can to her. I show her where I'm picking things up, and we work together for a couple of hours. A few times, I correct her, but mostly we work in silence, just the hissing of the paint cans and the high whine of cicadas.

Once, just once, I almost got caught.

I'd woken up at 2:00 a.m. the night before

our deadline, and the bed beside me was empty.

It wasn't the first time Claire had gone missing. But she had never missed a pressing night before. My hands shook as I shuffled through the pile of papers under the bed, finally finding the circle plans. I held onto a tiny hope that she would be there at the field, all antsy, smirking at me.

But she wasn't. It was just me and that wheat, barely lit by the moon.

We couldn't miss the deadline. I worked all night, fumbling around, tearing the plan along its folds as I whipped it open over and over. I stumbled over the presser, tangled up in its ropes. I squinted toward my chosen center stalk, which looked just like all the others. The air was cold on my arms.

I'd barely finished crushing the last section when the sky lightened and the sun began to rise. I ran back up to my car, the pressers flung awkwardly across my back. And just as I'd slammed the trunk door, I saw him.

It was the gas station owner. I'd seen him the day before when I filled my tank, leaning back against the small brick building. He was watching me now, returning my nod without a word.

I struggled to catch my breath. Maybe he hadn't seen. Together, we looked out at the field. It was hard not to wince at the crooked outlines, the messily crushed wheat. I'd missed a couple of stalks in the center, and they stood out like cowlicks. "Weird, huh?" I managed around the clench in my gut, pointing at the crop circle.

He didn't say anything. Just glanced at me, then away.

Over the course of the morning, neighbors and friends collected along the side of the road as usual. But the whole time, he was there. And when his buddies started laughing, talking about all the theories they'd always held, he just studied me, saying nothing.

By the time Claire showed up, I knew my career was over. "Hey, Danny," she said when she reached my side. "Sorry about that." She slung one arm over my shoulders. "Looks like it came out great."

The bile rose quickly in my throat. "What is wrong with you?" I hissed. "Are you crazy? I'm pretty sure that guy over there saw me. Do you understand what that means, or do I have to spell it out for you? Lionel's going to find out, and then I'm screwed."

Her eyes widened, two blue wounds. At

first, I wanted to reel all the words back in, bring Claire back. *It's not her fault,* I told myself. But I didn't quite believe it. I got into my car and drove away.

All that day, in the grocery store, during our cover job, the whispers crawled over me like spiders. Every time I turned, no one was there. Eventually, I convinced myself the gas station owner hadn't told anyone. Claire's good spirits were working overtime, dragging at me. She handled Lionel's check-in call, told him I was a champ, giggling softly as she told him about the one small bump in the road, nothing to be concerned about. By the end of the week, we'd moved on to a new farm in a new town. For weeks after that, I stayed awake every night, staring at the ceiling until I finally came up with my spray-painting method, the one that would allow me to work alone. Just in case.

The next few times I come by Sam's farm, it's the same: Nessa waiting on the porch, finger in a book, the other hand out for the plan so she can check our progress. Sometimes, she asks me questions that stick to me, pricking at the back of my mind while I set up the milking machine the next morning. How many of us are there? Are my parents lonely? Have any of my host families ever suspected? When she asks, my answers always seem incomplete, and all I want is the solidness of a folded-up sketch and my finger on the paint can.

And then, one night, when we're sitting on the porch steps, she says, "How bad is my dad, anyway?"

I turn to her, but she's staring out at the field. "I keep asking my mom," she says to the mountains hunched on the horizon, "but she always brushes me off. She says she doesn't want me to worry."

"Did you call your brother?" I ask. She's mentioned him a few times, the older brother who used to smirk when she snuck in past her curfew.

She snorts. "I doubt he knows anything. I'm pretty sure all they talk about now is the weather. He's just as clueless as I am. They must've told you something when they hired you, right? Some sort of reason for all this." She motions out at our work.

I remember sitting at Molly's kitchen table, the chicken heavy in my stomach. How desperately she needed to tell someone, and for them to tell no one else.

"Please, I need to know."

I swallow. "Yes, your mom told me. Stomach cancer. Apparently, it's not good." Her gaze could burn me, but when she looks away, back out into the field, it's even worse.

"No. It's not good." Her shoulders slump. She picks a stray blade of grass off her knee. "Charlie said it was a miracle he pulled through the last time. And now . . ." She covers her face, and I fumble for something, anything, to say. But when she brings her hands back down, her eyes are dry. "So, that's why. He's been obsessed with changing this town, and he's hoping this will —"

"Nessa? Is that you?" We both whip around to see Molly standing in the door, silhouetted against the kitchen. She pulls her nightgown closer when she sees me. "Hello, Daniel. I didn't realize you were working tonight."

Nessa stands, walks over to her. "Stomach?"

Molly freezes. Her eyes flit between Nessa's face and my own. I shouldn't have told Nessa. This is family business. I should've stayed out of it. Once again, Nessa'd managed to pry more out of me than I'd meant to give her.

Molly glances over her shoulder, but through the open door, we can all hear the faint sawing of Sam's snores. She eases the door closed. "I'm sorry I couldn't tell you, Nessa." She reaches out to smooth a stray hair from Nessa's face, tucks it behind her ear. "The doctors say — Well, you know what the doctors say. They've said it all before. Your dad, he's always been stronger than they think." The brightness in her voice flickers like the porch light.

"But, I mean . . ." Nessa says, pulling at her hair, messing it. "Stomach? He barely made it through prostate."

Something tightens around Molly's mouth. "Yes, well. He's beaten all the others, hasn't he?"

Nessa studies her for a moment, then draws Molly into her arms. "Oh, Mom."

CHAPTER NINE:
NESSA

I have no idea how to comfort my mother. She feels like a reed in my arms, thin and fragile. I scramble for the words she's always used to calm or soothe, but all I can think is, *He's dying. Again.*

I catch Daniel's eye over her shuddering shoulder. He shifts around on the stair and reaches for the can of paint I'd left there. Though I know I should, I can't do this alone.

"Here, come sit on the steps with us a minute," I say. His eyes widen a little, but he puts out a hand to help her sit down next to him.

She surveys the porch behind us, sighs, and says, "I keep meaning to find new porch chairs now those old ones have broken."

I laugh, because of course that's what she'd say, and the sound is harsh in the night. Mom leans her head on my shoulder, barely touching me.

On the night before I left for college, I walked up to my parents' closed door to ask what time we'd be leaving. I stopped short when I heard the rhythm of her murmurs. "Don't cry, Sam," she was saying. "Nessa will be just fine. She'll be great. She'll be perfect, I know it. Now, are you absolutely sure you put the last of her boxes in the car?"

I take her hand in mine and run my fingers over the veins mapped across the back of hers, counting the ways they branch. "Have you told Charlie?"

She pulls her hand away, holds the fingers up to her lips, and blows her breath out against them. I can tell she's imagining a cigarette. "No."

"Come on. You have to tell him."

"You know how things are between the two of them. It's never been the same since he left. And when I try to bring these things up with your brother, he just tries to diagnose him from clear across the country."

I shrink back in the face of the bald bitterness in her voice. "But what if . . ." I can't finish the thought.

She looks at me and smiles the softest, saddest smile. "Even if things went south for your father, what do you think would happen with both of them under one roof?"

I'd called Charlie on speakerphone as I drove back home a couple weeks ago. "I think something's wrong with Dad. Really wrong."

He sighed. He always knew exactly which bush I was beating around. "So you're going out there to find out for yourself. Don't you think we should wait until they're ready to tell us?"

"To hell with that. Mom waited way too long last time."

"Okay, so you're going out there to do what?" He was really pretty annoying.

"To find out what's wrong, to be there for them. And I think you should be there, too."

Even as I said it, I pictured every holiday he'd come home for, the sharp set of my dad's face, Charlie's fingers coiled in his fists like secrets. He was silent on the phone, and the road murmured beneath my tires for a moment before he said, "Do you really think that would help?"

My mom watches me think. "You see? There's no point in forcing a reunion. At least not yet."

No point. No point? It's all I can think about over the next couple of days. How could that be? It's like neither one of them has any idea they're actually the same person, separated by twenty-something years and three thousand miles. Right down to the way they order dinner, scanning the menu, folding it, and ordering the BLT. I used to walk in on them on spring mornings, comparing notes about the previous night's Sox game over bowls of cereal with little stale marshmallows in it. I would scurry to pour myself a bowl of it and pretend to give a shit about baseball.

Whenever the conversation turned to the farm, though, Charlie ducked down deeper into his breakfast. I'd be the one nodding along to Dad's never-ending quest to live in sync with the sun. And soon enough, I learned what he was talking about. Farming became more than just churning through chores, arguing with my brother about whose turn it was to do the milking before the school bus came. I learned what it was to look at a freshly tilled row at the end of the day and know that I did that. Me. And I started talking back during my Dad's morning ramblings, his hands dancing to the music of his plans.

All that time, though, it was supposed to be Charlie. We all knew that. Every farm in town, run by the son. You stuck with it, because if you didn't, there'd be no one else to take your place. And then what?

Us girls, meanwhile, had a couple of choices. We could get pregnant in our childhood bedrooms, laughing into our pillows while our boyfriends snuck out our windows, then waddling around trying to get high school diplomas over our full-term bellies. Reuniting in the bright brutality of the local Stop & Shop at the same time every week to plan Fourth of July parties and meal trains for whoever got pregnant, sick, or laid off.

Or you could go to college and get a new life. Come to town for bonfire reunions between semesters and then less and less once you'd graduated and your real life began. The rule was, you got married to someone in a city and did something else, maybe teaching or litigating. Only when you reached your forties and started thinking wistfully about everything were you allowed to come back, buy a plot of land, start your gray-haired back-to-basics farm, and struggle to sell rutabagas from an honor-system stand at the lip of your driveway.

My decision — to go to college in order to come back, to do the work my brother hated — is an odd one. I can see it in the particular cock of eyebrows when people ask what I'm up to.

That's one reason why Shawn and I are

so close: he's never really cared. And I'm reminded of that lovely fact every time I climb into his truck for our regular drives around town.

"Where to tonight, Loch Ness?" he says as I kick aside the Dunkin' Donuts cups and Happy Meal toys littering the passenger side floor.

"I'm thinking over to the lake? Supposed to be a meteor shower tonight, and that'd be a great place to watch it all from."

"You got it. As long as I'm home in an hour." He backs up our driveway, gravel kicking out from under his tires as he accelerates. This is the deal he's somehow struck with his wife, Melissa: one night a week when I'm in town, after their son's in bed, he can go hang out with his female best friend. As long as he's back in their bed by the time she rolls over to turn the light off. I can't necessarily blame her; it's a little weird, I'm sure, to have your husband driving around town at all hours with another woman. I wish she believed what every gossip in town knows — Shawn and I go way back, and any romantic potential died a quick and painless death before it began.

The first few minutes of the drive, we just watch the headlights slice through the night. Then, eyes still fixed on the road, he says,

"Did you hear about Tim Mahoney?"

"No, what about him?"

"He died a couple nights back. Heroin. They found him in his car, parked in his driveway."

I start to make those nondescript mumbles people do when they don't really know the deceased, but then an image of him flashes before me, baseball hat tipped sideways and kind and humid eyes. "I worked on a group project with him once junior year," I say instead. "Smart kid. Jesus."

Shawn lifts his hips slightly off his seat, his foot pressing the accelerator as he shifts his weight, and runs his hand down over his beard.

I flick the lock on my door back and forth, once, twice, then again, *one two three four five,* and the clicking is a constant until we pull up to the lake.

"Have you figured out anything more about your dad?" he asks as I slide up onto the hood of his truck. He leans back against the front bumper and lights a cigarette. The smoke filters the moon. I wonder if Melissa wants him to quit.

"Yeah. Stomach."

He winces. "That's not good."

"No." We sit in silence again. Bats swoop down over the water, commas against the sky. When we were kids, teachers always frowned over Shawn's name on their attendance list. He sat in the back, huddled over his desk, never taking a single note or raising his hand. He could always tell just what was simmering under your surface, though. We met at recess one day, sitting on the sidelines of a four-square game, sifting through the grass to find bugs. We used to spend almost every weekend at this lake, avoiding the practiced chaos of high school parties, sitting and talking.

"What are you going to do?"

I drum my fingers against the hood of the truck, warm like an animal under my hand. "I don't know. I've tried to corner my mom again a couple times since I found out, but she either pretends everything's okay or looks like she's about to fall apart. She refuses to tell Charlie."

He nods, the tip of his cigarette bouncing. "So, you have to do it."

"I guess so. The last time I did, he barely blinked before rattling on about the possible pathways a tumor can take through the body. That's how he said it, too — not 'my dad's body,' but 'the body.' The weirdest thing."

"It's how he copes, with distance. Always has." He takes another inhalation of smoke, then says through it, "He still needs to know."

"I just wish he would come out here and see for himself. Maybe it would be harder with him here, but maybe not." We used to cross our eyes at each other at the dinner table and stick up for each other from opposite ends of the school bus. Charlie, with his green eyes always clouded, with his thin careful fingers, was the other end of me.

Shawn stubs out his cigarette into the sole of his shoe and says what I've been thinking all along. "Why don't you just go get him? Look him in the eye and tell him. He'll come then."

There are a thousand reasons I haven't done this yet, but the main one is this: "Is that selfish of me?" I say. "To bring in the one person who can break my dad's heart, and to force that person to come back to a place where he doesn't feel comfortable, just because I need him here? It seems like it'd create so much drama, and it'd be all my fault."

"Ness." He turns to look at me straight on, gripping my shins to steady me. "He's your brother. You all need him here."

A couple of days later, I see Daniel at the general store. As a general rule, we are stilted and stiff around each other in public, not wanting to give the impression we spend late nights together but not really knowing how not to, either.

I walk up behind him where he's studying brands of bandages and tap his shoulder. "Hey," I say.

"Jesus! I didn't see you there."

I smirk. All those years of sneaking around on other people's private property have made him jumpy.

"Listen, I need you to come by our house later this afternoon. There's something I want to talk to you and Mom about."

He glances over his shoulder down the empty aisle. "I usually minimize time at clients' houses during the day," he says.

"Oh, please. We're the only unmarried people younger than forty in this town. People will just think we're dating." I laugh as his face downshifts into a grimace. "Just come by at four, okay? It won't take long. I promise."

At 3:55, Daniel sits at the kitchen table, his hands clasped in front of him and his feet tucked behind the front legs of the chair.

Mom, following just behind me, stops short at the sight of him. "Daniel. Can I get you something? Coffee? Soda?"

He shakes his head, and I guide her to another chair and sit down in a third, planting my palms on the table. "Actually, there's something I've been wanting to talk to you guys about." I clear my throat, and it feels like I'm asking their permission. "I'm going to go get Charlie."

Mom deflates. All she says is, "Yes. I suppose it's time."

My hands start to shake, and I grab the edges of my seat. Daniel stares at me, his mouth drawn into one corner. I meet his eyes. "And I was thinking maybe you could help me drive out there. It'd be so much faster with two people taking driving shifts, you know?"

I can hear his double take. "Drive? But wouldn't it be easier to fly?"

It's not the question I expected. I thought he'd be worried about leaving his circle, not about how we'd get from point A to point B. The compelling arguments I'd come up with to get him to come along all whisk away.

"Nessa doesn't fly," Mom supplies, a line she's said with authority over and over again to protect me from unanswerable questions, so I don't have to explain. I nod, and Daniel slowly starts to move his head with mine, pretending to understand.

"But," he asks softly, rolling the question across the table, "do we have time?"

"Yes," my mom tells herself. "We have time."

CHAPTER TEN:
DANIEL

I couldn't really tell you why I agreed to it. I've never left a job midstream, not ever — and if I did, I wouldn't come back. Too many questions to answer, too much attention. And I couldn't tell you why she chose me, out of a town full of people who remembered what she looked like as a toddler.

But she did. Pick me. And it felt like it'd already been decided. I could barely get a word in edgewise, much less deny Nessa and Molly their plan. They schemed and cracked cans of soda while I sat there silently and figured out how I would cover things up. Make sure no one found the circle while I was away, pinned it on me. There was no way I could start pressing before I left, that was for sure. But what if the paint wore away in the meantime? I wasn't sure how durable the stuff was. On second thought, maybe I'd better hope it'd wear off. I didn't know if I could trust Molly and Sam to come up with an explanation if anyone happened by at night and saw the paint when I wasn't there.

"You should tell the Shannons the truth," Molly said. "You're helping Nessa retrieve Charlie."

Nessa and I nodded. We needed an explanation for the two of us going and coming back at the same time.

Planning it from the safety of their kitchen was one thing, though. I decide to wait until the next morning to tell Connie Shannon, when Earl's already left the house, wordless as always, to get things started in the barn. This is the worst part of every job, letting down a family that was counting on your help for another season or two.

"I see." She sits down in stages, setting her hands on the kitchen table before dropping into the chair. "You're leaving with Nessa. And are you coming back?"

"Oh, yeah," I say, "definitely. It should only be a couple weeks, over to California and back with Charlie. It'll be faster with the two of us driving. I asked if she could just take a plane, but Nessa —"

"Doesn't fly. Yes." She fiddles with one of her earrings. "Sam must not be doing well."

It's not a question, but still, I clear my throat. There's nothing I can say here that wouldn't get spun out and redrawn with her friends.

I go with what we decided on. "Sam can't know what we're doing. He might refuse to see Charlie or call him and tell him not to come, or — you know."

Her mouth turns up a little. "He is stubborn."

"And we don't want people in town to know, either. It might get back to Sam. The story is a big early frost hit Nessa's old farm down in Georgia, and they need everyone to come back and help. And I've always wanted to see what the farm's about, so . . ."

"You're going with her."

This is the plan: make Connie part of our secret to distract her from what a strange story it really is. Her farmhand running a cross-country errand with a woman who, as far as Connie knows, I've only met a couple of times in the grocery store. It felt a little ridiculous and maybe a little scary, watching Molly's eyes twinkle at this part of the plan.

But it works. Connie firmly agrees. And smiles while she tells me a story about when she and Earl were new in town and Sam and Molly were the first to visit, with pasta salad and unsolicited farming advice. "Earl and Sam were shouting at each other for a good thirty minutes, and I thought poor Molly was going to sink straight into the floor, but by the time they left that night, the two of them were slapping each other's backs like we'd known them for years." She laughs, shakes her head. "It's nice of you to do this for them," she says.

I look down at my lap. "I've become a good long-distance driver working like this."

"Yes, I'm sure that's why," she says, and I could swear she winks.

This might be the first actual wink I've gotten. Usually, a woman in town will tow me over to some girl after church or at a holiday party and proudly announce that we both studied science in high school, or like the Beatles, or breathe oxygen. Then, she'll slink off to "check on the cheese and crackers." And the girl, who's definitely been through this more times than I have, will either try to make conversation for a few minutes, or she'll sigh, shrug at me like I'm in on the joke, and chew viciously on her cheese and crackers.

When Claire was here, it was all different, obviously. We were a package deal, a couple making our way across the country, farm by farm, duffel bags stacked in the back seat. She would come with me to those parties and church sermons, touching my waist in a way that felt completely foreign and welcome at the same time. She would grin slyly when our hosts asked when we were getting married, tapping the edge of her paper plate of swiss and cheddar. We were in no rush at that point. Nothing was rushed.

For a long time, Claire and I were just making crop circles together, nothing more. She was my partner from the very first project I ever worked on. She showed me where to stand to get the best view of the field, how to distribute my weight on the presser so I didn't lose my balance. Every time she touched me — on my shoulder or my arm mostly, but sometimes on the back of my neck — I felt it leave a mark, a shadow. But even though I'd driven hundreds of miles with her already, I couldn't make myself cross the space between us.

One day, the daughter at our cover job found me at the kitchen table. It was hours earlier than she usually woke up. She might've even been wearing lip gloss. She made herself a bowl of oatmeal and sat down next to me. She started asking where I was from, how I'd gotten into farming, and I gave her all the vague answers Claire and I had come up with. She giggled at everything I said, even when I wasn't trying to be funny. She took a bite of her oatmeal, and the spoon took all the lip gloss off.

After a few minutes, she pushed her bowl away and said, "Hey, do you want to go see a movie some night with me?"

I swallowed a glob of oatmeal whole and coughed around it, my eyes watering. "Um, I don't know. I have to be up pretty early in the mornings."

"Oh, come on," she said, halfway between teasing and begging. "That's the benefit of having two farmhands, right? That girl can handle herself for one single morning. My dad could hardly believe his luck with you guys, two helpers for the price of one. And I couldn't believe my luck, either."

I snorted into my coffee, and she laughed. I sighed. "Okay. Maybe."

"Cool," she said and floated back out of the kitchen, past Claire, who was standing in the doorway. Claire, whose eyes were, maybe, a little narrowed.

That night, I was almost asleep when the door creaked open and Claire slipped in. She ran across the floor in her bare feet and slid into my bed next to me. Without a word, she kissed me long and deep while my hands gripped her shoulders.

"You're mine, you're mine," she whispered into my neck hours later. And I was. She rolled over onto her back and stretched her tanned arms over her head. "You know," she said, running one finger over the bridge of my nose, "I knew I liked you the minute I saw you."

"Oh yeah?" I said. I pushed myself up on one elbow to stare down at her face. She brushed her hand over my cheek. I leaned into it to make it real.

"Yeah." She dropped her hand back to the bedspread. "You saw things, right from the beginning — things no one else had the patience to see. You sat there quietly and looked, when no one else would."

My skin warmed. It was a first, someone making my shyness sound like it was a good thing. The best thing.

"Like what?" I whispered.

"Oh, you know. Like how much I wanted a coffee." She pecked me on the nose and tried to laugh it off. But all that night, while she lay sleeping beside me, I ran her words through my head, over and over. *When no one else would.*

On my way in the door, Sam catches me by the elbow. "Hey, Danny. It's real nice of you to drive Nessa down to her old farm like

102

that. You know I'd do it myself if I could. But the circle. Are you sure . . ." Worry slips back and forth over his face. He doesn't know how much I know, about why he counts his days so carefully.

"It's not a problem, Sam. I'll be back soon, and the circle will still be finished by the end of the month."

He grins. "Excellent. Well, don't let me keep you from your planning. Nessa's over in the living room." He steps outside, raising one hand over his head as he walks down the porch steps.

Instantly, Nessa's at my side. "I thought he'd never leave. Come on. We've got a lot left to do." She leads me into the living room and pushes me toward the same armchair I sat in when I first met Sam and Molly. She perches on the arm of the nearby couch, and I can tell she's almost succeeded in forgetting the real reason behind this trip, about the cancer.

"So, did Connie buy it?" She tips toward me.

"Yep. She sure did."

Nessa claps her hands once. "Perfect. Now she'll tell the whole town I've gone to help the farm in Georgia. I've been thinking about what route we should take." She hauls an old laptop out of the tote bag at her feet, steadying it on her knees as it whirs to life. "Usually, I take the back roads, but I think it's better to be efficient this time and just do the interstates." Her hair puffs out from behind her ears as she bends over the keyboard, and she shoves it back with one hand.

I edge closer to her so I can see the screen. "You know, for not much more driving time, we could take a more scenic route if we cut down south a little," I say.

Twenty-four hours later, I'm walking back toward the Bartses' with my duffel bag pounding against my back. Nessa is waiting for me, a suitcase held together with bungee cords lying at her feet. Molly walks over with a grocery bag bulging with what looks like about twenty loaves of bread, and Sam stands on the porch, holding the railing.

"You ready to go?" Nessa asks, tugging the bag from my shoulder. She tosses our luggage in the back of her car. Once Molly's nestled her bread between our bags, Nessa slams the trunk shut. Several paint flakes drift off when she does, and it's clear her car is pretty much rust and air.

"I figured I could take the first shift, if that's okay with you," she says.

"Yeah, sure," I say.

She turns to hug Molly goodbye, her eyes squeezed tight. She whispers something in her mom's ear, and Molly smiles at her, lips closed. As Nessa vaults up the stairs to Sam, Molly steps in close.

"Be careful with her, okay?" she murmurs.

It's an odd way to ask me to look out for her daughter, but before I can figure out a response, Nessa is jogging past me to the car, saying, "Come on. We have to get moving if we're going to make it to Connecticut by dinnertime."

While Nessa turns her head to back the car up the driveway, I watch her parents through her filmy windshield. Molly goes up the stairs to Sam, who pulls her close. She buries her face in his neck.

Road trips sound exotic, but the reality is that one highway looks pretty much the same as every other, no matter where you are in the country: rusty, dented guardrails, big strips of burned-out tire rubber, generic pine trees, a video clip on repeat. This particular trip is just the same except for Nessa's presence. She keeps rambling on about farming techniques, only stopping when she gets out of the car at the run-down gas station in Massachusetts. When she slips into the passenger's seat, she reaches behind her for a pillow, rests her head against the window, and falls asleep almost immediately.

And I can relax again.

Mom used to always tell this story about me to her friends over glasses of wine. I was eight, and she'd invited a bunch of my classmates over for my birthday party. At some point in the middle of the chaos, she took a step back to watch the kids clambering all over everything — and noticed I wasn't one of them. In fact, I wasn't anywhere in the basement, dubbed Party Central by my parents and scattered with bowls of popcorn and empty pizza boxes. She leaped up the stairs two at a time. Barked at my dad to see if he'd seen me. He put down his newspaper and glasses, dazed, and told her I'd probably just gone to the bathroom. But the bathroom door was wide open. He followed her up the stairs to my bedroom, where they threw open the door.

And found me, huddled under the covers with a flashlight and a book.

My mom, imagining me snatched away from their quiet house on a quiet street, said, "Daniel! What are you doing here, you little rascal?" And then, thinking of the nights she'd spent after work turning the basement into a jungle, complete with dinosaurs, fit for a bunch of second graders, "Don't you know your guests are down there waiting for you?"

At which point, I put my book down and calmly said, "They're having more fun without me. And I'm having more fun without them."

"And that was the last time we ever threw a party for Daniel," my mom would say. Her friends, most of whom had already heard this story before, would break into loud, tipsy laughter. If I happened to be nearby, she would run her fingers over my shoulder, like she was thanking me for the punch line, for the happy, normal story from a happy, suburban life. But I cringed every time I heard it. Part of me always knew I would ruin her plans for my life one day.

A few miles past the rest stop, I call Lionel. As the phone rings, I come up with a story to explain why the circle's on hiatus: it's a bad season for my host family, and I haven't had time to make it back to the circle.

"How's the Barts circle coming?" he asks right away.

"Well, actually," I begin, but then I glance at Nessa, and something about the wrinkle in her sleeping forehead stops me. "It's coming fine," I say. Lionel's sigh sounds relieved. My teeth grind at the lie. "What's going on with everyone else's projects? Becca and Jim?"

He pauses for a second, long enough for me to know that something's not quite right. "Becca and Jim just finished theirs up in the wee hours this morning," he finally says. "Henry and Will are starting to scope out a new lead, too."

I wait for more. Nothing comes. "And?"

"And . . . nothing." He's trying to sound firm, but he doesn't quite make it. "Becca and Jim have alerted me to a couple of concerns, but it's nothing we haven't seen before. Par for the course, really."

I'm about to say something about there not being much of a "par" in our world, much less a "course," when he clears his throat. "I'm glad to hear everything's going well in Vermont." My fingers clench the steering wheel like I could choke off the guilt. "We'll speak again soon, I'm sure."

CHAPTER ELEVEN:
MOLLY

With Nessa gone, Sam stops his humming and tabletop drumming, in mourning for her. It's always been this way, ever since she first left home. She leaves a wake.

At dinner that night, I watch Sam pick through his broccoli ratatouille. It was a complicated recipe, and I'd filled the dusky hours with the snap of my knife against the cutting board, holding my breath to get the measurements just right.

"Come on now, honey," I say. "You need to eat something."

"Don't push me, for God's sake," he snaps.

I ball my napkin up in my lap and run through the responses in my head. *Your sadness does not give you license to snap at me. I wish you'd listened when I asked you to wear sunscreen.* I think of that envelope, already ground into the floor of the truck, pulpy and brown from the mud forever caking my shoes.

Instead, I spin my wedding ring around on my finger, the plain gold snagging at my skin.

"Do you remember," Sam says as he puts down his fork, "how long it used to take Charlie to get a meal down?"

Of course I do. I picture Charlie's worried face, biting his lip as he studied his mashed potatoes. It was as if he feared his small appetite was a personal failure. He used to watch Nessa plow through her plate, his chin resting in his little chubby hand. "We told him he couldn't have dessert until he'd finished dinner," I say.

"And he would perk right up, say 'Okay,' and get up and leave the table," Sam finishes. He reaches for my hand, and I let him take it. This is a marriage: telling stories worn so thin with use, the other can see straight through to the end.

"All right, now. Quit sulking and eat up. We've got to build up your strength," I say.

He grimaces, then starts shoveling broccoli in his mouth.

Late that night, I roll out of bed, slipping a kiss into the palm of Sam's hand as he swats a goodbye. I settle myself into the living room couch before dialing.

"Just like clockwork, Molls." Maggie's voice on the phone is a sweet memory of swing sets and sleepovers.

"Yes, as promised. Have you finished dinner already?"

"Nah, don't worry about it. I have to finish this deposition by tomorrow, so I'm just grabbing a dumpling from the nearest takeout container whenever I look up."

"This is the injunction you're working on?" I do my best to sound interested.

"Yup. The logging case. So many legal doctrines to throw, so little time," she says through slurpy chewing.

"Good thing they've got you to handle it."

"Anyway, enough of that," she says, and I can almost picture her pushing back from her paper-strewn kitchen table and pacing around their apartment. "How's Sam?"

"Well." I consider lying and pulling out the euphemisms we use around town, but I think better of it. "He's terrible." I hear her suck in her breath. "The doctors found another tumor."

"No. Oh no. Shit. Where?" Anyone else would've scolded me for not telling her sooner, as if my husband's pain were something that belonged to the world.

"Stomach."

"Oh, honey."

"Yeah. I know. And we thought . . ." My voice hitches. I roll the edge of my nightshirt tightly between my fingers.

"Cancer's a real motherfucker."

I smile in spite of everything. Maggie was raised by her father after her mother died. He always smelled of pot, the only adult I knew who talked to us like equals. He taught Maggie to swear.

"Sam's trying to stay positive. You know him."

"How are you doing?"

"I'm . . ." I watch as drops speckle my lap, like they're surfacing from some deep place. "I'm a wreck. I can't keep doing this. I just keep thinking I should've been a better wife to him. I should've loved him, all of this, more."

"Shut up," Maggie cuts in with the stern voice I imagine she uses on her defendants. "There's no better wife than you. Sam knows it, I know it — hell, I bet everyone in your town knows it. Your mistakes don't define your marriage."

This time, I do lie. "I suppose you're right."

It was early in our marriage. We were living above Sam's mother's garage in Nebraska while we saved for a piece of land wherever we could find it.

Sam was helping out on a neighbor's farm, and I was working as a teller at the local bank. Every morning, we would sit down at the kitchen table, and his mother would cook us poached eggs with wheat toast cut into even triangles. And every night, Sam would pull me close to his chest and recite our future while his fingers moved across my bare shoulders.

I would stare at the ceiling as he snored, wondering when my life had become so perfectly boxed in. Maggie was campaigning for women's rights and would call me from pay phones, tripping over words, and when we met for coffee, her eyes shifted everywhere. Many of our girlfriends were secretaries or teachers; some were in medical or law school. My mother, who had worked as a checkout girl in almost every shop in town after my father left, placed her hands on my cheeks before walking me down the aisle and said, "Are you sure?"

I had shaken her off, annoyed. Sam was meant to be a farmer, and I was meant to be with Sam. This was our great adventure, just us two. I would figure everything else out later.

Lately, though, I had begun wondering if

this was well and truly it. The world had seemed so fresh and open, leading us anywhere and everywhere at once. Everywhere was, apparently, right here. I clutched a silent dream in my belly to start a small business of my own, to be in charge — of what, I wasn't quite sure. When Sam spoke at night of our one-day children, he rested his hand absently on my abdomen, his palm just above the spot where my dream was lodged. The walls were narrowing further and further.

I wish I could say that time has blurred Thomas's face and he has melted into the parade of people who have marched through my life. If I were an artist, I could still paint him, his sharp chin, his dark bangs, and his sad eyes. All the women I worked with were in love with him, of course, and you could always tell when he was making his weekly deposit from all the nervous giggling.

Not me. My marriage was a cage, I thought, and if it kept me from campaigns and careers, it also exempted me from ever needing to flirt with anyone else. So when Thomas came to my window one crisp fall day and slid me his deposit slip, saying, "Thomas Grossman," I looked him in the eye and said evenly, "I know."

He raised his eyebrows. "My reputation

precedes me?"

I snorted. "Please. You're the most eligible bachelor to walk through those doors. I've heard your name so many times, my husband's starting to ask why I say it in my sleep."

A dimple surfaced on one of his cheeks, and I realized my carefree not-flirting was skirting dangerously close to inappropriate. I clasped my hands behind my waist and asked, "Will the deposit be all, Mr. Grossman?"

"Yes, Molly," he said soberly, peering at my name tag. "That'll do it."

The next few times he came into the bank, he marched straight to my booth, a wisp of a smile curling across his face. We never exchanged more than the necessary words, with an occasional sentence or two about the weather, but the other girls hated me nonetheless. Their whispers shivered up my neck every time Thomas came in the door. On our lunch breaks, I sat alone on a cold stone bench, picking at the tuna salad sandwiches my mother-in-law packed for me.

And so, one day, as he approached, I blurted, "I wish you'd go to one of the others. Can't you see they hate me for this?"

His mouth dropped open. He slipped something back into his pocket, then spun on his heel and walked right back out the door. He was well on his way to his car by the time I realized he'd never made his deposit. Our manager would surely pin the loss on me.

"Wait!" I cried as I slammed through the door. Thomas turned slowly. "Aren't you going to give us your check?" I said.

He laughed, wiping his hair back from his face. Only then did I notice the rain, a bit of drizzle misting his glasses. "Sure," he said, "but first —" He placed his hand on my forearm. His hands were large and fine-boned, like a pianist's.

"I'm sorry if I caused you any trouble with your coworkers." He sighed. "I guess it was just nice to have someone who hadn't singled me out as prey."

I pulled my arm away without meaning to. "Modest, aren't we?"

He grinned. "My sister says I come across as moody and enlightened, when really I'm just depressed."

"Your sister sounds like someone I'd like to meet." To my horror, I heard my coworkers' giggles coming out of my mouth.

"Let me make it up to you," he said. "I'll buy you coffee on your lunch break —

tomorrow, maybe? Just as a thank you," he added when my eyes widened.

I thought about the pigeon that stared at me on my solitary lunch breaks. I thought about Sam, working in the rain, mud creeping up his pant legs. I thought about the other girls, pretending to count out cash while they silently seethed.

I wish I had said no.

CHAPTER TWELVE:
DANIEL

The sky is dimming as we pull into a diner in Connecticut. The headlights sweep across the puddles, cigarette butts, fast food wrappers scattered over the parking lot. Just as I turn to Nessa and wonder if I should shake her awake, she opens her eyes and smiles at me. "We here already?"

A waitress with an unnaturally high and perky voice leads us to our table. I glance at Nessa, who hides her mouth behind her hand. When we sit down and the waitress trots away, Nessa says, "Man. I wonder what she's taking."

I stifle my laughter, but it doesn't really work, and the old couple sitting next to us scowl while I open the menu. Must be ruining their quiet night out. The waitress comes back with cups of water, and I can't even look at Nessa as she takes our order and squeaks, "Okay! Those will be right out!"

Nessa rolls her eyes and says, "She's giving me a headache," digs through her purse. I snicker, but then something rattles in her hand, and over the lip of her purse, I can see a prescription bottle, familiar and orange. She pokes one finger into the bottle, pinches out a beige pill, slips it carefully into her mouth, sip of water. A practiced motion, routine.

And now I've got a headache, too, pressing behind my eyes. Please, please don't let it be oxy. "Um, Advil not strong enough?"

She raises her eyebrows for a split second. Maybe it was too bold of me to ask. "Oh, you know." She slips the bottle back into a pocket in her bag. "The doctor prescribes them. For my migraines."

But I don't know. At all, really. I suddenly wonder what I was thinking, leaving a project to head off on a chase with some girl I only just met. I'll have to call Lionel again soon and cross my fingers that my story holds up. I hope to God I didn't agree to this just because she watches my mouth when I talk like my words are magic. Just because her words ring in my head long after they're spoken. Just because of those eyes.

She clears her throat, and I look down to see I've twisted my straw wrapper into a tiny little pellet. "Hey," she says. "I'm not a pill popper or anything."

"Oh. No, obviously not."

"A kid in my class just overdosed. I know how nasty that shit is. How much it messes with your life."

Thankfully, the waitress chooses that moment to return with our hamburgers and french fries. The smell of meat and hot oil reminds me of how hungry I am. Nessa crunches on her pickle.

When we've finished eating, I toss my napkin on the table. "So," I say, "college?"

"Oh great, Twenty Questions," she says, smiling her half smile so I can't quite tell if she's joking. "UNH. Full ride. I started out as an English major, but in my first lit class, the professor kept saying 'Can you unpack that for us?' like her words were luggage or something and this was her home. It sure wasn't mine, so I switched to animal science." She tilts her chin up, and I can tell she's told this story before.

"And now you're out working in California, way on the other side of the country," I say, looking down at my water and stirring my straw.

She takes a sip of her Coke. "One of our seasonal interns in Georgia mentioned the foraging culture out there, and I had to see it. It sounds kind of ridiculous, I know, but people get really intense and professional about it, guarding their territory and all that."

"Plus, I bet it's nice to be close to Charlie."

She shrugs. "Every few weeks, I go down to San Francisco, and Zach cooks dinner for us."

"Zach?"

"His husband." She takes another sip, her eyes daring me to react.

"Cool. Your parents, they didn't mention he's married."

"No. They don't know." She sighs. "Charlie's convinced the real reason Dad won't talk to him is because he's gay. He came out to my parents a couple weeks before he left, and he doesn't believe that Dad would be so offended just because he left the farm. But . . ." She chews her lip, wiggles her straw wrapper back and forth on the table like a snake. "Charlie always holed up in his room studying while we all did the chores, and my mom would defend him and say we've all got our strengths. Farmers, though, we assume outsiders think they're better or smarter than us. Or worse, that they picture us standing in the middle of a field of wheat, proud to provide food for our country. Bread basket of America shit."

She braces her hands on the table like it's a podium. "What they don't show in truck commercials is that it's really hard work. And you do that work every day because who else will? And at the end of the night, you crawl into bed, and you're in so much pain, and just before you close your eyes, you think —"

"That there's nowhere else you'd rather be." The words slip out of me. For a second, I'm afraid I've stopped her, dammed up her voice.

But her eyes refocus on my face. "Yes. That's exactly it. Anyway. Charlie became one of those outsiders over the years. He chose something else. And that's always been fine with me and Mom — I mean, clearly, he's happier there — but Dad always wanted to share that feeling with Charlie, and he never got to."

"He's got you, though," I say as her eyes begin to fill.

"Yeah." She dashes the edge of her sleeve across her face. "Yes. Of course he does. Should we get the check?"

At the motel across the street, we share a room with two double beds. It's cheaper that way. While Nessa showers, I shove myself as far down under the covers as possible. I lie there, listening to the pipes clank and watching shadows move across the ceiling. The shower valves screech shut, and Nessa comes out in a towel and a cloud of steam. She makes her way over to her suitcase, tousling her fingers through her hair. She opens her toiletry bag and runs her fingers over the toothpaste, the bottles, whispering something. I see her reach for one corner of her towel, and I turn my back to her and close my eyes for good measure. I hear the towel drop damply to the floor. Maybe sharing a room wasn't such a good idea, after all.

I clear my throat. "Are you going to call Charlie? Let him know we're coming?"

"Not a chance. He'd tell us to turn right around." Her voice is muffled by the shirt she's pulling on.

"Okay, I'm decent," she says.

I glance over, but she's already tucked under the shiny brown hotel bedspread. She reaches for the remote, and the TV clicks to life. She finds a local news show, and at every mention of crime or violence or disease, she pulls at a chunk of her hair. I turn back to my side and let the news anchors' voices drift into background noise as I close my eyes. Soon enough, I'll be back in Vermont. I'll finish the circle and go find a new life near Claire. For some reason, the thought doesn't comfort me as much as it usually does.

"Hey," Nessa says, sitting upright and pointing at the screen. "It's another circle."

Sure enough, there's a woman clutching her mic at the edge of a field, looking confused and a little dismayed as a crowd of people mumble behind her. "That's right, Fred," she's saying. "Just this morning, a farmer in Delaware alerted us to a formation that appeared in his wheat field, seemingly overnight." She gestures behind her, and an inset of an aerial photo appears in the corner of the screen, three interlocking circles pressed into the greenness.

Becca and Jim must be psyched. It's not often the news crews spring for an aerial shot. And on their first solo project, no less. They're a quiet couple, married, just started coming to meetings about a year ago. Jim spends the whole time furiously taking notes. According to Leslie, who they'd been shadowing for months, the two of them mastered the methods faster than anyone she'd seen.

"That must be the guy who did it, right?" Nessa nods at the screen.

And then I see him. A man standing behind the reporter. While everyone else is either talking to their neighbor or staring at the field, he's looking straight into the camera. He's wearing a clean white shirt with the sleeves rolled up to his elbows and a loosened tie, and his arms are crossed. And he's almost, barely, smirking.

Ray.

Nessa's waiting for me to answer. "Be right back," I choke, and I race to the bathroom. I lock the door behind me. I fill the sink with cold water, my heart thumping in my ears. When the sink is finally full, I turn off the faucet and thrust my head into the water. Almost immediately, my pulse slows.

I was there for Ray's first meeting. He had been fired the week before from some sort of finance position. His wife was starting to lose patience with his late nights on the computer, filling the gap his job had left with online farming RPG games and forum threads. One of those threads had directed him to Lionel, and then he showed up all bleary-eyed, his T-shirt wrinkled. He sat in the back and stared at his hands. But he didn't stay quiet for long.

This must've been what Lionel was worried about, what he refused to tell me. Shit.

CHAPTER THIRTEEN:
NESSA

I startle awake in the middle of the night, and it takes me a minute to figure out where I am. That the night-light flickering in the bathroom doorway is not dawn in Vermont or the semi-ironic lava lamp in Scott's bedroom.

I was dreaming of Scott. He sat on his thrift-store couch while tears traced down his face.

I'm still feeling guilty about him, about the breakup call I made on my way to Vermont, not quite paying attention to his responses while I squinted at road signs. *We were just having fun,* I told myself. We crunched our way through the forest with our eyes on our feet, searching the wetly rotting leaves and logs for those telltale mushroom bumps. Nights ordering pizza and watching PBS through a film of his artisanal pot smoke. Our time together filled space. It had run its course.

They've always been that way, the relationships I find myself in. Even with Shawn.

When Shawn asked if I wanted to grab dinner the week before I left for college, I figured it would be just another night of drive-through burgers by the lake. The first sign of trouble was when he came to pick me up in a pressed button-down and khakis. I looked down at my jeans and T-shirt. My burbling stomach sounded like a warning. Things got even worse when he parked in the lot of the town's one and only sit-down restaurant, a steak house with a salad bar the size of a small sedan.

"This okay?" Shawn said before we left his truck.

"Yeah. Um, Shawn," I started, then coughed a little. "Is this a date?"

He studied his palms, resting in his lap. "Do you want it to be?"

I was about to say no, hell no, but then he looked up, and there was hope in his eyes. "Sure," I said. "Why not?"

It was a disaster from the start. We couldn't even figure out how to position ourselves around each other and almost ended up sitting side by side in a booth before Shawn shook his head and took the chair across the table instead. "Our waiter is kinda hot," I blurted before I could stop myself, the way I would on any other night with Shawn, even though the kid waiting on us was only passingly attractive, with a sprinkling of acne across his chin. Shawn smiled painfully. When he dropped me off at the end of the night, I walked up the path as quickly as I could and didn't notice that he was trying to escort me to the door until I was halfway there.

On the front porch, in the moment of truth, I bit my lip and looked up at him.

"This isn't working," Shawn said.

At last, I could breathe again. I laughed. "We're much better as friends," I said. *You know way too much about me* is what I thought.

"I'm not sure what I was thinking," he said. I gave him a hug so I wouldn't have to look him in the eye and see if he was bluffing. He patted my back, and I sighed. My boyfriends could only skim the surface of me. Dipping any deeper would never do, and that's why Shawn and I could not be a thing.

I shift to one side and am almost startled to see Daniel in his bed. His face is as bunched up as his sheets. What could he be dreaming about? I haven't figured him out yet. It might take me all the way to California to do so.

■ ■ ■ ■

The next morning, we wake up with the sunrise leaking into our room and get ready mostly in silence, passing the cheap granola bars I'd packed from home. Daniel takes the first shift driving. A few minutes into the drive, he calls one of his crop circle friends to check in on things. He clenches the phone and glances at me as they talk about the man from the news report last night and what it means. I flick the lock on the door back and forth, once, twice, three times. It's my fault he's here, not finishing his circle. Why didn't it occur to me that he might get in trouble for this? I want to ask him more, like it's another night out in the field, and tell him he can turn around and go back if he needs to. His face when he hangs up doesn't exactly invite questions, though.

It's not until we've been on the road for an hour and the sugar's pounding in my head that I break. I tap the window to crack the quiet, an opening shot. "That girl you used to work with, the one who taught you about making crop circles."

Daniel shifts his hands on the steering wheel. "Claire."

I wait a few seconds, but he doesn't offer anything other than this perfectly normal name. "You guys were together."

He pauses again, then pulls on one earlobe. "Yes."

"But you're not anymore."

He's silent. The windshield wipers squeak, sweeping away the fine drizzle on the windshield. "She was a high-functioning alcoholic." A muscle pulses in his jaw like a cornered mouse. "I used to laugh at all her Irish coffees in the morning. But then I started to notice. She would always offer to go check our progress or to man the tractor or something, and she'd pull a flask out of her pocket when she thought I wasn't looking."

I maneuver in my seat so I'm facing him with my feet pulled up, one knee pressed up against the dashboard. I can tell he wants to say more, maybe has even forgotten I'm here. I don't speak for fear of reminding him.

"Farming is dangerous enough when you're sober," he says.

"Drinking sure doesn't make it safer," I supply when his pause stretches on.

Daniel shakes his head quickly, erasing his words and mine. "It was more than that." The muscle pulses again. "I wanted her to be happy. Happy and healthy."

I nod, although he doesn't see me. His eyes are fixed on the road.

"I started taking her to meetings. I'd drop her off, and she'd act like she was humoring me. She knew she could blow our cover if something happened while we were working on a circle, so she agreed to it. That's what mattered to her more than anything. The work."

He tilts his head one way, then the other, the joints in his neck popping softly. "And it worked, at first. She was real quiet whenever I picked her up afterward. She'd work harder than ever those nights, so fast, I couldn't keep up with her."

He smiles a little, and I try to picture it, this guy with his intense focus, with his shoulders tensed up to his ears all night in the cornfield. Did he laugh with Claire, catching his voice in one hand so it wouldn't reach the sleeping houses beyond?

"She got her six-month chip, and then it was time for us to move. They had an AA group in the new town, too, but Claire said she was fine, didn't need to stand up in a room of strangers and tell them about her first beer when she was fourteen. And I believed her. This one night, she kept pushing and pushing, and we worked for hours planning out our pattern. We snuck back into our cover job's house like always, to grab an hour or so of sleep. And when I woke up, she was gone." His voice stops short, like a radio flipped off in the middle of a song.

I can't watch his face fall apart. I straighten out in my seat and lean my forehead against the window.

We pass an exit on the freeway, and there's a man standing by the on-ramp, his thumb held out halfheartedly. The wind from passing cars blows over his muddy features and through his hair. I wonder if he's doing it on purpose, hitchhiking in a spot where he can't possibly be picked up.

"She didn't leave a note or anything?" I say, watching the guardrail ribboning by.

"No. Haven't heard a word from her since."

I glance over at him. He is biting at a hangnail, chewing and chewing. I have no idea if he's telling the truth.

CHAPTER FOURTEEN: MOLLY

I hang up the phone before Maggie can ask if I've talked to Sam about the bakery, telling her I'm fine, of course she's right, it's not my fault, and I'll talk to her same time next week. I feel adrift without the tether of her voice. I should get back to bed, as sleep is like raindrops in a drought, something to be funneled into good use. Instead, I stay curled up on the couch, the deep silence of the house churning in my ears.

It was only supposed to be lunch, an innocent daylight meal between friends — acquaintances, really. That's why I didn't tell Sam. His mother still packed me a sandwich that morning, and I clutched the brown paper bag as I walked to work, each step a beat, *it's just lunch, it's just lunch.* By the time I got to the bank, the top of the bag was falling apart, shriveled with my sweat.

I checked the clock every ten minutes that morning. At 11:56, I sprang toward the door, certain I could feel everyone's stares against my back.

When I saw Thomas leaning against his car in the parking lot, my heart was a living thing, a rabbit scrabbling in my throat. It sank and died again when I remembered the last time I felt that way: waiting for Sam in the student union and watching him walk toward me in his cluster of friends.

"This was a mistake," I started to say when I reached Thomas, but he cut in with, "Thanks for agreeing to this. I'm still getting my bearings around here, and eating lunch by myself was getting old." And what else could I do when he opened the car door?

He drove us to his favorite café in the next town over, asking questions on the way about my job that I tried to answer as an ordinary person would, level as the plains. When the hostess showed us to our table, he touched his hand briefly to my shoulder.

He waited until we'd gotten our sandwiches to motion toward my ring finger and say, "You're married. What's your husband like?"

Relief spilled down my back. Yes, Sam. Here was something safe to talk about, a conversation between friends. I told him about the class where we met, weekend nights with him and Maggie. I told him about when he proposed our senior year, over shrimp scampi at a restaurant he couldn't afford, running his finger under the necktie drawn too tight against his throat. I told him about living with my mother-in-law, that, in truth, I didn't know who would be doing our laundry and cooking our meals if not for her.

And then I asked him about his family, just to be polite. His face lit up like a window on a cold day as he talked about his sister, his nieces and nephews. He could recite each of the kids' favorite foods, what they wanted to be when they grew up. At least one of them, I suspected, wanted to be like their adoring, adored uncle.

"What about your parents?" I asked mid-laugh.

He wiped his mouth with his napkin, draping it carefully back over his lap before answering. "They died in a car wreck."

"Oh, how terrible. I am so sorry." In that moment, I had never been sorrier in my life, watching the lines creep across this stranger's face.

"Me, too. But it won't bring them back." He cleared his throat, holding a fist to his chest. "I'm so glad I have my sister and her kids. They're my family now. Sometimes I worry I'm around too much." He looked down at his fist.

If Thomas were one of my girlfriends, I would've patted him on the arm and worked up the courage to fold him into a hug. I settled for, "I'm sure that's not true. It's impossible for them not to love you."

Immediately, I knew I'd said too much. What did I know about how his family felt? Thomas blushed from his neck to the tips of his ears, but he smiled a real, luminous smile. "You're right. I'm probably overthinking it."

By the time we finished talking, our cups held nothing but an inch of soda-flavored melted ice, and our waitress hovered anxiously around our table. We tumbled wincing out into the midday, drunk on new friendship and lost time.

When we'd reached his car, he said, "So, same time tomorrow?"

And I, not thinking, said, "Of course."

It went on for two months, those twice-weekly lunches. I told Sam I'd made a friend and left it at that. He was so pleased, he didn't even ask about her. The guilt collected on me like snow, but somehow, I couldn't find the strength to stay away. I didn't want to.

Then, one afternoon. After pizza, I slipped into his passenger's seat, and his face was so sweetly open, so simply happy. And somehow, I found my hands on his neck, pulling him to me. And his mouth was on mine, strange and right. Our tongues reaching for each other. And we were tearing at buttons and collars, fumbling at zippers, his lips by my ear.

We went to a motel room, I suppose, though the details are unfocused now. All I can recall is the stark white ceiling and the stiff, starchy sheets. Afterward, I turned away from him, feeling his eyes on my neck. I heard him shifting to reach for me, and I said, one last time, "This was a mistake."

He didn't interrupt me. I peeked over my shoulder to be sure he'd heard me. He was up on one elbow, looking at me, and I thought he might reply, but instead, he sat up rigidly, as if reciting the motions to himself. He eased out of bed and collected his clothes from across the floor. In the light spilling through the curtains, I saw a scar slashed across his back. I decided not to ask about it. I decided not to care.

"I'm sorry," he said to the floor, rubbing his jaw. "I never meant . . . well. I'll leave you alone now. Do you . . . need money for a cab?"

"No." My voice came out raspy. More softly, I said, "Please don't tell anyone about this."

"I swear."

I stared up at the ceiling and willed the tears blurring the edges not to spill down my cheeks. When I heard the door latch gently behind him, there was no hope for it. The sobs came in waves, flooding my insides clean. I let them come.

It was an hour before I could roll over and pick up the phone. There was only one thing I could think to do.

"Hello?" Maggie said.

"It's me. I've done something terrible," I managed before the next wave towed me under.

"Where are you." It was a statement, not a question. A command. At the time, she was still working in the next town over, so soon enough, she swept in the door in her trench coat, gathering my clothes. She perched on the edge of the bed, drew the sheets back from my face, and said, "This is what we're going to do."

That evening, when Sam walked into our

bedroom to shower before dinner, I was waiting for him, wearing Maggie's mascara.

"Hi, love," he said as he stripped off his undershirt. "How was your day?"

"I have the most wonderful news," I said, hoping the tremor in my voice passed for excitement. "I made a few phone calls and found a plot of land for sale in Vermont for just the right price."

Sam froze, then turned one degree at a time to face me, a cartoonish picture of shock that was supposed to make me laugh.

I forged ahead. "I know Vermont doesn't have the most arable land in the world, all those rocks and everything, but I've heard corn does well there, and you're always talking about buying a few dairy cows. We could even try maple sugaring if you like. And — what's wrong? Is it too far away?"

Sam sat down next to me on the bed and took one of my hands, running the pads of his thumbs over my knuckles. "No, of course not. You're right, it's a great idea. But are you sure it's what you want? Giving up your job and . . . well, everything?" He looked up at me finally, and his eyes were rimmed with tears. I realized with a great painful gulp that I had underestimated this man.

I laid my other hand on his cheek. "I'd do

it in a heartbeat for you."

He grinned then. "Ready to be a farmer's wife, eh?"

I smiled back. "Of course. Why wouldn't I be?"

CHAPTER FIFTEEN: DANIEL

I wasn't sure how much to tell Nessa, how far I could go while still keeping my eyes on the road. I decided on less than all of it.

It didn't do me much good either way. I can tell Nessa's getting annoyed with me and my unimpressive answers. But no matter how many rest stops she points out, I stay in the driver's seat. I need something to focus on.

At my first circlers meeting, that something was the scrap of paper that mysterious woman had given me, folded up into nothing in my pocket. I figured the meeting would be held somewhere dank and stony, or at least in an unmarked building. It turned out to be in a church basement, cheerily hiding in plain sight.

"I'm Claire." A small woman with bright-blond hair appeared in front of me, holding her hand out.

I scanned the room as I shook it, searching for that woman from the field. "Daniel. I'm going to that farming camp down the road, and —"

"Oh, you must be the one Zoe recruited. She's not here tonight," she said, "but you're welcome to stay for a bit if you'd like. The first part of the meeting is always open to newcomers. You have to become a paying member and sign the compact before we let you in on the juicy stuff."

I studied her face, waiting for her to burst out laughing and reveal it was all one big joke on me. She looked right back.

"Okay, sure. I guess I could hang around a little."

She beamed. "Great! There's cookies and coffee over there on the table, and you can grab a seat wherever when you're ready."

Following orders, I offered to get her something before stacking a few Oreos on a paper napkin and surveying my options. There were a couple of rows of metal folding chairs arranged in a semicircle. I picked one on the edge of the outer ring, behind an overweight man in a loose-fitting suit sitting next to a woman in a ratty T-shirt. There were small groups of people scattered around the room, chatting. I wondered if I took a wrong turn and wound up at a church council meeting by accident.

But then, everyone took their seats. Claire picked the chair next to mine. A man in a gray sweater walked up to the podium, his thick glasses reflecting the overhead lights. "Good evening, circlers," he said.

"Good evening," everyone around me replied.

"That's Lionel," Claire whispered, her words brushing over my ear, "the grand poo-bah of the circlers." Was she serious? That was his official title? Her eyes danced, and I bit the question back.

"Now, I understand we have a new observer with us today," Lionel continued. Suddenly, he focused his eyes on me.

Claire elbowed me, and I swiped at the cookie crumbs in the corner of my mouth.

"Yeah, hi, I'm Daniel. Good, uh, evening."

Lionel smiled. "Don't worry, Daniel. It's just our customary greeting, not an oath. And welcome! We start our meetings off by reviewing some circle forms and new techniques, then we have the closed part of our meetings, where we talk about our current and recent projects. Claire will let you know when it's time to leave. Sound good?"

I nodded, feeling the eyes of the whole room on me. I couldn't help but wonder if maybe he could've told me all this in private, before the meeting started.

"Great. Karen, please pass around the circle form handout. Today, we'll be reviewing fractals."

Twenty minutes later, I'd curled the photocopied handout into a tight tube and was crunching the end into my thigh. I couldn't believe how much crop circle making was turning out to be like geometry class.

Lionel was just launching into a hearty discussion on proper angles and footings when Claire poked me in the leg. "Yeah, this is the boring part," she whispered. "Meet me tomorrow morning by the entrance to your camp, and I'll show you why we do all this."

I told her I would, trying not to look uncomfortable as she nudged me. As if I was used to getting touched by shiny-haired women in crop circle meetings.

When my alarm finally rang just before dawn, I snapped out of bed to silence it. I scribbled a note to our camp counselor on the back of a receipt — "family emergency, be back soon," enough to let him know I was alive — and left it on my pillow.

I walked down the quarter-mile driveway of the camp to find a truck idling by the side of the road. Claire swung the back door open from her spot in the passenger's seat.

"Morning," Zoe said from behind the wheel as I climbed in. She was silent while Claire explained the plan.

"We're doing what's known as the Santa Claus approach," Claire said, turning in her seat to face me. I nodded, and she continued. "A bunch of circles close to each other in quick succession. Like the one you saw the other night — the one Zoe worked on — and now this one we're heading to today. It tends to throw folks off our scent and make them think there's aliens in the area or something. After all, how could one person be responsible for so many circles in such a short amount of time? Like Santa Claus, get it?" I nodded again. She grinned. "It won't do anything to convince the people who already know about the organization and that there's more than one of us. For those of them who think it's just some local troublemaker behind the circle in their town, though, it works like a charm."

Thirty minutes later, light was just starting to seep across the sky when Zoe pulled the truck down a dirt road into a thick patch of woods across from another farm. Two men were gathering up their wood planks in the field, and they waved to Zoe as they loaded them into their car and drove away. In the wheat, there was a Venn diagram of collapsed stalks, shimmering in the dew.

"Perfect. We got here just in time," Claire said, and I struggled not to read into her smile, the excitement in her eyes.

"I heard you made it to the meeting," Zoe said, her first words since I'd gotten into the truck. "Good for you."

"Zoe was the one who first brought me into the group, too. Her designs are spectacular," Claire said.

"Well. Shall we get ready for the good part?" Zoe brushed her hands together. I could hear the whisper of her calluses.

"Absolutely. Follow us." The two women walked down the road a few hundred feet. Claire's thick braid swayed with every step. They slipped back into the woods. I followed them behind a bush, where we hunkered down on our haunches, facing the road. I watched for a few minutes, but there was nothing but silent asphalt and, every so often, a bellowing cow.

I cleared my throat. "What are we —"

"Shh. Look, here they come."

Sure enough, a truck appeared on the horizon, engine growling louder as it got closer. It sped by the circle, and I thought it was gone. But just before the bend in the road, it slowed, pulled a U-turn, and eased back in a huge, mechanical double take. The engine stilled, and the door slowly opened. The driver stood on the strip of gravel between field and road, hands on his hips. After a few minutes, a decision. He vaulted back into his truck, slammed the door, and peeled out.

I chuckled hesitantly. Were we laughing at him? "That was sorta cool. Thanks, guys. I should probably —"

I started to rise, but Claire held up one hand. "Hold on. It's only just getting started."

I sank back down. A few minutes later, the truck was back, followed by two others. They pulled to a stop. Four men jumped out of each and lined the road. Their mouths open, they rubbed their jaws. The breeze carried a confetti of their words to us.

"Well I —"

"I can't believe —"

"What the —"

"Do you think —"

"Did you hear about the one in —"

Soon, they fell silent. They stared a few minutes. Then, one of them burst out laughing, and it was the perfect laugh, pure and clear in the new morning. Another one joined him, and the rest looked at each other, grinning and shaking their heads. And one of them said, "I'll be goddamned."

"You see?" Claire whispered, eyes fixed on the crowd. "Magic."

I saw.

When the men stepped apart to dial on their cell phones, Claire and Zoe rose and hugged each other. We eased back into the woods until we were back at the truck, far from the farmers' view. Claire threw her arms wide. "That was the best one yet," she said.

Zoe smiled. "I love it when they laugh."

"It was unreal. Thanks for showing me, guys." I was a little embarrassed by the earnestness in my voice, but Claire just linked her arm through mine as Zoe unlocked the truck. A woodpecker clattered its beak against a tree above us, and I concentrated on the sharp tapping. And Claire's arm, small and sinewy, roped with mine.

When we parked in front of my camp, I looked back and forth between the two women and said, "So, when's the next meeting?"

The camp counselor shook his head and ticked my name off the list on his clipboard when I stepped back into my cabin, but he wasn't paid enough to really care where I'd

148

been. I slipped right into an argument with my bunkmates over football players, and it was like I'd never left.

But all day, while we tilled the soil in the fields and flung cow pies at each other in the barn, I was picturing that morning. The men de-gruffed by disbelief, the circles dancing as a breeze brushed the wheat. And Claire, drinking it in like water.

When I drove back down the next summer, after graduation, my heart pounded all the way from my parents' house to Delaware. I'd planned it so I would arrive just in time for another circlers meeting — found Lionel's number where Claire had programmed it into my phone and checked and double-checked the place and time he gave me. I got there early, so I spent a half hour or so at the fast-food place across the way. I sat in the window, wiggling my chair back and forth on its uneven legs and eating chicken nuggets. I watched people file into the church basement, some glancing over their shoulders, some laughing and slapping each other's backs.

And then there was Claire. Her hair blazed clean against the church siding as she bent her head closer to Lionel, who was speaking into her ear. I crumpled the chicken wrapper in my fist and stood.

I pushed the church door open, and just when I wanted to turn around and leave again, go back home, Claire saw me.

"Hey, look who it is!" she said. Nobody looked. "You came back." She sounded excited, but then, maybe she always did.

"Daniel," I said.

"That's right, Daniel. I'm Claire," she said, and I didn't tell her I remembered. "Come on. Come sit with me," she said, towing me by the arm toward her chair, the same one as last time, back right corner.

"What brings you back here?" she asked when we were sitting. "You were here for summer camp or something last year, right? Is that where you're at right now?"

"Actually, I graduated. All done with high school. I thought I'd try doing this for a while." I hoped she couldn't tell I'd been thinking about her almost every night and most mornings, too.

She just smiled and bit into her Oreo. The crumbs flew into my lap. "That's great. We're always looking for new recruits. Plus, now I won't be the baby of the group anymore." Her smile grew, and I looked away, up at the ceiling.

"Would you —" I said. "I mean, do you think I could shadow you or something? Tag along?" It seemed impossible to even ask, but there was a brand-new duffel bag stuffed with old clothes in the back of my car, and my parents barely knew where I was. Maybe this was nothing in comparison.

Claire dropped the rest of her cookie into her lap. "I don't know. I mean, I'm not a great teacher. You really need someone more experienced than me to show you how it's done."

"Oh, come on. You seemed to know your stuff last time, and now you've got a whole extra year of experience, right?" I bit my lip. I'd practiced this on the car ride down.

Claire glanced at the podium and crossed her legs. "I guess I did just lose my partner. She got a full-time job offer she couldn't pass up. It's always easier to do this in pairs." She paused, and I held my breath. "Okay, sure," she said. "Let's do it."

I couldn't wipe the goofy grin off my face if I'd wanted to.

CHAPTER SIXTEEN: NESSA

By the time we reach Kentucky a couple of days later, Daniel's hands are claws on the steering wheel. I've tried sleeping through it all, but the silence is just too damn loud, and I'm afraid to turn on the radio.

"It's time to make a pit stop. Take this exit up here."

Daniel huffs out through his nose a little but complies. I bounce in my seat as we pull up to the Mammoth Cave National Park entrance.

"Have you ever been here?"

"No." Daniel scowls as he searches for a parking spot, but it's a relief to hear his voice.

"It's amazing. It'll make all your problems seem much smaller. I promise."

After the accident, I drove straight here from Georgia. While the tour carried on around me, I stood in the night-black cave and closed my eyes and breathed until I could no longer see the ambulance lights pulsing behind my eyelids.

Daniel doesn't need to hear that story.

He looks skeptical when he takes in the splendor of the brown-carpeted visitor's center, surrounded by retirees taking gray-haired selfies. Our tour guide ushers us down to the mouth of the cave, and the stream of cool air from inside hits our faces like an intake of breath. Inside, it's all darkness, a huge, gaping hole carved into the earth with steps curving down into it. And I hear him say, "Wow."

We step inside, and the stony walls arch over our heads, and my face aches from the grinning. We fall behind the pack of our tour group, stick our hands out over the guardrails, and run our fingers over the walls, wet like they're perspiring from the dense, damp air. Our eyes adjust to the dim. The cave swallows everything the spotlights at our feet can throw at it. Our hushed voices vanish into the darkness.

The tour guide's narration echoes weakly, explaining how the caves were first discovered. I step toward him, and Daniel's hand is on my elbow.

"Wait," he whispers. He leans his head back, face turned toward the stalactites dripping high above us. He closes his eyes. I can just see the fringe of his eyelashes, his throat moving under his stubbled skin. His neck is a road, his Adam's apple a waypoint, and I want to run my finger over it. I turn my head, embarrassed.

When he looks at me, his eyes are bright. "You were right," he says, and I tuck the words away. I duck my head and move first one foot, then the other, my shoes scraping along the uneven earth.

He lets us catch up with the group then and exclaims at all the right times, making thoughtful noises in response to the tour guide. Every so often, he touches my arm softly, brushing his fingers against my elbow as he points at a rock formation. I try to see what he is seeing. I try not to stare at his hands. When the tour guide turns off the spotlights so we can see what it was like for the discoverers, his hand trips down my arm. It lands, and his fingers are laced with my own.

I have no idea what the guide says for the rest of the tour. My thoughts are pulled to Daniel's palm, big and warm on mine. The air feels wet on my face now, too heavy to breathe. I can't remember the last time someone touched me for this long. I always pull away, worried about what it means, what it says, what I'll have to do to clean up after it. He doesn't seem to notice, down here in the dark. My hand is just something he's carrying.

The tour ends, and we climb back into the unforgiving sun. He lets go to shield his eyes. I feel strange and weightless. I tell him I'm going to get some snacks. He sits on a bench outside the visitor's center.

In the bathroom, I turn the sink faucet on as hot as it will go and let the water run through my fingers until the blood rises to just beneath my skin, like it's a membrane I could burst with one fingernail. I stare at my face in the mirror, but there's nothing new there, puffy eyes and sunburn.

Quietly, one at a time, I count. One. Two. Three. By the time I get to seven, I've almost returned to normal, my heartbeat slowed. A woman with gelled-up hair walks in the door, and I startle, spraying water all over her Grand Canyon sweatshirt.

"Oh no! I'm so sorry —" I pull stacks of paper towels from the dispenser.

"That's all right, honey. Don't worry about it." I realize as she leans closer that she was on our tour. She kept asking the tour guide personal questions and making him second-guess his life choices. "First date jitters, I see," she says, staring at my shaking hands. She smiles.

"No, no, we're not —" I say to the stall door as it clamps shut behind her. My mind whirls, brushing over and over against what she must be thinking. What did it look like, down there in the cave, when I was too distracted to see other people noticing? I take a deep, shaky breath and close my eyes. *It doesn't matter what she thought,* I tell myself sternly. *There is nothing there to see.*

Daniel is still sitting on that bench, staring off into space. I've forgotten the snacks, but he doesn't mention it as I sit down next to him.

I'm about to go back to the car and press my head between my knees when he says, "Claire was a lot more than an alcoholic."

He runs a bracelet between his fingers, something old and worn, something straight out of arts and crafts hour. "She was smart and hard on herself. She taught me everything I know. She would get so mad at you over nothing, and then, an hour later, she'd be writing you a five-page love letter."

I pull a chunk of hair out from behind my ear and start twisting.

He stares off into the parking lot again.

I say, "It sounds like you really loved her."

He shrugs, but a smile creeps in, wringing out my chest as it goes. "People used to ask

156

us when we were getting married. But the one time I got close to it, she asked if that was what I wanted, a wife and a house, someone to write holiday cards while I wrestled with the Christmas tree. And I said no." His mouth sets in a line, underlining the lie.

Two boys, brown-haired brothers, are outside the door to the visitor's center, waiting for their parents. They've found two sticks the size of their arms and are, naturally, using them as swords. Splinters of bark fly off them as they clack and jab, shrapnel that hits the occasional passing adult. Their mom finally emerges, stuffing change into her purse, and growls "Boys" without looking up. The two giggle, drop their weapons, and start poking each other instead.

"And you really haven't heard anything from her since you left?" I say, sticking my own finger into the wound.

"No." His voice is so final that I turn to face him again. This time, he's looking at me, only at me. "She's gone. She died."

CHAPTER SEVENTEEN:
MOLLY

The first time we went to see Dr. Cooper, I couldn't sleep the night before. My eyes grew drier each time the red numbers on our alarm clock changed. I had lists of questions to ask, notes to take, miracle cures to research, and I added to them with every turn Sam took in his sleep. I imagined him wrestling with the great black web of the tumor, and I needed something that would allow me to reach inside him and pluck it all out, every last sticky thread.

I had laid out everything we needed right by the front door: Sam's good shoes, a handful of the granola bars he liked with the chocolate chips in them, a fresh notepad, and several pens. In the waiting room, we sat with our hands balled tightly in our laps. Sam's foot tapped a manic, looping rhythm on the scuffed linoleum.

This morning, we slept through the alarm, set before sunrise so we could make the first appointment at the clinic an hour away. I offered to drive so Sam could nap, and after he climbed into the passenger's seat, he frowned and reached down at his feet. When he straightened, he held the envelope, pinched between his pointer finger and thumb as though it held an odor. I felt my pulse all the way in my temples. He flipped the envelope over and peered at the return address. My thumbnails dug into the vinyl flesh of the gearshift. I would, I decided, explain it all, how I'd only been curious, how I knew he'd want to support me even though we couldn't afford it, how I wasn't sure why I hadn't told him, except that I couldn't pile this on top of his doctor's appointments and treatment plans, the pills he'd had to take every day for the past few weeks to strip out the tumor.

He tossed the envelope over his shoulder into the back seat. "Those junk mailers are relentless," he said.

I kept my exhale measured, but I couldn't reply, and Sam stayed awake the whole drive, gazing out the window.

Now, he snores softly in the hard-edged chair next to mine in the waiting room. With him safely asleep, I flip blindly through a magazine about celebrities I don't recognize, its pages faded at the seams. I smile at the woman in the chair opposite us who's trying very hard not to cry, but I'm afraid it comes out as more of a grimace. At any moment, that's who we could become. And so, the envelope remains unopened.

Sam has already had his response scan this morning, and we're waiting for Dr. Cooper to give us the results. At our last scan, the one where they found the tumor, Dr. Cooper laid his sterile-gloved hand over mine and told me he was cautiously optimistic. For now, my fear is nothing but a kernel lodged in my throat. I can speak around it.

"Sam?" The nurse, Irene, appears in the doorway.

I elbow Sam in the ribs, and he wakes with a start. Irene smiles a smile as tight as her raked-back hair and leads us down the hallway. I take my usual seat, the extra chair for mothers and spouses, while Sam climbs up onto the examining table. The pages of my notepad now ripple with scribbled notes, and I'd nearly forgotten to bring it this morning.

The paper on the table rustles as Sam shifts from one leg to the other. I lay my hand on his knee. "I'm sure it will be okay," I say. "Remember what he said last time: optimistic."

He stills. "Hmm? Oh, right. I was just

wondering where the hell I'm going to find those parts to fix the combine." He sighs. "Just wish the harvest would hurry up and get here. Maybe the Cadburys will let me help out with the haying." His eyes light up, and I know he's itching to put his tractor to good use.

I am about to tell him I'm sure they'd love to have him when the door eases open and Dr. Cooper's head pops around it. "All ready in here?" he says.

"You bet," Sam says and tries to look comfortable as he leans back on his elbows.

Dr. Cooper walks over to his desk, pulling at the cuffs of his shirt under his white jacket. He perches on his little stool, a bird waiting to take flight, and I wonder why he hasn't met our eyes yet. The kernel grows.

He takes a deep breath, the button at his throat straining with it. "There's no easy way to say this." *Don't say it,* I beg him silently. "The treatments don't seem to be working this time around." He finally looks at Sam, and I can almost read the prognosis in his frown lines.

Still, I must ask, so I pose my pen above a blank sheet of paper. "What do we try next?"

He looks at me, and I wish he hadn't. "I'm afraid there's not much we can do. The tumor appears to be very aggressive. It's not responding to our usual treatment. In fact, it's metastasized. Surgical removal would be extremely dangerous at this point, and I wouldn't recommend it."

For a moment, I feel sorry for this man. What his days must be like, telling people over and over the one thing they cannot hear.

He keeps talking, starting in on what we can expect and what our new life will be like. I turn to Sam, but he is a plastic version of himself, immobile.

When Dr. Cooper at last stops talking, I look at my notepad and find the only words I've written are *palliative care.* An odd word, *palliative.* As if the letters themselves could smooth over those things that infect you. Round things out and carry you home.

"It's a lot to take in, I know," Dr. Cooper is saying. He takes his glasses off and pinches the bridge of his nose. It makes him look smaller. How could I have ever trusted so small a man to shoulder Sam?

"You two should go home and discuss this together. When you're ready to talk, please don't hesitate to give me a call."

Without a word, Sam walks out the door. The squeak of his church shoes against the tile is enough to break me. Instead, I get up to follow, scrabbling around for a polite goodbye.

Before I come up with anything, Dr. Cooper says, his voice lowered, "You should know, with how extensively this has spread, Sam's likely in a lot of pain. He'll probably want to go back to his farm like everything is normal, but he really should go easy on himself."

I nod. I don't know how I could even begin to enforce such a thing. "How long does he have?" I ask, more fragile than I'd like.

I can tell from the downturn of his mouth that he's already told us this. Perhaps he thinks this information should've been more than a faint echo against the walls. "It's hard to say. Certainly less than six months. I would hope more than one month."

He's staring at me, but I can't muster a response. I let the door slam shut behind me. I scurry down the hallway after my husband.

There is no one else in the elevator with us, and I'm grateful for that one small dignity as the green-lit numbers tick down. I reach for Sam's hand, and he threads his fingers through mine automatically. I can feel his pulse in his thumb, strong and true, and he squeezes tightly.

"We'll get a second opinion," I say, staring at our fuzzy reflection in the metal doors. The smudge that is Sam's face doesn't move, so I clear my throat. "Maybe we can go down to Boston. Or I bet Charlie knows someone who can help. He did that rotation in onc—"

"No." His voice is bitten and firm.

In an instant, I can see him, his thin-skinned head sunk into the pillow I just purchased for him last week. Wasting away in our bed. I squeeze my eyes closed tight against the image.

"You can't seriously be giving up," I say. "Dr. Cooper's only been practicing five years, and I know we used to say that was a good thing because he'd know all about the latest medical treatments, but I was reading about this new thing called immunotherapy, and he didn't even mention that, so —"

"Molly." Sam looks me in the eye, and there's a crack in his voice. "We've known for a long time that this thing was going to take me. I'll keep fighting if you want me to" — he squeezes my fingers again — "but please don't make me."

"You can't be serious," I repeat. The jaws of the elevator open onto the hospital lobby, and Sam drops my hand and walks toward the parking lot. I start to follow him, but then I pause, watching him get smaller and farther away. From a distance, I can see he walks with a small limp now, listing toward his right side. I wonder how long I hadn't noticed it.

CHAPTER EIGHTEEN: DANIEL

That last night, everything seemed fine at first. Claire and I lay in bed together. We had just finished the plans for our tenth circle, and the farmer had approved them, clapping me on the shoulder. I ran my fingers over Claire's arm and the ridge of the scar she'd gotten as a kid falling off a horse. She giggled a little and pressed her face into my chest.

"Oh! I almost forgot," she said, sitting up. "I got us something to celebrate."

I felt a little queasy as she leaned over and rustled through a plastic bag under the nightstand. Sure enough, she resurfaced with a sweating bottle of cheap white wine hoisted over her head.

"Claire," I began.

"What?" she said. "Ten crop circles is a big deal. In circler terms, we're practically common-law married. We have to commemorate it." She waggled the bottle back and forth. The liquid swished.

"Maybe we should consummate instead of commemorate," I tried, a cheesy last resort. I raised one eyebrow and ran my hand up her arm.

She pulled away. "Maybe later. I spent good money on this, so let's drink it." Her smile looked dangerous, on the edge.

"Are you sure that's such a great idea?"

"Please." She rolled her eyes. "A sip or two won't hurt. If it makes you feel better, I'll let you drink most of it." She reached back into the bag and pulled out a cork-screw, glinting in the moonlight.

"Claire," I said. "You can't."

She stood up. "I'm not a kid. Maybe you should find something better to do than babysit me. It gives me the creeps, you watching me."

The words burrowed in and found their target. "Maybe I should." She paused at that, as surprised as I was. I couldn't stop. "If you're so dead set on becoming a disaster all over again, be my guest."

She turned on her heel, shoved the door open with her shoulder, and was gone. I was supposed to follow her and bring her back, the way I always did. I knew she wanted me to hold her by the shoulders and remind her of everything she'd accomplished.

But I was tired. I was done. She had her exact specifications plotted out, and they didn't include me. So I lay back down and tried to sleep.

A couple of weeks later, I'd given up on finding her, stopped driving miles and miles every day, every night. I lay in bed, staring at nothing. I inhaled deep, picked up my phone from the floor next to my bed. I pulled up the websites for the local newspapers for all ten jobs we'd worked, her hometown in Oregon. And I started searching for her name.

I did this every morning for months, only letting my head drop back to the pillow when the results came up empty. The plans for that tenth circle collected dust and hair in their folds under the bed. I kept avoiding the farmer who'd wanted the circle, skirting around him in town until he finally got the message and gave up. When Lionel didn't call to check in, I wondered what he knew. I kept dialing his number, hanging up before it started to ring.

And then, one cold morning, there she was. Claire Marie Phillips. Twenty-four. Survived by her parents, Kathleen and Roger, and her sister, Elaine. Services to be held the following Friday at the family church in Oregon. The one Claire used to tell me about, with the priest who glared down at her when she squirmed.

I spent the next few days rolling these words around in my mind, stark against the glow of my phone screen. Every night, when I got into bed, I had no idea where I'd been or what I'd done that day. All I could think about were those words. They said she died suddenly and peacefully, like it was even possible for both to be true at once. An ideal death.

I knew it was more likely she died in a car accident. She always insisted on driving. It was how I found out. She started down the wrong side of the road one morning after she took a sip from her thermos. I had snatched the cup out of its holder as she swerved, to keep it from spilling. Her face went from indignant to afraid when I smelled the sharpness of bourbon.

Or maybe. Maybe she got into something deeper in those weeks, something harsher. Maybe she died of an overdose. I wondered if it happened in a snowbank — she always did want to go to Colorado. Or was she in the sun in California?

I could've looked it up, I know that. I knew there would probably be news stories. I knew the descriptions to look for in the police blotters. But I couldn't get myself to do it. As long as I didn't know the details, the impossible sentence in her obituary could still be true. It could've still been sudden. And peaceful.

At night, in my head, she was there with me, looking for new projects on her phone or draped over my chest with her hair on my arm. It was like someone split open my torso and emptied it out, organ by organ, over and over.

After about a week, on the morning of her funeral, my cover job family sat me down on their living room couch and told me that something was clearly going on, and they didn't know what it was, but I'd missed the last three feedings. They wondered if it had something to do with Claire. I'd told them she had to leave suddenly because of a family illness, but they seemed unconvinced. The wife suggested softly that I must need some time to cope with whatever had happened. She touched my knee as they told me they would welcome me back once I'd done whatever it was I needed to do.

When I was packing, I found a green woven bracelet under the bed. She'd made it on one of our longer drives, dirty bare feet up on the dashboard, one end of the cord looped around her toe as her fingers moved through the thread. As she worked, she had told me how she'd learned to make them at the expensive sleepaway camp her parents had made her go to.

I stuffed the bracelet into my pocket. Loaded my bags into my car, shook the husband's hand. I'd been driving for an hour before I realized I was going west, toward Oregon.

I stopped at a strip mall twenty miles outside her hometown and bought the cheapest black suit I could find. By the time I reached the church, the polyester had scratched an angry line into the back of my neck.

Stepping through those heavy wooden doors was and wasn't like every other funeral I'd been to. There were a few over the years that Claire and I had gone to because we didn't want to be the only people in town who didn't. We would stand in the back and watch as the parents dissolved over the course of the service, falling in on themselves. Claire would hold my hand, our palms glued together with sweat. When it was finally over, we would bust back out into the world and smile at each other. *Not us,* we thought to ourselves. We were alive and relieved.

This church was bigger and fancier than

the others we'd been in, but there was the same dust in the air, the same faces gray with grief. I could almost forget where I was except for the oversized photo propped on an easel by the coffin.

It was Claire, all right. Claire at eighteen, her smile stiff, her senior school photo. She was in a white shirt with her hair smoothed down. It might've been the most recent photo her parents had. She said her parents weren't really the type to whip out their cameras on Christmas. They preferred shiny, prepackaged studio portraits.

I stepped toward the back row of pews to find a seat and saw Lionel with another circler, Leslie, their outfits as stiffly new as my own. So he did know, then. Claire would've called him as soon as she'd left. Another hiccup for her to explain away, the circle always priority number one. And me a distant second. I slid in next to them.

The service began, the priest droning on about a woman he clearly didn't care to remember. I couldn't stop staring at her parents. They sat straight, shoulders square, her blond hair swept off her neck, his beard neatly trimmed. But as the priest began to talk about her new place with God, her mother raised one hand to her face and sank her head toward her husband, whose shoulders shook.

I clenched my hand around the bracelet in my pocket and pulled out my phone, found the most recent picture I'd taken of her. We'd just finished a feeding, and her cheeks were red and damp, head thrown back with glee. I spent the rest of the service trying to remember the sound of her voice.

As soon as it ended and people started to inch their way toward the front to pay their respects, the three of us slipped out the back door. I was glad for the rain on my face as Leslie sniffed and wiped at her cheeks. She turned to me and told me how she couldn't even imagine my loss, her eyes darting sideways. I thanked her, hoping that would be enough.

Lionel adjusted his glasses and cleared his throat. "Yes," he said, "take all the time you need. And when you're ready to come back" — Leslie touched his arm and started shaking her head, but he moved away — "we'll find a suitable circler partner for you."

The word *suitable* rang in my ears, louder than the church bells. I couldn't imagine a more unsuitable partner than Claire, with her impatience and her grand plans impossible to execute. But I didn't want to stand in a field in the middle of the night with anyone else. I told him no. I'd work alone now.

Lionel looked unconvinced. "Are you sure? It's a hard thing to do by yourself. Harder than you might think."

"Yup," I said. It was better than screaming, *What did she tell you? Where did she go?*

He turned to Leslie, who was still pleading silently with him. After a long beat, he sighed and held out his hand. "Well then. You give me a call when you're ready."

I shook his hand, found it cool and rough. My throat was closing up, and the only thing I could say was, "Thank you."

This is what I tell Nessa, my words echoing in the courtyard. I'm sure if I looked, there'd be tourists staring, wondering at their luck today to see some guy falling apart. I don't look. I'm holding the bracelet tightly in my fist, and Nessa keeps glancing at it. I loosen my grip, finger by finger, and lay the bracelet down on the bench beside me. The threads have turned a worn olive color by now, and they're fraying into nothing at the ends.

Nessa taps her fingers on her knee. "I'm . . . I don't know. 'Sorry' doesn't really seem to cut it."

I try to smile. "It's okay. Or it's not, but — I know what you mean." I nudge her with my shoulder. Somehow, I know my stories are safe with her. For a second, it's unsettling, how comfortable I feel around this person I only met a few weeks ago.

Before I can think too hard about it, she squeezes my arm once and stands. "All right, well, I guess we'd better keep moving, right? Can I start driving again?"

I fall asleep immediately in the passenger's seat and dream of nothing at all. I wake up to Nessa tentatively poking my arm. "I think you might want to hear this," she says and turns up the volume on the radio.

"— simply impossible for patterns like that to be man-made. The symmetry is too complex to engineer. Not to mention the way the wheat stalks are bent — could not be replicated by humans or any machine we're familiar with on our planet."

I settle back into my seat and smile. Dr. Sherman, noted crop circle researcher. At our meetings, we affectionately call him "the ringmaster," the person responsible for keeping the mystery alive. He's devoted his life to proving we don't exist. He's constantly publishing articles and doing interviews about the alien masterpieces, intro-

175

ducing the world at large to our work. Once, Lionel approached him at a paranormal conference in Tucson and mildly suggested that the myth could be even stronger if he formed an alliance with the circlers. The two students Dr. Sherman was traveling with — disciples or handlers, it wasn't clear — had to hold him back from punching Lionel in the face.

"Interesting theory, Dr. Sherman," the radio host says. "Actually, we've got somebody on the line here who's got a totally different story. Mr. Haley? Are you there?"

"Yup, I'm here, Stacey. And please, call me Ray."

My eyes snap open, and a sound escapes from my throat. Nessa glances at me.

"Ray, why don't you tell our listeners a little bit about yourself and what you told me when you called in this morning." The host can barely contain herself. She knows what she's about to unleash.

"Yeah, sure. I work for a financial planning firm here in DC. A big one, though you've probably never heard of it. And I know for a fact that circle in Maryland you're talking about was not made by aliens." He pauses for dramatic effect, and I resist the urge to rip the radio out of the dashboard with my bare hands. "It was made by me."

Dr. Sherman huffs. "Excuse me, sir, but who do you —"

"And that's not all." Ray clears his throat. "What if I told you there was a secret society of people all across the country responsible for making every single crop circle you've ever heard of and a lot of ones you haven't?"

Now, Nessa turns her head fully and looks at me. And she must not like what she sees, because she starts to pull over onto the dusty shoulder of the road. But just before she puts the car in Park, the host laughs. It's that loud, honking, demanding laugh that all radio hosts seem to have, and after a few seconds, Dr. Sherman joins her.

"Wait, wait," the host says. "I'm sorry. What? You guys, I swear this is unscripted. He did not bring that part up when I talked to him earlier. You're saying there's some underground club that just goes around making crop circles? I mean, I'm not saying I buy the whole alien thing, either" — at this, there's a brief hiccup in Dr. Sherman's chuckles — "but come on, man. What, do you have punch cards? A secret handshake?"

"It's true. You can look it all up on You-Tube," Ray tries, but now the host is laughing again. He pushes on. "Look, you want me to name names? I can do that. There's Li—"

"Whoa, hold on," the host says. "The station won't be happy with me if I let you list off people's names. It's a liability or something."

"Liability? That's bullshit. These people should be liable. Especially Li—"

The host hangs up on him before he can get any further, the dial tone droning until the sound engineer catches on and cuts the audio.

"Oops, I guess we lost him." The host finally recovers herself. "Dr. Sherman, thank you so much for joining us. And now, back to the music," she says over Dr. Sherman's reply. "You're listening to Stacey Monroe, Monroe's Moves at Four, on WKCD."

"Thank God they didn't take that seriously," Nessa says, turning the volume back down. "And hey, nobody's listening to this radio station in the middle of nowhere at 4:30 anyway, right?"

"Right," I say. Except that nowadays, there's a good chance someone will find the audio file and upload it to their online compilation of Hilarious Radio Fails. And Lionel is definitely going to hear it then.

I reach for the bracelet, old habit, but my

178

pocket is flat and empty. I left it lying there on the bench.

Chapter Nineteen: Nessa

When we reach Texas, a collection of empty sandwich wrappers and paper coffee cups rattles on the floor of the passenger's seat, and Daniel is no longer talking about Claire. He seems slowly to have returned to himself, chuckling at my stories and answering my questions with multiple words at a time.

For a couple of days, I braced myself every time he laughed or when we walked into a fast-food place, waiting for his hand on me, for that odd warmth to run through me. Whatever made him reach for me in the caves must be gone now, though. He has not touched me once. I was certain I didn't want him to, but there's a sadness in my belly, a nervous bubble as we pass signs advertising half gallons of iced tea free with every bucket of ribs.

Maybe, though, my nerves are more about Charlie than Daniel. Now that we're getting closer, I wonder if this was such a good idea. I probably should've called Charlie when we left Vermont to give him some warning.

Once, when we were in high school and Charlie was home from college on break, Shawn and I wrestled him out of bed on the night before his birthday. We'd come up with this plan the week before on one of our drives to the lake. We made him get dressed in an outfit I'd picked out: dark jeans he'd almost outgrown and a black T-shirt of his that I'd ripped when I borrowed it. He did all this while Shawn dangled one of the papers he was working on for class in an opened pair of scissors. Shawn stifled giggles as he whispered, "Do what we say, or Aristotle gets it!"

Charlie groaned the whole time, only stopping when we crept down the stairs and out of the house, obediently stepping over the creaky floorboards I pointed out. We hustled him into the back seat of the truck, and I tied one of Mom's dish towels around his eyes while Shawn eased the truck back up the driveway, headlights off.

It took almost an hour for us to get to the city, Charlie's pleas for mercy — or at least a location — getting more and more half-hearted as we went. Finally, we pulled up in front of the nightclub. I could barely stand still as I pulled his blindfold off, the bass line of his favorite song from his favorite punk band thrumming angrily through the crisp spring air.

He blinked at the band's name on the marquee. I bit my fingernails, and his face fell a little. He smiled weakly at me and said, "Cool. Thanks, Nessa."

"So, I know it's a school night and you've got finals and everything, but it's your birthday tomorrow, and you love this band, and I couldn't let you turn it down." It came out in a rush, and I gasped for air.

He raised one hand to the back of his neck, stabbing his fingers through the hair there, and I grabbed him by the elbow and towed him to the entrance. I plastered on my most winning smile as I flashed our fake IDs at the bouncer, but he was just a skinny college kid who barely glanced at us before nodding us in.

Inside, everything was dark, black walls and black floor. Even the stage had just a single spotlight on the lead singer's sweaty head. I couldn't understand the lyrics over his husky screaming and the insistent pounding of the drums and bass. Charlie was bobbing his head to the beat, and he walked with purpose into the thrashing mass of people at the band's feet. I watched my brother melt into the crowd and wondered for a second if I'd ever find him again.

Shawn poked my shoulder. "Come on. Let's find a spot at the bar," he said.

The songs all sounded the same to me, one long, loud mash, so it was hard to tell how much time had passed when I told Shawn I was worried we'd made a mistake, coming here. "I mean, I thought he'd be psyched," I said, drawing my finger through the beads of water collecting on the sides of my soda. "Maybe this just isn't his scene. Maybe he only likes the music on CD."

Shawn scanned the room as he drew a long gulp from his beer. "I don't know about that," he said, pointing over my shoulder.

I turned on my stool and there he was, Charlie, standing at the edge of the crowd. Another guy, small, light, and blond, was leaning in to yell something in his ear. As his mouth moved, Charlie's whole face lightened, unfurrowed, his eyes wide. He spoke back, his hands moving to explain something, and I pretended I could hear him over the band. He leaned toward the guy, and I turned back to Shawn, grinning.

"Guess I was right after all," I said. He

rolled his eyes, then laughed like I knew he would.

"So, have you told your parents about your plans yet?" I asked as the band played its encore. Shawn had been collecting brochures for out-of-state colleges and storing them under his mattress, looking up financial aid packages on the family computer when no one was around.

He tilted his glass to inspect the remains of his beer. "No. It's a stupid idea anyway. They need me here."

"But you can't do that. You need to go!" I followed his eyes to my hand, clutching his forearm. "Sorry," I said and pulled it back.

Shawn looked at me, squinting a little, and it made me uneasy. "Nessa," he said, "do you —"

"Get the fuck off me, you motherfucker." The scream drove straight through my neck.

I spun around. The people at the back of the crowd had turned away from the stage, staring at my brother as he stumbled toward the bar. Before I could register that he'd been shoved and that I was furious, Shawn's stool clattered to the floor. He held the blond guy by the collar. The guy's face was mean and twisted before Shawn punched it.

I flew off my barstool and toward the

fight, threading my way through the crowd. Finally, I reached my brother and touched the shredded sleeve of his T-shirt while the bouncer hauled Shawn away from the guy, who was now clawing and flailing back at Shawn.

"What the hell," I said. I couldn't see Charlie's face, but I felt him shaking.

"Let's go," Shawn said, ducking away from the bouncer's pushing hands and herding us out the door. The blond guy spat on the sticky ground as we left.

Outside, Charlie's face was blooming red.

"Jesus Christ. Are you —"

"I'm fine," Charlie said, yanking out of my grip. "Where's the truck?"

I drove home, Shawn asleep with his mouth open in the passenger's seat and Charlie staring out the window in the back. Every time I looked in the rearview mirror, I found another way he'd been hurt in the light from passing cars.

We were almost home when Charlie cleared his throat and said, "There's something I should tell you."

"It's okay," I said, meeting his eyes in the mirror. "I already knew." He glanced down into his lap, and I tried not to cry. "I'm so sorry, Charlie." I never should've dragged him to that place.

He looked back out the window and said nothing. Shawn stretched awake, spreading his hands across the dashboard. One of his eyes was already swelling up.

We waited until Shawn had pulled out of the driveway before we went back into the house. My ears felt plugged with cotton, dulling the squealing mating calls of the frogs in the nearby pond. I turned to Charlie, but he walked toward the door, his head down. I followed him into the house and watched him climb the stairs to his room, stepping nimbly over those creaky floorboards. He shut the door behind him, and I stared at it, wondering about all the things I didn't know.

Behind me, a cough. I spun around in the dark, hands flailing into a vaguely defensive position around my face. Before I had time to consider my next move, my dad's shape grew out of the shadows, his long legs extending from the living room sofa.

"Did you guys give Charlie a good time?"

"I — I —"

"It's all right. He needs a break. I won't tell Mom." He raised one hand in a truce, and even in the dark, I could tell he was smiling.

I collapsed onto the couch. "He got into a fight."

He stiffened. "What? Charlie?"

"Yeah." I couldn't say more. I wasn't sure how much they knew, and on certain things, my loyalty ran to Charlie.

Dad was silent for a moment. "Is he okay?"

I thought of Charlie's jaw working back and forth in the rearview mirror, of his hands clenched tight in his lap. "I don't know," I whispered.

He sighed. "Sometimes I worry about that boy. He's not a fighter, not like you." He patted my knee.

I wish now that I had told him there was more than one way to fight back, that we are, each of us, stronger than we appear. I laid my hand over his, squeezed it, and said, "We're gonna have to come up with a story for Mom."

CHAPTER TWENTY:
MOLLY

After the appointment, Sam pulled into the driveway, put the truck in Park, and said, "I'm going to go take the tractor around the fields, make sure you can't see the markings. Got to check on that rye in the back, too."

By the time I remembered Dr. Cooper's warning, he'd already kissed my cheek and left the truck. He walked up to the house and kicked his shoes off on the porch. A moment later, he reemerged in his work boots, leaning heavily on the porch railing as he walked down the stairs. As he moved toward the fields, my hand touched the damp spot on my face where his lips once were. My other hand reached for the glove box, but out of the corner of my eye, I spotted the envelope, wedged behind a seat belt in the back where Sam had tossed it. It shook a finger at me. *Shame, shame, shame on you,* it said.

I got out of the truck. Sam's shoes were exactly where he stepped out of them, as if he'd dissolved and they carried on without him. I ignored the twinge in my lower back as I leaned over to retrieve them.

I've been meaning to make a casserole for Allison Remy ever since I ran into her at the feed supply store. It's the right thing to do, the expected thing. So today, I find myself in front of our dusty bookshelf. Instead of pulling out a cookbook, though, I reach for a story to take me somewhere else. I grab a thick paperback of Charlie's, its spine striped with cracks like scars. A movie ticket stub drifts from its pages to the floor.

Sam has always kept all his ticket stubs. They used to collect in great, slippery piles on his nightstand, falling to the floor every time he slapped at his alarm clock. When I threatened to throw them all away, he started tucking them into books, sneaking one off the shelf and replacing it before he even took his jacket off when we got home.

I kneel down to pick up the stub. It's for the movie we saw the night Nessa left for college. Ordinarily, in late summer, Sam would go straight to bed after dinner while I washed dishes so he could sleep off one long day and roll into the next. That night, he laid his fork down next to his plate and announced he was taking me out. He wouldn't even let me clear the table first, just pulled me out the door.

Of course, as soon as the lights went down, Sam fell asleep, his head tilted back against the seat. The theater was mostly empty, so I was alone under the actors' stares. I wiggled my fingers in Sam's loose, warm grip and finished off an entire bucket of popcorn by myself. When we left the theater, I felt bloated from the salt and sated for the first time in months.

There's probably a ticket in every book on this shelf. Small slips of paper holding small, quiet memories that I will find in the years to come, wandering over to find one of Nessa's old picture books or a mystery Sam used to read over and over, gasping at the plot twists every time.

I stand up. Reach for another one. Pause, and then another. And tear them all down. I am an earthquake, a thunderstorm, a tornado, ripping handfuls of books from the shelves and throwing them to the ground. The tickets try to flee, fluttering from the pages in a gentle flurry. I bury them with more books until finally, the shelves are all empty, and I join the books on the floor, my face in my hands.

■ ■ ■ ■

The children were small, and I had just put Nessa down for a nap. Sam and Charlie were sitting on the floor together, Sam tapping his chin as Charlie detailed all the wrongdoings his plastic dinosaurs had exacted on each other. Sam heard me in the doorway and winked at me from over Charlie's head.

And something in my chest finally twisted and tore.

"Charlie, sweets. It's time for your nap." I laid one hand on his shoulder, the bones under his skin no bigger than a chicken's.

"Okay, Mama." He hugged me briefly and firmly, as if more for my benefit than for his, before scampering upstairs to his room.

Sam's eyes widened. "Well, we did something right with that one."

"I'm not sure we had anything to do with it," I said, sitting down next to him. Charlie was born quickly, obligingly, his eyes wide open and mouth shut tight. And then we were three, him and Sam and me.

"There's something I need to tell you," I said, staring at the thin, worn carpet.

"Okay, sure," Sam said when I didn't continue. His voice shaking a bit, he said,

"What is it? Did something happen with Nessa?"

"No, no." I looked up in time to watch relief clear his face. I didn't give myself a chance to think then, just pushed the words out like afterbirth. "I was with someone else. Another man."

He froze. He blinked. It occurred to me that in all our time together, I had never seen Sam yell, not at swerving drivers or stray plastic dinosaurs. I straightened my shoulders, waiting for it now.

When he spoke, it was quietly. "When?"

"It was years ago, before we moved here," I said quickly. It was eight years, three months, and two weeks ago. "It meant nothing, Sam. You and the children, you're all that matters to me."

"Now," he said. "We're all that matters to you *now.*" That something in my chest began to bleed. "Why are you telling me this?" His mouth trembled at the edges.

I knew my mouth was open only from the air scraping over my tongue. I clamped my lips closed. "I couldn't bear it, you not knowing, not anymore. I'm so sorry," I said, because I realized then that I hadn't said it yet. I reached for him.

He stiffened and wrenched away.

"What was his name?" he said to the wall.

"It doesn't matter, I hardly remember —"

"What. Was. His. Name."

I didn't recognize his face, all sharp corners.

There was a dried fleck of Play-Doh ground into the carpet, falsely blue and bright. I picked at it with chipped fingernails. "His name was Thomas Grossman," I whispered.

He stood, his knees cracking. I stayed cross-legged at his feet like a child. When I looked up, he was gone, the screen door swinging shut behind him.

I don't know how long I stayed there on the floor. The room turned golden with the setting sun, then darker with the dusk. I tried to imagine where I would go if he never came back, what I would do. It was like turning the key with no gas in the engine, turning and turning with no movement.

The door wheezed back open, and Sam stepped inside. His face was sweaty and smeared with dirt. He stared at me. "How long has she been crying?"

And for the first time, I heard it, Nessa's wails tumbling down the stairs. "I — I don't —"

He took the stairs two at a time, his boots thumping on the wood. I ran up after him, the bannister skimming under my fingers. He threw the door open, and there she was, clutching the top rail of her crib, her face red and raw, her mouth hinged open.

Sam ran to the crib and scooped her up with one arm. His hand smoothed circles into her tiny back. Her cries eased down to a shudder and a hiccup as she laced her fingers through his beard. He swayed back and forth, bending his head toward her and crossing his eyes. She giggled.

I backed out of the room. Nessa was born screaming, her face almost purple with it. They handed her to me with her hands in fists, and though I could barely see her through the fog of exhaustion, I knew she was perfect. When Sam eased her from my arms, she fell silent.

I stepped softly down the hall to Charlie's room and peeked around his door. He was squatting on the floor, waging quiet battles with his dinosaurs. He looked up at me with wide, worried eyes. "Are you sad, Mama?" he asked.

"No, Charlie," I said, and he hurtled toward me, throwing his arms around my knees. "Everything is just fine."

"I changed Nessa's diaper," Sam said behind me. When I looked up, he was already gone, his footsteps echoing down the stairwell.

I unlaced Charlie's arms and sent him back to his toys before I followed Sam down. He stood in the kitchen, his hands on the counter, staring out the window.

"Sam, I —"

"Don't," he said. He did not turn around.

It was like that for three days, hot anger radiating from him every time I stepped near him. He smiled for the kids, holding Nessa close and listening patiently to Charlie's stories. He would not look at me. I moved a pillow and a blanket down to the couch without saying a word and lay there every night. I stared at the rust-colored water stains on the ceiling. *At least he's still here,* I told myself and picked at a fraying seam in the blanket. *At least he hasn't left yet.*

On the fourth day, I woke to find him sitting at the kitchen table, a mug of coffee cupped between his palms. There was a second cup steaming feebly in front of the chair across from him. I sat down.

"There was no one else?" he said.

I shook my head.

"And it was just once?"

I nodded. "Sam, I was just lonely and confused and lost. I didn't know that this was what it would be like, that I would love it this much." I touched his arm, and though he still would not look at me, he did not move away.

Finally, he turned to me, and I forced myself to meet his eyes, so painfully green. "I will forgive you. For her sake." He pointed to the bulky plastic high chair looming at the end of the table. "For both of them."

"Okay," I said and tried not to smile, tried not to cry.

I've made a mess, the books flayed open, the tickets scattered. With the bookshelf empty, I can see the cobwebs stretched in its corners. Sam will be back any minute now from his morning rounds. I reach for a stub, this one for a movie we saw just last week, when all we felt was so much promise. I lay it in an open book, slap it shut, and slide it back onto the shelf. And begin again.

We eat dinner in silence, our silverware scraping and clicking against our plates. Sam pauses every once in a while to stare over my shoulder and out the window, chewing slowly. I can't think of anything to say.

A knock comes at the door. Sam glances up as I push back from the table. It's possible he smiles, but I turn away before I can see. The knock comes again, more tentative this time, a tapping of fingertips as I reach for the doorknob.

"Yes," I say loudly through the closed door, then, pulling it open, "What is it?"

Lisa Zinke stands on the doorstep, her hand slightly raised, looking somehow surprised to find us there. She's wearing a T-shirt advertising some small local brewery, and their big golden retriever lunges toward our driveway from the end of the leash in her hand. The Zinkes are one of the few summer families in Munsen, driving in from Manhattan every June to rent the Mc-Manns' old farmhouse.

She collects herself, tucking some hair behind her ear. "Oh, hi, Molly," she says. "I hope this isn't an awkward question." She stops, and I clutch the edge of the door. She knows, somehow, about Sam. Maybe she saw him walking through the fields today and could tell from the slope of his spine what was amiss.

"I was walking by with Henry here. I usually take the main roads, but I figured we'd try a different route," she continues. As if on cue, the dog snaps at a passing gnat, his teeth clacking shut. I blink against the zinging of my thoughts. "He stopped to go potty at the edge of your field — sorry about that,

197

but no permanent damage, I'm sure. So, anyway, I was standing there staring into your field — off in the distance, you know, not anything creepy."

A mosquito bites my ankle, and I brush at the sting with my other foot. Now that it's clear this isn't about Sam, I want to beg this woman to get to her point.

"Anyway, I couldn't help but notice there are some weird-looking sort of glowing dots out in your field, and I was wondering if you knew they were there and also what they are?"

I freeze, the toes of one foot pressed against my ankle bone. The circle markings. Now that Lisa's finished, she stands there with her head slightly tilted to the side, the perfect picture of honest curiosity. I consider telling the truth: that my husband hatched an eccentric plan and is carrying it through, despite the many other things on our plate. Perhaps she would find it funny, in a small-town sort of way, and we could lean toward each other from either side of the threshold and laugh.

"That's a good question, Lisa."

Sam's voice startles me, and I turn to see him lumbering toward us. He shoots me a glance that begs me to play along. I step to one side to make room for him.

"Have you heard about the cutworms we've been dealing with out in the cornfields this year?"

Lisa nods eagerly and steps closer, one hand on the doorjamb.

"They're nasty things, but I hate spraying for them, so I thought I'd try something new. See, I've been painting my stalks at the first sign of damage, and I'm hoping to find some sort of pattern to where they pop up."

"Ah," Lisa says, her face bright. "And the paint is glow-in-the-dark, it looks like? So you can see it at night?"

"That's right," he crows, and she looks like she's won a trophy.

I smuggle a smile behind one hand. This is an absurd story, a strategy that would never work on a full-scale working farm. Lisa is all too willing to believe it, though. By the time the crop circle is finished, she will be gone, and this will become one of the charming rural stories she tells her friends back home. Sam steps outside to scratch Henry behind his ears and ask her how her summer's going. I touch his shoulder as he passes and close the door gently behind him.

CHAPTER TWENTY-ONE: DANIEL

We pass through Nevada, billboards for casinos sprouting up from the desert. Nessa curls and uncurls herself, legs folding and unfolding, shifting back and forth. By the time we get to California, she crouches with her feet under her, tapping a quick, steady beat on the window. At night, the sheets and comforters rustle for hours on her double bed. She apologizes in loud whispers whenever I clear my throat or show any other signs of life.

"Things you should know about Charlie," she says now, drumming on the steering wheel in that same rhythm. She turns her head to make sure I'm listening, and I scan the road for oncoming traffic. "He can be kind of standoffish. Usually Zach does most of the talking. God help you if something vaguely medical comes up, though. That's the only time he'll really talk your ear off."

She rattles on. Really, I'm listening, but as

I stare out the window, all I can think about is Sam's circle. On cue, my phone starts buzzing, Lionel's number scrolling across the screen for the third time today. I hit Ignore again. This trip was a huge mistake. I was supposed to finish marking the circle within a couple of weeks and then do all the pressing right away, in one night, before anyone noticed the markings. That was the process I agreed to with Lionel when I said I'd be doing it alone. Has anybody seen the markings yet? Have they wondered why some of Sam's cornstalks look a little off? Are they talking about it?

Uneasily, I think of our last circlers meeting. It was two months ago, in Ohio, yet another church basement. It'd been a slow season for us, so almost everyone was there. The overhead fan couldn't keep up with the accumulated heat of all thirty-five of us. Becca was sitting next to me, the evening agenda folded accordion-style into a fan, flapping frantically at her face. In front of me, the Mason twins were arguing with Wilson Davis, a retired lawyer who was spending his golden years as a circler, combining his two biggest hobbies: dirt and geometry. The twins were fresh out of college, and no one knew exactly where they were from or what their long-term plans were. What we did know about them was that they actually believed in aliens. They became circlers so they could make their own evidence to support their theories.

"Don't you see?" one of the twins said to Wilson. "The CIA's instructions could only be meant for taking photos of UFOs."

Wilson smiled and shook his head. "I suppose there's no way for me to win this one, is there?"

"What a couple of morons," Ray said, just loud enough for them to hear. He was sitting behind me, leaning forward between the chairs. The twins glanced over at him, but they knew by now to ignore him. Ray had been showing up for some of the projects in the region for the past year or so. He never helped much, just asked questions from the sidelines and refused to whisper. "Who's really gonna hear me out here in the middle of nowhere?" he'd say.

The rest of the group had been talking about taking him off the email list. They wanted me to approach Lionel about it, because for some reason, they thought he respected my opinion. Wilson looked at me and raised his eyebrows like *See? See what we're dealing with?*

Luckily, Lionel chose that moment to begin, allowing me to ignore Wilson. "Now,

I know I haven't received many requests lately," he said. He leaned into the podium. "Becca and Jim have found a lead in Maryland and will be working with him this summer. It's their very first project, so let's all congratulate them."

Everyone clapped while Lionel smiled. But before the applause petered out, Ray began to speak over it.

"Here's what I don't get," he said. He had one arm slung across the empty chair next to him and held the other one lazily in the air, for show. Lionel had been avoiding calling on him lately, as more and more circlers started ignoring him and his questions grew more and more frustrated. "Why do we bother waiting for requests?"

Ray leaned forward, grinning. Becca's fan stilled. "I've been coming along to these meetings, even popping into a couple of reveals, and it's cool and all, but we can't devote months to this shit, getting cover jobs and all that. Some of us have day jobs, families to support." He looked around the room, but no one met his eyes. None of us had that, actually. Just him.

"I saw this field on my drive over, and it'd be perfect. I could just sneak in there one night with one of you guys, and it'd all be done in a couple hours. None of this messing around in the town."

"Circlers do not trespass," Lionel said, clipped and clear. "We do not break any rules. We do not want police investigations. We do not need notoriety."

"But it would add to the mystery, if even the farm owner didn't —"

"Enough!" Lionel slammed his palm against the podium. "We follow the protocol. Period. Now, does anyone else have any questions?" In the silence that followed, we were all aware of Ray's glower.

We should've seen it coming. What he was going to do with that anger, that resentment. Part of me is irrationally mad at Lionel. He should've bent the rules that one time, let Ray have his fun.

Because now, if someone sees those markings in Sam's field, if they figure out it was me when the circle's all done, if they've seen the latest viral video of the radio interview with the local lunatic, if Ray manages to list our names somewhere. Now it won't just be that one circle in Vermont that loses its myth. It won't just be me that loses face. It'll become another piece of evidence that the circle — that all circles — are made by us, by a finite group of people on the fringes. Nothing more than glorified social engineers, doodlers. I'll have put us all at risk.

We stop two hours from Charlie's place so Nessa can get a coffee. We sit at a rickety table inside the empty midafternoon café. Nessa's hands shake as she tears open a sugar packet.

"Nervous?"

"Not at all," she says, closing her eyes to inhale the steam. She opens one eye. "Well, maybe a little."

"You didn't text him or anything?" In my family, unannounced visits are not a good thing. My mom ends up spending more time fluffing pillows than actually sitting with the visitor.

Nessa shakes her head, no big deal. "He's probably expecting to hear from me, but not in person."

Every family's different. Maybe she's right about hers. "It'll be okay," I say, touching her arm. I remember the way her fingers moved a little when I grabbed them in the cave, like I was holding them back from something.

I put my hand back in my lap. She finishes her coffee in a few big gulps. "Shall we?"

Charlie lives in a rent-controlled apartment

in Haight-Ashbury, and even I'm a little nervous when Nessa parks in front of his building. It's more of a house, really, with cats and plants in the windows, flaking brown paint. She has to jiggle the doorknob and shove with her shoulder to get the door open, but inside, the light streams in through stained-glass windows, painting the tile floor red, yellow, green.

"Pretty cool, huh?" Nessa says. I trace the carvings on the wooden railing as I follow her up the stairs.

We stop in front of a red door, two pairs of running shoes lined up parallel beside it. Nessa looks at me expectantly. I smile and try to make it look reassuring. She takes a deep breath, tugs at her collar, and knocks.

For all Nessa's told me, I expect someone to open the door, grunt, and throw us back out. But instead, it's a skinny, olive-skinned man with dark hair, whose mouth drops into a mildly surprised O.

"Zach!" she cries.

"Nessa," he says. He hugs her close. "What are you doing here?"

"Just got back from Vermont and wanted to stop by on my way up north," she says breezily as Zach yells over his shoulder for Charlie.

She darts past Zach, who turns to me with

his hand outstretched. "I'm sorry, you are
. . . ?"

"Daniel. I'm a — friend of Nessa's."

"Ah." He grins.

I want to tell him that I only hesitated
because I'm working for her dad. I'm
someone he contacted to make a crop circle
in his field, not really your garden-variety
friend. Something tells me that wouldn't go
over well.

I follow him into the apartment, where
Nessa's hugging Charlie. He's got his
blond, curly head tucked down into her
shoulder, but he looks up when he hears us.

"Charlie," Zach says, laying one hand on
his back, "this is Daniel. He's a friend of
Nessa's." Even I can hear the air quotes
around the word "friend."

"Another one?" He looks down at her in
mock surprise.

"Oh, shut up," she says, finally letting go
of him to smack him on the arm. "He was
working on the Shannons' farm and very
nicely offered to help me drive out here."
She turns to me like she's asked a question.

"Got it." He pauses. "We've only got one
guest bed, so —"

"I'll sleep on the couch," I say hurriedly.
"Or the floor, or wherever. Anywhere's fine."

If this was a test, I've passed. Charlie looks

at Zach, who turns to me and says, "Well. Can I get you anything? Water, beer?"

Nessa and Zach wedge themselves into a beat-up leather love seat. She props her bare feet up on the coffee table to tell him about the caves, our perky waitress, a hitchhiker we apparently passed at some point.

"Can you believe people still do that?" she says as Charlie turns to me from the other end of the couch.

"I hope she didn't grill you too hard on the way over here," he says with a half smile. "Three thousand miles is a long time to be in the car with my sister."

"Oh, well . . ." I say, shuffling around for words that aren't a lie but aren't the whole truth, either. After the caves, Nessa hasn't brought up Claire at all, and I'm still not sure how much I should've told her.

"It's okay," he says. "I know. She has a way of figuring you out." He watches her throw her arms wide to re-create the hugeness of the caves for Zach while he laughs.

Charlie may have been the aloof person Nessa described when he was a kid. Maybe neighbors and teachers always marveled at how much more talkative and friendly she was than her older brother. But his eyes are so soft on Nessa and Zach that I have to look away.

Charlie and Zach insist that I sleep on their air mattress on the guest room floor instead of on the couch. "I have to get up at 5:00 a.m. on Monday to get to the clinic," Charlie says, "and no farmer wants to wake up that early on their vacation." I consider joking that no farmer can sleep past the sunrise, but I just lug my bag into the room after Nessa.

Zach's already unfolded the mattress onto the strip of floor next to the bed, and Nessa plugs it in. The motor whirs as the mattress swells.

"I'll sleep there," I say, tossing her pillow onto the bed.

"Nah," she says, snatching it back. "I like sleeping on these things. It reminds me of when Charlie and I used to sneak out and sleep under the stars when we thought our parents weren't looking." She flops back on the mattress to demonstrate, her arms flung over her head, pieces of hair stuck to the plastic with static.

"Well, at least put some sheets on it," I say, looking away from the line of white skin where her shirt has lifted. I pick up the stack at the foot of the bed, old, faded floral. I hand her a corner, and we stretch it onto the mattress.

"So," I say, "when are you going to tell him?"

She sighs, sits back on her heels. "Tonight, I guess," she says. "Or maybe tomorrow morning. I've got to catch him alone, you know?"

She looks down at her nails, picks at them. The skin around them is red and irritated. I come around the mattress and grab her hand before it gets worse.

"Hey. It'll be okay." The words sound even faker than they did the first time I'd said them, in the café. But she touches her head to my shoulder, a little lean.

"I know," she whispers.

CHAPTER TWENTY-TWO: NESSA

According to the Post-it Note on the Formica countertop, Charlie and Zach have already gone to buy dinner supplies. I hold the note up to Daniel and say, "Wanna take a walk?" I need steady motion to match the constant spinning in my head.

Charlie lives a few blocks from a park on top of a hill, so we walk in that direction, my lungs burning as we climb. We pass a middle-aged woman practically skipping to keep up with a tall, scrawny kid, her son, carrying overstuffed fabric grocery bags. She's talking as quickly as she walks, and the look he throws us is full of desperation. I try to wait until they've turned the corner to laugh, but I don't quite make it. Daniel shakes his head and grins as I bend over, the laughter clearing out my skull.

We start walking again, and I nudge him in the ribs. "Tell me about your parents."

"What about them?" he says, looking at

me sideways.

"I don't know. What do they do? What do they look like? Does your mom make you carry her groceries?" I shoot him a mischievous look, and finally, he chuckles.

"My mom's a therapist, and she likes to do therapy. I'm serious," he says as I raise an eyebrow at this, a woman with no hobbies. "On the weekends, she volunteers at a teen rehab center. You have to be careful what you say to her — she stashes everything in a file in her head. Her dad was a farmer, actually, but she tries to hide from that in her office. Unfortunately, she ended up marrying someone who loves to get his hands dirty. My dad's a science professor at the state university. Entomologist — bugs. He likes to take walks in the woods. At least, he did when I was home."

We've reached the edge of the park, and we follow the path to the center. A line of kids walk by, strung together, hand-in-hand, led by their skinny blond teacher. Two dogs fight over a stick, their owner watching as he talks into his phone.

"How often do you talk to them?"

He looks up at the sky. "Every month. Sometimes less, depending on if it's harvest season or finals period for my dad."

"I can't remember the last time I went

more than two weeks without talking to my parents."

"Uh-huh." He watches a woman wiggle her fingers at her baby on a blanket on the grass.

I bite my lip, hard. He probably didn't need a reminder of how he neglects his parents.

"I'm sorry," I say, tugging at his elbow. "I've got no filter when I'm stressed out. Or ever."

"Yeah. It's all right." He looks down at me. His eyes are deep and brown. Something passes through the air between us. The base of my neck tingles, electric.

I drop his arm. "Well, there's the view," I say with relief as we crest the hill.

"It's not the worst I've seen," he says.

I smile. In fact, it's pretty amazing. The street at the bottom of the hill is lined with gingerbread houses, the sides of each painted a different shade of pastel, like Easter eggs waiting to be found in the middle of the city. Behind them, the skyline is ribbed with office buildings thrusting their suited accountants and cargo-shorted techies farther and farther into the sky.

"Welcome to San Francisco," I say, sweeping my arm out. Immediately, the gesture feels fake, forced, but Daniel touches my shoulder, and we continue on down the path.

When we get back to the apartment, Charlie and Zach are in the kitchen, unloading boxes of pasta and packets of meat from paper bags. Charlie wiggles an eyebrow suggestively at me, but I roll my eyes.

"What's for dinner?" I say, opening a box of crackers they've left on the counter.

"Spaghetti with meatballs," Zach says. He pulls a bundle of basil out of the bag with a flourish that sends the fresh, green scent my way.

"It's his family's recipe," Charlie says. He leans in and plants a kiss on Zach's cheek, and Zach smiles back at him.

"I'll help." Daniel steps around the counter to peer into the remaining bags.

"And I won't." Charlie walks over to the living room.

I collapse into the couch next to him, the box of crackers still in my hands.

"First, we need some music." Zach turns on the stereo, and a slicked-over wedding band version of "Ain't No Mountain High Enough" starts to play. He nods his head to the beat as he walks back into the kitchen.

"Isn't this a cover?" I say.

"Yeah, and a bad one at that. He's got terrible taste in music, my husband." Charlie says the last word like a touchstone, like a prize.

I haven't seen them since their wedding at the city hall, where they stood with their hands clasped together and their eyes shining. We'd hugged goodbye outside the Chinese restaurant where we'd eaten afterward, and I told them I'd see them soon. The restaurant had been mostly empty, a Tuesday night Charlie happened to have off, and part of me couldn't believe the story, that he'd just woken up that morning — my last in town — and told Zach he wanted to get married that day.

I lean over so our shoulders are touching, like they used to in the barn while Dad told us how this cow or that was feeling today. "You look good," I say. "Marriage agrees with you."

"Zach agrees with me," he corrects. "But marriage isn't so bad, either." He's in a good mood. I have to tell him tonight.

"So." He turns to me, green eyes like mine studying my face. "Who is this guy, seriously?" He pitches his voice low, but Daniel is far away anyway, his head bent over as he dices tomatoes into cubes.

I hesitate. Daniel is so vigilant about covering his tracks, but I know Charlie

215

would never tell. I set the cracker box down on the coffee table. "Dad hired him, actually. To make a crop circle in their field."

He smirks but then stares at me when I don't laugh along.

"Yeah," I continue. "Apparently, it's a thing, making crop circles. They've got meetings and everything. Dad found a video online, if you can imagine that, him on the internet. I guess one of his farming friends saw the link and sent it his way." I tap his knee with mine. His eyes don't leave my face.

"Why?"

I shake my head. "Who knows? You know what happens when he gets one of his ideas. Remember the year he made that farm stand at the end of the driveway? He made, like, two dollars, and the sweet corn just sat there and rotted until Mom made him close it down." I laugh a little, but Charlie doesn't.

"Won't that hurt their yields, damaging the fields like that?"

"Daniel says you can still harvest the corn after the circle's all done." I glance up at Daniel, who has moved on from tomatoes to onions and is singing along to the music, painfully.

"Huh." Charlie sits back in the couch and

studies Daniel with narrowed eyes.

I need to tell him tonight. I need to explain why Dad wants to do this now, why he didn't even bother to ask how it would affect his future yields.

Tonight. Not right now.

We sit down at the table, Zach placing a wooden salad bowl on the blue-and-white tablecloth. Charlie distributes glasses of beer, and Daniel brings over a steaming pot of pasta.

"Cheers," Charlie says, raising his glass as everyone settles into their chairs. "To new friends," he says as he tips the glass toward Daniel, who lifts his own in reply, "and to family." He looks right at Zach as he says it.

Zach reaches over and pats me on the arm, and everyone digs in. The beer, when I sip it, is so bitter, it makes my tongue ache.

Chapter Twenty-Three: Molly

It happens quickly. I'm sitting at the kitchen table after I've finished the day's cleaning, a cookbook spread in front of me. It will have to be simple, I decide, just plain roasted chicken breasts. I sigh as I walk toward the fridge, making a mental checklist for my next trip to the grocery store.

The door flings open. There is Sam, his face pinched. He staggers to the table. I rush to help him, but he shakes me off. He collapses into a chair. It bucks back a little under his weight.

"Sam? Sam, what's wrong?"

He looks at me, then screws his eyes shut, shaking his head.

"I'm calling the doctor," I say. I pull Dr. Cooper's card out of my wallet. It's soft with wear, with the number of times I've worried my fingers along the edges. I can still read his home phone number where he'd scrawled it on the back. The phone shakes as I pick it up, and so does my finger, finding the numbers. As the phone rings, jangling rudely, the thought is faint: it's as if the doctor's words gave Sam's body permission to fold.

"Hello?" His voice is light with laughter. I picture him feeding his daughter, wiping mashed peas from his cheek where she'd flung them. Or sitting in his living room with friends, a glass of wine resting in his fingertips.

Sam sinks his head into his arms, folded on the table.

I clear my throat. "Dr. Cooper? It's Molly Barts. Sorry to interrupt. Sam just came in from the field and, well, he's having trouble staying upright."

He sighs, breath pushing roundly through the receiver. I bite my lip, ready for him to scold me for letting Sam work, but his voice is warm. "All right. I'm sorry, Molly. Here's what we're going to do." His words are so like Maggie's in that years-ago dim motel room that I could cry.

When I come back from the drugstore, Sam is still stretched out on the sofa where I left him, his legs dangling over one arm and his head propped up on the other. He's taken off his boots and placed them neatly on the braided rug, side by side.

"Dr. Cooper got you the good stuff," I say. I rattle the paper bag over my head with one hand while I lay the other on his forehead. "He said this'll knock you right out."

He smiles thinly. "Wait," he says, pulling himself up by the back of the sofa. He winces, and I reach for him as he shuffles toward the bathroom. I stand in the doorway, and he grips the edge of the medicine cabinet and eases it open.

He paws the medicine bottles down from the shelves into the sink, orange, rattling. Xeloda for the colon and stomach. Toposar for the prostate. Prednisone for the rash that came with Xeloda. Codeine for the pain. On and on, until the sink is full.

Then he gasps for air, his shoulders rising with it. He fumbles with a bottle until it's open. I do not move to help him. He upends it over the toilet, a great shower of pills plopping into the bowl like white noise. At first, I raise one hand to stop him, the waterfall of hundreds of dollars we've spent that he's about to pour down the drain and the strict disposal instructions he's ignoring. His face, though, is almost gleeful, and then I understand. He will never have to take these pills again. Save for his new pain medication, he can stop the rattling of the medicine cabinet. He can pretend, at least for a little while, that he is healthy again.

Finally, the sink is empty, the pills all dumped. He gestures to me, and I pick my way through the bottles now rolling on the floor, my feet catching a couple and sending them spinning out, ricocheting against the baseboards.

I half expect the toilet to be full to the brim, but it's just a sad little heap of pills slowly dissolving. A litany of side effects runs through my head — nausea, diarrhea, fatigue, weight loss — the way Sam tried to chuckle as he pulled out fistfuls of his beautiful hair on the Toposar. Schedules, eat with a meal, take with fluids. Sam reaches for my hand. It's hard to tell who is holding on more tightly. The toilet flushes with one heaving gulp. And they're gone, all of them.

In the silence afterward, I squeeze Sam's hand. "Dr. Cooper wants you to stop working and go on bed rest as soon as possible."

"Yeah," he says, "I know. I've got to keep going until I can't bend over and tie my shoes anymore." He's still staring at the toilet, at the water rippling and hissing in there.

"Yes," I whisper, an echo. "I know." He

looks up at me and smiles — a shadow of his usual grin, but a smile nonetheless. I think, perhaps, we can do this together.

CHAPTER TWENTY-FOUR: DANIEL

"These two, huh?" Zach mutters as he pours me another beer, then grins at Nessa and Charlie. Their heads are bent together over Nessa's phone, and Charlie's got his arm across the back of her chair. She's showing him the pictures she took of their old school photos, blown up on canvas in the hallways of Sam and Molly's house. A breeze eases through the open window behind them and lifts bits of her hair from her face as she laughs.

Charlie takes the phone from her hand, turns it so Zach can see his striped turtle-neck, thick glasses, gap-filled smile. "It's a good thing we can't have biological kids," he says. "Can you imagine the unfortunate-ness that would result if you crossed my awkward years with yours?"

Nessa's eyes meet mine from across the table. Zach stands up and walks behind Charlie, placing his hand on his shoulder as he leans in closer to the phone. Charlie reaches up and touches his fingers before continuing to swipe.

My chair screeches against the floor when I stand to gather plates and pots. Zach starts to join me, but I shake my head and wave him back to his seat, like my mom used to do. I carry the stack to their kitchen and start scrubbing. A film of bubbles collects in the bottom of the sink. Even over the hiss of their water pipes, I can hear the three of them laughing.

When I've finished the Tetris game of carefully fitting everything into the drying rack, Nessa and Charlie are tilting their chairs back, balancing them on two legs while she tells a story that apparently ended with a split chin and several stitches. I waggle my phone in the air.

"I'm going to go make a phone call," I say.

Nessa nods, her hands pausing mid-gesture before I walk out the door.

Out in the street, I dial Lionel's number. It's long past time.

"So, about Becca and Jim's news report," I say after reassuring him that everything's still on track in Vermont.

"Ray. I still have no idea what he was doing there, and I don't like it. Becca and Jim

224

are pretty shaken up about it."

I pause, hoping he'll say he's heard the radio clip and I don't have to break the news. No such luck. "There's more," I say.

"Oh?"

"I, um. I heard him give an interview on the radio. He claimed he'd made the circle. And that there's a secret society of people just like him. He threatened to name names."

"Damn it." It's the first time I've heard him swear, and it's sharp, acid.

"The host laughed him off before he could get very far. And it was a little local station in the middle of nowhere, no syndication or anything."

"Still," he says, "he's endangering all of us. He's become a threat, and it's time to take appropriate measures."

Appropriate measures. I know what he's talking about, although it's only been discussed at a couple of meetings, never acted on. In most cases, if someone gets caught or seems a little too chatty, they'll get cut out of the group, plain and simple. But if they're intentional about it — if it looks like we're all about to be exposed — the group will fight back. They'll leak a story to the press claiming that the misbehaving member, acting on his own, was responsible for several recent circles across the country. The story will include quotes from the owners of those farms saying they recognize the circler as someone they caught trespassing on their land in the weeks before a circle appeared in their field. All farmers have to sign an agreement to tell and change any cover story we give them, at any time, so it'll be easy enough for Lionel to feed them quotes to give to the reporter when she calls. And she will call, eager for the crazy kind of human interest story that'll help her go viral.

And then, instead of an interviewee who might blow the cover on all of us, the ex-circler becomes a trespasser. Who is now trying to defuse his liability for property damages by making up a story about an army of circlers — one the American public won't be fooled into believing, no matter how many times he tells it, now that they've seen the farmers he's harmed. And while the mystery and life will get sucked out of those farmers' circles, pinned to a run-of-the-mill prankster, it's all for the greater good. Because the next time a circle appears, it will be in the middle of that prankster's very public grappling with small claims courts. Leaving the town to wonder: if he's not responsible for this one, then who

— or what — is?

"This means I've got a good deal of work to do tonight," Lionel says. "I'd better sign off. Thank you for alerting me, Daniel."

After he hangs up, at first, I'm weightless. Lionel will take care of it. Of course he will. But then, the now-familiar fear comes back. Sam's markings can no longer be traced back to the group, it's true, now that Ray's claims will be discounted. Still, they're clear proof that his circle was man-made, and I left them out there. Just swaying in the breeze for anyone to see. If they're discovered, I could live with the excommunication. I could eventually get over losing Claire's chance at London.

But what if Lionel decides that's not enough? What if he leaks my name, too, as punishment for being so careless? What if my face ends up plastered all over the Live at Five news report?

My steps are picking up speed with my thoughts, practically jogging now. I slow to a stop at the edge of a dingy puddle and take a deep breath before dialing again.

"Hello?" My mom's voice is gravelly. She must've fallen asleep on the couch under a blanket of psychology journals.

"Hey, Mom."

"Daniel? What day is it?" I hear her get up

to check the calendar on their fridge. I can picture it hanging there, my mom's scribble all over the pages.

"No, it's not our usual day," I say as her fingers flip through the months. "I just thought I'd check in."

"Oh," she says. Then, with a buried smile, "Well. Let me go get your dad." She muffles the phone against her chest, but I can tell when she's climbing the stairs. There's confusion in my dad's voice when she wakes him from his place in front of the baseball game. I'm feeling pretty stupid by the time they've fumbled the speakerphone on.

"Daniel?"

"Yeah, hi."

"It's not the fifth yet, is it?"

"He just called to *check in,*" my mom says.

I imagine her eyes conveying the italics to him. I stifle a sigh.

"Cool! Great!" His voice is suddenly alert. "Did Mom tell you about her new client?"

She gets in a few minutes of details just vague enough to still be ethical, some college kid with an anxiety disorder and her parents, before my dad's curiosity gets the better of him. "So, where are you now?" he asks.

"California, actually. I'm helping out a friend."

"A friend?" my mom asks.

"Yup."

"Oh. But won't you miss the —" She cuts herself off, biting back her internal alignment to frost dates.

"We'll be back in time to harvest the corn, I'm sure. It's just a quick trip," I reassure her.

Silence. Then my dad says, "Oh! Keep an eye out for the valley elderberry longhorn beetle. They only live in the Central Valley, and they're beautiful, like little strawberries."

"Okay."

"And be careful." Against my will, I hear the hurt in my mom's voice, all the layers of things she wants to say but thinks she can't. The ways she wishes I could still be a kid, kept safe by the sheer power of her will.

"Yeah."

"Send me a photo of that beetle if you find one!"

"I will, Dad."

Silence fills the phone line for a moment before my mom says, "Well, we won't keep you any longer. We love you, Daniel. Be good." And she clicks the phone off.

She hasn't really forgiven me. We were chopping onions for dinner one Friday night. Every few minutes, she would reach over and pull my fingers from the path of my blade. I'm not sure what she was more afraid of: that I would never learn to cook for myself, or that I'd cut myself in the process of her teaching me.

"So, sweetie," she said, "how was your day?"

I thought about droning teachers, the guys playing finger football with a Cheeto at lunch, track practice. I shrugged. "All right. You?"

"I ran into Sally at the Compost Collective booth at the farmers market, and their members list is coming along, so that's great. And all my patients are dealing with the holidays just fine, which is a little miracle."

"Mmm." I squinted through my onion tears. Dad once told me all about the chemical compound in the onion that makes you cry. He drew pictures and everything, but I couldn't for the life of me remember any of it.

"How's Jess? Has she started applying to colleges yet?" Jess was my halfhearted girlfriend and automatic prom date, who thought it was her civic duty to drag me to football games every Saturday.

"Uh, I think so."

"You guys think you're going to wind up at the same school?" She kept her eyes on the pile of vegetables on her side of the board, but she smiled to herself.

"Umm. I dunno." I laid my knife on the board. "Actually, Mom, I was thinking I might want to work on a farm again." I had to keep the real work, the crop circles, a secret even from her. That was the rule.

"Okay." She chewed her lip. "Didn't you get enough of that at camp? You want to go back?"

"No, Mom, I mean . . ." I sighed. "I mean I want to do that instead of college. There's this website I found last night that lists all these farms across the country that are looking for help, and I thought it would be great to just go from one to the next for a while."

"For a while." She put down her knife and pressed one finger on its handle to stop the rattling of the blade. "For a while? Daniel, you've worked so hard in school, and now you're giving up on it? Don't you realize how important a college degree is nowadays? Don't you want —"

I shook my head. "No, Mom. I don't."

She stared at me for a beat, then said quietly, "I forbid it." She planted one fist on her hip and turned away.

The front door flung open. "Hi, folks,"

my dad said cheerfully. Then he saw her face. "Honey? Honey, what's wrong?"

That night, I drove circles through the town, music blaring. I stopped at a drive-through for dinner, but the french fries grew cold in the bag. It was well past my curfew when I finally pulled back into our driveway.

My dad sat at the dinner table, biting a pencil and staring at the day's Sudoku. I tried to walk past him without a word, but he pulled out the chair next to him and said, "Sit."

He pushed the newspaper away from him, then turned to look at me. "There's something you need to understand about your mother," he started.

"Yeah, I know," I said, frustration burning in my cheeks. "She hated growing up on a farm and wants me to do something else."

"No. Your mother loved her childhood." He studied me for a moment. "I don't want to speak ill of the dead, but you remember what your grandpa was like after he came to live with us, right?"

I shrugged. When Grandpa broke his hip and couldn't farm anymore, there was no one left to help him. His wife had been gone since my mom was little, and my mom sure as hell wasn't going to take over a dairy farm. So he had to sell it and move in with us.

He was always my favorite grandparent. When I was a kid, he used to slip me candies and a wink when he thought no one was looking. My mom would roll her eyes, saying nothing, and I was giddy over the unexpected sugar. But after he sold the farm, he spent most of his days holed up in the guest bedroom. At dinner, he would scowl at me and poke my skinny arm, telling my parents I was turning into a pansy-ass. The first few times, my parents made me leave the room so they could scold him, tell him not to talk about their son that way. Eventually, I started catching their eye and shaking my head a little, begging them not to bother. When he died, there was a little relief in my mom's face behind her tears.

"He missed farming," I said. "It was his whole life. I can't blame him if he was miserable without it."

He sighed. "That's not the whole truth. Your grandpa didn't sell the farm just because he was injured and couldn't work anymore. For years, he'd barely been getting by." He folded his hands and stared down at them. "We sent him checks, but he would return every single one. That farm was mortgaged to the hilt, and he had to drain his savings to pay for his hip surgery. When he came home from the hospital, the bank decided to foreclose."

I pictured my grandpa then, the way he used to fling me over his shoulder with one strong arm while I squealed. Even after he moved in with us, he woke up before sunrise every morning, grumbling over his weather radio while he drank his coffee. My mom would watch him from the kitchen doorway.

"We need you to understand this, Daniel. He gave everything to that farm, it's true. But in return, that place destroyed him. All his life, he struggled to make the margins work, to support your mom with what little they were willing to pay for his milk. And in the end, it fell apart."

I ran my toe over the grout between the floor tiles.

My dad placed one hand on my shoulder. "Your mother doesn't want that to happen to you. She worked hard to get you away from it."

"Don't you think I'm old enough to make that decision for myself?"

He smiled sadly. "Yes. I guess you are."

The whole call took less than five minutes, just long enough for me to circle the block once. I shove the phone back in my pocket.

Nessa's laughter falls out the window above me. I can see Zach crossing behind her and gathering her into a hug. I climb back up the front steps.

Chapter Twenty-Five:
Nessa

"I'm heading to bed," Zach says, stretching his arms over his head like it's a luxury as he stands up from the table.

"I'll be in soon," Charlie says after Zach leans in to kiss him good night.

"Nah, take your time." Zach smiles at me. I guess that's my cue to talk to Charlie. My stomach is already turning.

"Yeah, I'm pretty tired, too," Daniel says.

He squeezes my shoulder on his way past, and I can feel Charlie staring at me. I refuse to look at him.

He raises his glass, lacy with dregs of beer foam. "Well, I'm going to get another one of these."

"Me, too, please." I push my glass into his other hand.

He pauses. "Are you sure?"

Now I meet his eyes, feel my chin rise and jaw set. "I've only had one."

He closes his fingers around the glass and

takes them into the kitchen. I move to the couch and perch on the arm, its blocky IKEA corners digging into my tailbone.

"Zach's all moved in, then?" I say, shuffling through the stack of magazines on the coffee table.

"Yeah," he says. He hands me a full glass and sits down on the cushions. "It only took a couple weeks." He starts to tell a story about the group of friends banded together by takeout and beer who helped carry boxes.

I'm having trouble focusing over the pressure in my head. *Tell him. You have to tell him.*

When he pauses, I say, "Hey." He stops and looks up at me, eyes wide and waiting. The words are stuck. I stare down at the glass, growing warm in my hands. The liquid sloshes back and forth, and I place my hand over the lip of the glass, not wanting to stain his new couch. His new life.

"Is it Dad?" he says, and it's not really a question. His words from my drive home still ring in my head, asking what exactly I was planning to do to help, why I was going home, practical and true but not quite right.

I take a swallow of the beer and let it swish down my throat. "Yes."

He sets his glass on a coaster. I move down to the couch next to him, our legs barely touching. "Where is it now?" he says, staring out into the dimly lit room.

"Stomach," I say.

Headlights from passing cars unfurl across the walls, distorting over his face. Somewhere below us, a woman is screaming happily, drunkenly, about the score of the Giants game.

He looks down at his lap. "They'll probably put him on chemo again." His words are clipped and clear, like he's taking an oral examination. "The side effects won't be great, but they'll want to stick with what works for now. Maybe immunotherapy eventually, but —"

"Charlie." I grit my teeth without meaning to. "Mom and Dad are having a really tough time." He looks up. "You and I both know they would never ask you to come home, but I am."

My hands are clenched around my glass. I don't loosen my grip for fear of dropping it. I can picture where the floor would smack its edge, the explosion of sharp-edged, glittering shards, the dusting of tiny pieces that he would never really be able to clean up, not entirely, so every once in a while, he'd stand up from the couch and feel a bite in the soles of his feet, look down, and see the glass winking from a cut in his callus and wonder how that happened.

I set the glass down on the bare wood of the coffee table. Beer spills over the side, and I wipe it up with my hand, but it leaves a smear.

"You know I can't do that," he finally says.

I lick the beer remains off my fingers and turn to him. "I know you say that. And I know you think Dad is some horrible person who won't be able to handle your — you and Zach." His eyes glisten in the evening light, and he's getting that old pink stain that used to spread from his neck to his ears to his cheekbones. I push on anyway. "What if this is — if this is it?" I swallow hard around the catch in my breath. "Wouldn't you regret it, not coming home?"

"He doesn't want to see me," he says. "Trust me. And anyway, this is my home." He motions toward their closed bedroom door, at the finger of light poking through the crack in the bottom.

"Okay." I set my palms firmly on my thighs, for lack of a better place to put them. "You have this whole story you tell yourself where Dad was just looking for an excuse to get rid of you after you came out. I so don't think that's true." My voice is swelling and filling the room. The light in their bedroom clicks off. "That farm is the only thing he thinks he can leave us. And when you decided it wasn't enough for you, it was like —"

"Christ." He says it softly, but he pushes himself off the couch and walks toward the kitchen. Though his feet are bare, I can feel every footstep through the floorboards beneath me. He throws the refrigerator door open, and it hums. He stands there for a couple of minutes, his face hidden and his hand tensed, motionless, over the top of the door.

When he walks back to the couch, his hair is standing on end the way it does when he's been pulling on it, curls silhouetted. He sits next to me, and his weight makes a dip in the cushions I have to fight not to roll into.

"Do you know what he said when I left?" he says. I shake my head. "It was a couple of weeks after I'd come out to them. The night after I told them about med school. You were off at Shawn's house or something. I'd just finished packing up all my stuff, and I was starting to feel a little guilty, looking at all those family photos on my bureau, all that. So I went downstairs to say sorry — not for leaving, but for how we'd fought about it."

He pauses. The morning after his birthday

concert, when he dropped me off at school, he'd apologized to me. "Sorry for ruining it all. I know you guys just wanted me to have a good time." I stared at him from the passenger's seat of his sedan. His eyes were puffy, as if he hadn't slept at all, and he stared stiffly out the windshield. I wasn't sure how to tell him not to apologize.

"I heard Mom and Dad talking in the kitchen," he says. "It sounded serious, so I stopped halfway down the stairs. She was telling him it would be okay. Farming is hard, and it wouldn't do anyone any good to force me to do it." He smiles faintly. "And anyway, she said, they'd always have you, Nessa, to take care of things." His smile pinches in at the corners. I wonder how often he's heard us weighed against each other, our relative weaknesses held squintingly up to the light. I wonder how often he's done it himself.

"Dad said, 'I know, you're right, like always.' " He rotates the coaster a few degrees, fingertips white with the pressure. "And then Dad said, he said, 'Besides, I'm not sure this is the right place for his type anyway.' " His mouth is screwed up all the way to one side now. "My 'type,' " he repeats, looking at me this time.

I put my hand on his shoulder. The world

of this room moves loopy around me. I close my eyes against it. I try to picture anything cruel coming out of my dad's mouth, the same one that sings songs with made-up lyrics. I think of the other things he could have meant, how Charlie could have misinterpreted. He just knew Charlie wasn't meant for farming and was trying to make himself feel better about it, that must be it. The dirt and dust would have dulled Charlie, beaten him down until he was just an imitation, a fragment of himself.

I know that's not what he meant, though. And even if I could convince myself, I could never say so to Charlie. This is what he hears every time he thinks of home. He will never go back. Not even for Mom's sake.

I reach for his hand. It feels wrong, out of place in our language of nudges and elbowings. His fingers lace with mine and pull tight.

"You're pretty great, you know," I say for the first time.

"You, too," he says. He pecks the side of my head, a quick pressure near my temple, and then it's gone. He picks up our glasses and carries them to the kitchen. The sink gurgles as he pours the beer down the drain.

CHAPTER TWENTY-SIX:
DANIEL

Nessa swears sharply under her breath when the guest room door creaks on its hinges and as she fumbles through her suitcase in the dark. When she accidentally walks into the bed on her way to her mattress, I give up.

"Don't worry about it," I say, and she stifles a shriek.

"Shit! Sorry," she whispers.

When the air mattress's plasticky shifting has stopped, I say, "Did you tell him?"

"Yeah," she says, her voice flat. "He's not coming home."

In the light through the curtains, I can see her staring at the ceiling. I should probably just let her be. "Did you tell him it was stomach?" I ask stupidly.

"Yes." She swallows hard enough that I can hear it. "Apparently . . ." She pauses. "I guess my dad said some pretty bad things about him before he left for med school.

Not to his face," she says, though she sounds unconvinced that the detail matters. "Charlie overheard him. But it — well, it makes it pretty hard for him to go back."

I turn onto my back and close my eyes, like I'll find the right thing to say inside my eyelids.

"We should leave in the morning," she says.

I think of Zach, the way his voice picked up speed while he and Nessa made our Sunday plans. We would go to Golden Gate Park, they said, since I'd never been. Walk through secondhand bookstores and eat a late garlicky brunch. Charlie pulled out his phone while they talked, checking his emails, but he smiled in all the right places.

"Okay," I whisper. "Sounds good."

She turns away, toward the wall. "Good night," she says.

"Good night." And we settle in for a long night of listening to each other breathe in the dark.

When I wake up the next morning, the air mattress is already folded away and tucked under the bed. Nessa sits against the wall, staring blankly at a book. It's *Anne of Green Gables*, the same one she was reading back on her parents' porch.

"I didn't know you brought that with you," I say after I've cleared the sleep from my throat.

She stuffs the book into her bag and reaches for her phone. "I found this story on an extraterrestrial forum this morning. I don't think you have to worry about that Ray guy anymore." She tosses the phone to me. It lands facedown on the bed.

I flip the phone over and am about to tease her for finding those forums when I see the headline: "Local Eccentric Responsible for Rash of Crop Circles."

I scan the article. Lionel did a good job — the list of circles includes all the ones from the past year where the town held some fragment of doubt. The one near Des Moines, where the local newspaper decided it must've been some big senior prank from the graduating high school class. The one in Montana, where everyone in town rolled their eyes and assumed the farm owner was just trying to draw attention to his new hemp field. (It didn't help that he managed to mention the evils of cotton in every post-reveal interview.) And, of course, the circle in Maryland. Poor Becca and Jim. They'll have to wait for their next project to really see the wonder they can give to a town.

Lionel clearly found the right reporter,

too. You can almost hear the writer chuckling as she describes Ray's attempts to shrug off his responsibility by inventing a group of people who supposedly work with him. Of course, she included the quotes from farm owners describing sketchy encounters with Ray. There's also a quote from Ray himself, who's changed his tune and now insists that he never stepped foot on those farms, that he's never even made a circle, he just sat in on a few circler meetings. The article closes with a few quotes from a prominent psychiatrist who says Ray might be a schizophrenic suffering from delusions and should be approached with caution, because people like that can be dangerous.

I expect Nessa to look as relieved as I feel when I hand the phone back to her. But her eyes slide down across the floor. She still isn't getting what she needed out of this trip. Charlie's still staying behind. No circle can fix that.

"So he's just another crazy person now," she says. "I'm all packed and ready to go."

"Yep." I push my way out of the covers.

When we leave the room with our bags over our shoulders, I'm prepared to apologize to Zach and promise to visit later — soon, maybe. But he's screwing the lids onto two travel mugs, Charlie rummaging in the cupboard behind him for protein bars. Of course. Charlie would've told him. Maybe even last night, while I was grilling Nessa.

Charlie pushes a couple of bars in through the zipper on Nessa's bag.

"We'd better get back," she says.

He tucks his hands in his back pockets. She dumps her bag on the ground, throws her arms around his neck. After a second, he spreads his palms across her back, then pulls her in close. Zach and I smile tightly at each other. When Nessa pulls away, there are wet spots on the shoulder of Charlie's T-shirt.

"It was great to meet you, Daniel," Charlie says as Zach nods along.

"Yeah, you, too," I say, but he's already turned back to Nessa.

"Tell Mom and Dad I . . . Well, tell them hi for me."

"I will." She reaches for his hand, squeezes, and it's weirdly intimate.

Charlie coughs and pulls away, and we're out the door, coffee forgotten.

When we get to the car, I move toward the driver's side, but Nessa shakes her head. She doesn't check the rearview mirror as she pulls away down the road, crests the hill we walked last night. She doesn't say a single word until we're back in Nevada, pulling over to change places.

Her eyes are bright when we pass each other. "Let's go to Vegas," she says.

On the way to California, we refused to drive through Las Vegas, agreeing on a looping route that avoided its crowds and noise. But her hands are clasped in front of her like a little kid, so I say, "Okay."

My muscles clench as soon as the flashing lights and overpasses appear on the horizon.

"I can't believe neither of us has been here before," Nessa says, drumming her hands on the dashboard. "It's an entire city built around fun."

Exactly, I think but don't say.

Soon enough, I pull into the entrance of the hotel Nessa'd looked up, insisting on paying for the room herself this time instead of splitting it. A small man in a bright-red vest with gold plastic buttons takes the car keys and hands me a valet ticket, and another man whisks our bags out of the trunk before I can even ask if I can park the car myself.

"Casino first?" she says, already walking away.

"Uh, sure." My hand touches my wallet, stuffed safely in my back pocket.

The doors slide shut behind us, and we're sealed off in a glass and metal box of stale air-conditioning. There are no windows — I read about this once, the casinos shutting out all hints of the outside world. The room is filled with rows of clinking slot machines, each one with a white-haired woman or tie-loosened guy sitting in front of it, staring dully at their results. The air is crowded with the screech and whoop of sugary booze-filled conversations. Panic rises in my throat.

"Oops, sorry!" A high voice in my ear as a group of girls in shiny dresses stumble past, pushing me into Nessa. She hasn't moved, either. Her eyes are wide and darting. She's chewing her lip so hard, I check for blood.

She startles as I move closer, refocusing on my face. And she laughs, her head back, and a few slot machiners turn and stare at us. I grin and wave at them.

"Okay, so this was a huge mistake," she says after she's recovered. "Come on. Let's see if we can find their restaurant. I'm starving." She pulls me back out into the hot, dry air by my elbow.

Neither of us speaks as we dig into our steaks, but it's a calmer silence than before. It's 5:30 when we sit down, early still, and we're the only people under fifty in the restaurant. She raises her eyebrows at me when the woman at the next table over asks how much salt they use in their hamburger meat.

Halfway through the meal, Nessa puts down her fork and knife, lines them up under the rim of her plate. She bends the straw in her electric blue rum punch back and forth.

"I can do this," she says.

"Do what?" I say when she doesn't continue.

"Help my dad and my mom by myself, without Charlie. He was right. It probably would've just stressed my parents out, him being there."

I put my own fork down and wipe my hands on my napkin, but she doesn't look up from her drink. She smiles firmly.

"I called my parents last night." I'm not sure why I say this, except to surprise her out of this.

"Really?" Her smile is real this time. She's picturing a warm family conversation, maybe wishing for one herself. That's not something I can give her.

"It didn't go too well."

"What? Why?"

I push at the edge of my plate, turning it a couple of degrees. "It wasn't my usual call time, so I caught them off guard. We hung up after four minutes. I think they're afraid of taking up too much space in my life." I don't realize it's true until the words fall out.

She taps on the tines of her fork three times, pauses, then three more. "Well, I'm sure they were still happy. They love you."

"You're right," I say, and I smile at her. "They do."

CHAPTER TWENTY-SEVEN: MOLLY

This morning, after Sam has eaten his breakfast, I unwrap a dose of fentanyl. They're little white torpedo pills on a stick, and Dr. Cooper's steady voice on the phone explained that Sam has to suck on them like candy until they've dissolved completely. They help with the breakthrough pain, the sharp reminders that will poke through the extended-release fentanyl patch he has to wear every day now, just under the hem of his shirtsleeve.

"How's that lollipop?" I say brightly as I stand over him and wait for him to pop the bare stick out of his mouth and into my hand.

He still spends his morning out in the field, and I spend it hovering near windows, holding my breath until he passes into view. At one point, I move out to sit in the truck with a cigarette, hoping he doesn't notice the threads of smoke rising out of the window, my breath vanishing cleanly into the air. There's a hypocrisy in it, I suppose, inhaling something that could give me the very disease my husband is dying of. I just can't bring myself to care. I can't very well quit now, when everything else is falling apart. I need these moments alone, with nothing else before me.

I push the driver's seat back into a recline and reach for the envelope, turning it over and over while the seat belt clasp digs into my hip. Every time I see it, I remember learning about Schrödinger's cat in an entry-level philosophy class I took in college. I leave it closed. Even if the letter was an acceptance from the development organization, there's not much point in pursuing it now.

During his midmorning break, he checks his email on the computer. I hear the printer whirring away and smile — Sam never did get used to reading messages from his friends on the screen. He prefers to print them out and hold them between his hands. He slowly sits down at the kitchen table, his eyes fixed on the stapled pile of papers he's carrying. "Nessa just sent this to me," he says. He presses one trembling finger to the paper.

I lean over his shoulder to read. There's a

lengthy news article copied and pasted below Nessa's message. She writes, *Hey, Dad! Wasn't sure if you were following this story or not, but it had Daniel pretty worried for a while there. Thought I'd send it along to you to let you know it's all been handled. All systems go! xoxo.* The article's headline, in big, bold print, is "Local Eccentric Responsible for Rash of Crop Circles."

"Well," I say when I've finished reading. "It sounds like that man was a real —" I stop myself before saying "kook." After all, I remind myself, his claims of a secret society were all true. "A real blabbermouth," I finish. "Good thing no one seems to believe him." I start to step away.

"What if they all laugh?" he says. He looks up at me and bites his lip. "What if this article gets popular and then everyone in town assumes our circle is just another one of his — another prank from this, this 'eccentric'?"

I pause and run through the article again, then point triumphantly at a line toward the end. "Look at what she says here, though, about all those damages he might be liable for. No one in their right mind would keep making crop circles if they knew they'd have to pay for it. I bet you no amateurs would want to start breaking into new farms, either. Which means" — I nudge his shoulder and cock one eyebrow — "something more mysterious must be at play out in our cornfield. Maybe even something from another planet."

"You're right," he says. The relief in his face is so like Nessa's every time I soothed a worry that I turn away and begin washing the dishes from breakfast.

A few moments later, he says, "You know, you don't have to watch me while I'm out there."

I freeze, my hands buried in the hot, soapy water. Fleetingly, I wonder if I'm caught. Did he see me from afar through the windshield, wasting time? When I turn around, though, there's no reproach in his face. He's only grinning.

"Oh, I don't, do I?" I say. I whisk my hands through the dish towel and grasp at the box of fentanyl, though I don't need to read it to know what it says. It's a prop, and I hold it out toward him. "Side effects include confusion, weakness, dizziness, and shortness of breath. It's bad enough you insisted on working through the chemo, with all the side effects of those pills. What if something happens to you out there?"

"Then at least I can say I went down doing what I love." It was his standard response in our early days, when I kept him up at night asking about machinery, imagining the great, heavy gears and wheezing exhaust pipes, the many ways I could lose him. He always followed it with the same teasing smile. This time, though, his voice is sharper, and his smile is thinner and falls away quickly.

He sighs, pulling me into his arms, into the spot where my head fits just exactly. I listen to his breath rattle up through his ribs. "Listen, honey," he says, patient and low. "I need it to be normal for just a little while longer. Okay?" He dislodges one arm, reaches for the lacy curtain above the sink, and draws it closed. Of course, there are plenty of other windows I could watch him through, but I don't say so.

"All right. Fine," I say, though of course it isn't. I pull myself upward and shake out my shoulders. He is gone, out the door.

It almost works, our day of pretend. I quicken my step every time I walk by the window. When I see him sit down on the porch steps at lunchtime, I carry his sandwich out to him on a flimsy paper plate. I even manage a convincing smile when I sit down next to him. For a moment, we stare out at the farm together, at the green corduroy rows of corn, the soybeans just a blur behind them, and the clouds' shadows skidding across the mountains beyond.

Sam's hands are unsteady as he reaches for the sandwich. When he looks up, his face is drained and drawn.

"What is it?" I say.

He puts the sandwich back down and buries his face in his hands.

I set my hands on the step on either side of me, splinters of wood digging into my palms.

He looks up at me. "I'm not sure," he says, and my throat jams shut. I scan his skin for cuts and damage. "I was sitting on the tractor, and next thing I knew, I — wasn't." He spreads his hands open on his lap, palms up, as if he's asking for something. "The tractor wasn't moving. I'd just put it in Park. Since I landed with such a dead weight, I think the worst I'll see is just a nasty bruise."

I can't say anything. There's an apology in his eyes. I lay my hands over one of his.

"I think it's time for us to call Nessa," he says quietly, looking at our fingers.

I pause to let myself catch up. "She'll be home soon. We should wait until she gets here."

He sighs. "She's going to need some time to deal with the news."

"You're right," I say, though I wish he weren't. I wish we could continue putting off and pretending. "I'll do it," I say, and the words hit the ground like round stones, lying there.

I wait until Sam's asleep that night. I wait much longer than that, really. I sit on the couch and stare at the phone, and for a brief, shameful moment, I wish I were calling Charlie instead.

Nessa was always like her father, all emotion and action bundled together by translucent skin. She's a cluster of raw nerves shooting pain and joy alike straight to her heart, and it was my job to sheathe them all, to shield her. Charlie kept his reactions close to the bone, balled up like wadded tissue.

Or he used to anyway. When he was with us.

I rub my chin once, vigorously, the friction pulling me back, and dial her number. As the phone rings, I wonder what on earth I'll say.

She picks up on the fourth ring, and her voice is light and easy. She's had a good day, and I'm glad for that.

"What's up, Mom?" she says, and almost, I tell her not much, that this call is no different from the thousands we've made before, exchanging weather reports and dinner recipes.

Then, with a start, I remember where she is and why. Those plans we made feel like another era, though it was less than two weeks ago we huddled around the kitchen table. A small flame of hope flickers near my breastbone. "Have you seen Charlie yet?"

"Yeah." She sighs, and the flame puffs out. "He's not coming home."

I bite my lip, chewing off a flake of skin there. "It's okay, sweets. Thank you for trying."

There is silence for a moment, as if she's allowing me time to collect myself. Then, quietly, "How's Dad?"

"He's not so good. The doctor, he said the chemo's not working this time." Her breath stutters, and it's my turn to pause. I consider stopping altogether, but then, she'll find out for herself soon enough and will only be angry with me for keeping it from her. I remember the last time. "He doesn't want to try anything else. And the doctor said — he said he's in a lot of pain."

I brace myself for her tears, spilling straight from the phone down my ear canal and into my chest.

"I'll be home as soon as I can," she says instead.

"Okay." I don't protest. My voice would trip and hitch too much. I hang up the phone before it gets worse and toss the receiver toward the other end of the couch, away.

I walk toward the kitchen and whip the curtains open again. The tractor sits in the middle of the field, a black lump accusing me of something. We'd had a banner year when we bought it, sun and rain together coaxing the corn and beans from the soil, the cows more productive than we'd ever seen. Sam's smile was so wide the first time he drove it that I almost forgot our truck was rusting out and Nessa needed braces. The kids scrabbled up the tires and into his lap. We were happy, the four of us.

That boy will be back soon, bending the field into something else altogether, some shared vision of his and Sam's, no longer what we made of it. I shut my eyes and close the curtain again.

CHAPTER TWENTY-EIGHT: NESSA

The lights of the city flash endlessly around me from the balcony of our hotel room, bright, relentless colors not found in nature. I press my hands to my face, my exhales condensing hot on my fingers, but they're still there, insisting on Technicolor. My phone is on the table in front of me where I dropped it. I know I need to call Charlie. I know my mom doesn't have it in her.

The door slides open behind me.

"You were right. The reality show about out-of-work rodeo clowns was just as boring as it sounded," Daniel says, laughing. "Want to pick something else?"

"Sure," I say, and there must be something not quite right in my voice, because he steps out onto the balcony.

"Was that Charlie?"

"No." I pick up my phone and let it dangle from my fingertips, swinging back and forth. Its glass face catches the flashing lights and makes them flicker. They're almost pleasant that way, like Christmas decorations on a white picket fence.

He sits on the metal chair next to mine, not saying anything.

"The treatments aren't working. He's dying," I say.

"Shit," he says, and something else too, probably "sorry." He runs one hand over his face.

I stare back out into the city, its swinging doors and swinging hips and neon drinks. This place I dragged us to, so far from home. I've never gambled, never got so drunk I couldn't see, and I wanted to find out if I could lose myself to the lights, become wide open with laughter. If, for once, I could lose the mask.

"Let's go back inside," he says, plucking at my arm. "I'll find us something dumb to watch." He leads me through the door with his hand on my back, and I can feel its weight between my shoulder blades.

He sits next to me on the hotel couch and flips through the channels. It's surprising to me how much it helps, getting lost in the lives of strangers who don't matter. Scott the forager exclusively watched late-night cartoons starring talking meatballs that made me feel slightly unhinged. He sneered at reality TV, and so did I, but now I found it soothing, the problems packaged neatly into thirty-minute story lines.

During a commercial break, Daniel darts off down the hallway to the vending machine, returning with an armful of brightly colored junk food. The fake cheese and salt is sharp, numbing my tongue.

He falls asleep at hour three, but I can't bring myself to turn it off. I can't be alone. So instead, I study his face, pale in the pulsing glow of the TV. Asleep, he is peaceful, empty of his quiet, jumpy energy.

My dad never liked any of my boyfriends. There were a couple in high school with long hair who would take me out into the field and try first to tell me about the stars and second to stick their hands up my shirt. Before they could do cither, though, they had to sit on my parents' couch while my dad sat across from them in his armchair, his legs spread wide. He asked them about their parents and their farms and how school was going. Charlie would smirk supportively from behind Dad's back, shaking his head while he made himself a sandwich.

Late at night, though, when I was back in bed and the boys had driven home, I could hear Dad talking to Mom downstairs. His voice rumbled up through the floorboards, a low growl. It would go on for minutes at a time, sometimes, before my mom piped in. Eventually, I turned on my side and crammed my quilt up around my ears into a cushioned cave.

Two photos from my parents' wedding hung in the stairwell of the house. One was the formal portrait, his hand resting stiffly on her waist, in a fancy gold frame that my mom had long ago given up on keeping clean. It was a gift from my grandma — not Dad's mom, pillowy, Midwestern — the other grandma, the one we saw twice a year, all sharp angles, her face pinched with worry.

The second photo was smaller, in a thin, wood frame. It's from their reception, in some church basement with tulle draped behind them. Dad has his arm laid across the top of Mom's chair, and he's staring at her, smiling like he can't quite believe it. Her hand is spread across her chest, her fingers splayed across her lace neckline. Her head is thrown back in laughter, her mouth open with it.

It's this second picture I used to touch gently, like a good luck charm, on my way downstairs to breakfast. They were just abstracts to me then, shinier versions of the same people who packed my lunch and helped me with my homework. It wasn't until recently that the picture would stop me in my tracks. How young they were, how happy and complete.

The sky is growing gray again by the time I stand up from the couch and walk out on the balcony, wincing as the door squeals closed behind me. Charlie will be awake by now. It takes a few rings, but he picks up, grunting a little from his lunges, in the middle of stretching for his preclinic morning run.

"Dad's dying," my voice says before I can stop it.

He's silent. "What do you mean?"

"Mom called me yesterday. The chemo's not working."

He catches his bearings. "Okay, so they'll want to try immunotherapy, then. Or maybe surgery. There's been a lot of progress in —"

"She says he doesn't want to try anything else."

He clears his throat.

"Okay," I say, pushing forward. "I just thought you should know."

"Yeah. Thanks," he says eventually, his voice rough.

Daniel is awake when I open the door.

"How'd it go?" he says.

I stop, not really sure what to say or how to describe it. I stare at him for a moment, the circles under his eyes, and imagine what my dad would've thought if I'd brought him home. Would he have admired him, called him a hard worker as he does now? Or would his voice still hum as deep as bedrock through the floorboards of my bedroom?

"Should we see if they've put breakfast stuff out?" I want to sound cheerful, but it comes out wrong, all flinty.

Daniel smiles anyway and heaves himself up from the couch. "Sure," he says, holding his hand out.

I take it in my own, because I'm not sure what else to do.

CHAPTER TWENTY-NINE: MOLLY

Somehow, still, the cupboards go empty, and the refrigerator goes bare and stale. The meals are a blur of sandwiches and leftovers, sometimes ferried up to bed and sometimes eaten quietly at the table. Eventually, the grocery store becomes inevitable.

"Sam?" I say. He takes his fentanyl before anything else in the morning, his head still on the pillow. He smiles up at me, and I could almost convince myself it was the same old smile, save for that silly white stick poking out of one corner.

"I'm going to run some errands," I say.

"Maybe pick up some low tunnels and fabric? I want to try to build a winter garden."

My fists clench, nails biting into the pads of my palms. Is this it? Has the cancer started nibbling at his brain, made him forget? He winks, and I slap him lightly on the shoulder.

"I'll be back in an hour," I say on my way out the door. "Call me if you need anything."

The grocery store is so very bright, unchanging with its scuffed tile floors. I find myself lost in the cereal aisle, a song from when the kids were in high school tinkling over the loudspeaker as I pick out the sugary flavor that will make Sam smile the widest.

I read an article in a magazine once where a woman was describing what depression felt like. She said it was like being suspended in a cold, cloudy pond. You could see the sun shining, but from far away, a place you cannot reach. I stare at the cheerful cartoon frog on the box in my hands and wonder where the line is between grief and depression. Or if it matters.

"Hello, again." The voice is far too close, and I jump, the box falling to the ground with a thud. She bends over to pick it up, and her red ponytail shifts sideways.

"Hi, Allison," I say, managing to smile as she hands the box to me. It's dented now, the frog's face distorted, but Sam won't mind. It might even make him laugh. I slip the box into my cart.

"I know it's only been a few weeks, but I feel like I haven't seen you in ages," she says. "We've just been so busy with the girls home and everything. Speaking of which, I heard Nessa was around for a while. Must have been so nice to see her."

"Yes, she just surprised us with a little visit," I say.

"And rumor has it she stole the Shannons' farmhand." Her eyes crinkle merrily.

"Oh, well." I look down at my cart, nearly empty. "She told him they were dealing with an early frost at the farm she used to work at, and he wanted to lend a hand." The story sounds untrue even to me, but Allison turns and runs her fingers over a row of cereal boxes, tap-tap-tap, already moving on.

"Listen," she says, "I was serious about wanting to help with your garden. I know it's not the right time of year yet, but maybe we could get together soon and start planning? I really do miss it." Her face is bright and hopeful, verging on begging. I can barely remember being embarrassed by things like the state of our front lawn.

"Sure," I say. I push my cart back and forth, as if to rock a baby to sleep.

She claps her hands a little. "Wonderful! Oh, and" — she glances up and down the aisle, then leans in closer, though no one else is here — "how's Sam?"

"Well," I start, prepared with my usual

vague answer. But then, why bother? "He's not well, actually." My voice wavers a bit, but it's surprising how good it feels to tell someone without needing to cushion their fall.

One of Allison's hands flies to her mouth. "No," she says, her voice muffled. She turns to put her basket on the floor, and before I can step away, her arms are clasped around my neck. They're soft and cool, and they smell like deodorant, powdery. "I am so, so sorry," she whispers in my ear, as if her closeness could heal me. "He is such a wonderful man."

I nod, and my chin digs into her shoulder.

She backs up, bracing my upper arms between her hands, and glances at my halfhearted cart. "Don't worry a thing about food, okay? I'll organize a meal train," she says. I smile thinly, my heart sinking. "I'll come by tonight with something. And I'll bring a pencil and some paper, too, so we can talk flowers. Take your mind off of things." She smiles, and her ponytail bobs. Problem solved.

I think of the cigarette I will smoke in the parking lot, not caring who sees.

I come home with an army of plastic bags, lining the counters with their tipsy weight. I fill the fridge and cupboards with steaks, frozen home fries, hamburger meat, Twinkies, and bacon. All the foods that Dr. Cooper gently suggested (and the internet not-so-gently demanded) Sam should avoid.

I've just finished stuffing the last of the granola and the jiggly boneless chicken breasts in the trash when Sam walks up. He stands in the doorway, wrists resting on either side, and watches as I shove the lid of the trash bin down.

I stand and push aside a strand of my hair with my forearm. "I was thinking about making some chicken-fried steak for dinner tonight."

He grins. "It's like you read my mind."

My cheeks warm, and I turn to the sink to start tidying up the dishes from breakfast. He comes up behind me and snakes his arms around my middle. I lean back, and his ribs ridge up against my spine. His arms are still solid and firm, enough to hold me together. I touch his hand with soapy fingers, and the warm water slips down over my belly.

"By the way," I say, chipper, "I ran into Allison at the grocery store. She's organizing a meal train for us, and she said she'd kick it off by bringing us something tonight."

He groans. "Not the Tupperware Brigade."

I turn to him and wink. "My bets are she brings her famous buffalo chicken." It's cruel to joke about her kindness, I know, but at least for now, it's still the two of us against everyone else.

"And my bets are I spend half the night in the bathroom as a result."

"Why do you think I'm planning on making steak?" My smile grows. "I'll have to make some more room in the trash can for that chicken, though." I tap my chin thoughtfully.

Sam roars with laughter. He's still laughing when he walks back up the stairs to bed, and I can almost convince myself that's why he clings to the bannister for support.

The phone rings, and I snatch it up before it can wake Sam.

"Hi, Molly. It's Connie. Connie Shannon."

"Connie! Yes! Hello! How are things going on the farm? I hope it's not been too much trouble with Daniel gone." My shoulders tense with shame, for what, I'm not sure — for my daughter stealing away her much-needed farmhand, for the stories she's had to tell in town to explain his disappearance.

"Oh — no." She falters a little bit, barely enough for me to hear the lie. "We've been managing just fine."

"I know you were hoping Earl would be able to ease up on the work now, with his bad back and all," I can't help but say.

"You know Earl," she says quickly. "He insists he's got at least another season or two in him, and I guess now I believe him." She laughs, two high breaths. "Look at me, babbling about my own husband when it's yours I'm calling about."

I knead one knuckle into my temple and close my eyes. She works fast, that Allison.

"I'm so sorry to hear he's unwell again," Connie says. "Is there anything we can do for him? Or for you? I'm happy to hop by and spruce things up around there — you know, if you're too busy with appointments and things . . ."

"That's sweet of you to offer, but I think we're fine for now." I open my eyes and start collecting the flotsam that has, in fact, begun to collect on our coffee table, the tissues and paper pharmacy bags.

"All right," she says. "Well. You let me know if that changes, okay?"

"Of course. I will." I soften. Connie is always the first to offer. She bustles in at the first rumor of distress, silently sweeping and straightening. She loves gossiping as much as the rest of us, but she'll never tell a soul about the closed-door arguments and tears she overhears during those cleaning sessions.

"By the way, you haven't heard any updates from Nessa about when she and Daniel will be back, have you?" She says it casually, but her hope gives itself away. "He hasn't been in touch, and we're a bit worried, to tell the truth."

"I've spoken to her, yes. They should be home within the week, I expect."

"Good! That's good." She pauses. "I found something a little weird while I was cleaning his room last night. I pulled out the bed so I could vacuum, and there was this folded-up sheet of paper tucked behind the headboard. I know I should've let it be, but I opened it up without thinking, and it was this — drawing, I guess? Only it didn't look like anything I recognized. It was all abstract and loopy, almost."

The handful of trash I've been collecting falls to the floor. It sounds like the crop circle plans I'd seen Daniel pull from his pocket over and over again, at our kitchen table and outside our bedroom window at night. I assumed he'd brought them with him. I think of Sam's face while he read

Nessa's email, how afraid he was that the town wouldn't believe him and would laugh at him. I silently curse Daniel for his recklessness.

"Actually," I say, the story tumbling into place, "he was helping me out with a quilt design I've been having trouble with." I drop my voice so it's low and secretive. "I'm sure you know he was around here quite a bit to visit with Nessa. They're just friends, of course." She giggles. I'll have to apologize to Nessa for this. "He mentioned geometry was his best subject in school, and I'd been puzzling over this pattern for weeks, so I asked if he could help me draft the pattern. That must've been what you found." I clutch the back of the sofa. It sounds like a serviceable lie to me, but then, I'm not exactly known around town for my quilting. The few I've made for Nessa and Charlie were simple blocks sewn messily together.

"I see," she says. "I'll have to drop it off the next time I see you so you can sneak a peek at what he's come up with. It looks pretty complicated."

"Oh dear. We'll see if I'm up for the challenge. I have to go. Someone seems to be knocking on our window. Bye, now." I hang up and step carefully toward the rapping in our kitchen.

"Anybody home?" Allison cups her hands around her eyes and peers in.

I steel myself and open the door. "You're just in time. I was just slicing up this morning's bread." I motion to the table, where I've laid out a stack of thick slices and my mother-in-law's old butter dish.

"You didn't have to do that," she says, depositing a glass dish of something aggressively orange into the fridge. She sits and helps herself. Crumbs scatter over the notepad she lays out in front of her. "Mmm." She closes her eyes, and I feel a small glow of pride in spite of myself. "You've outdone yourself with this one. You really should think about opening a bakery. I bet people would come from all around," she says, squinting appraisingly at me and shaking the crust like a finger. A piece of it falls off and tumbles to the floor. When I bend to pick it up from under the table, I sweep my palm across my cheeks as if to clear away the flush.

"Sam would ordinarily love to join us, but he's asleep upstairs. The medication makes him so tired, you know." This much is true. He'll be genuinely disappointed I didn't wake him. Much as he dislikes the meals in the meal train, he adores the company that comes with them, loves being fussed over and exchanging town gossip.

Allison makes a valiant effort to cover up her own disappointment, waving my apologies aside.

I touch the notepad. "What's this?"

She flips to a page filled with penciled diagrams, words crossed out and rewritten several times over. "I was just doing some brainstorming for that garden." My eyes widen, and she laughs. "I know it looks a little overwhelming, but trust me, this is one of those things you only have to do right once and then —"

We both hear the uneven thumps of Sam's feet on the stairs at the same time. Allison's face lights up in anticipation. As he descends into view, her mouth drops open into a wide, horrified circle.

I suppose it is a bit alarming, from her point of view. He would've filled out that sweater nicely a couple of months ago. He wouldn't have needed a sweater at all, in fact, in these warm late-summer afternoons. His cheeks are sinking in, deflating. His face is pale except for two spots of dark pink surfacing from the effort of walking the stairs. People in town are used to seeing him fluctuate, the chemo sapping him of any excess for weeks, months at a time. It's never this fast, though. Never this final.

Allison snaps her mouth shut, but not before Sam sees. His eager smile falters a little, and he pauses. I hurry to his side and give him my hand, knowing full well he can make it down himself and would usually, in fact, be annoyed with me for helping. I press his knuckles gently.

Allison appears to have collected herself. "Well, look who decided to honor us with his presence. If it isn't the queen of Sheba himself," she teases.

Sam leans over to embrace her. "What's the fastest redhead in town doing in my kitchen?"

She tosses her hair over her shoulder and laughs as he pulls out a chair. The two of them launch into a discussion of the town plans to build a new parking lot for the grocery store while I run my finger over the list of flowers Allison has written down, names I don't recognize smudging slightly under the pressure of my thumb. Delphinium. Hyacinth. Coreopsis. Penstemon. Clematis. For some of them, she's noted the Latin names or particular color varieties.

By the time I've reached the bottom of the list, imagining their twisting stems and spindly leaves, Sam's chuckles have grown softer and more punctuated with sighs. I lean across the table and say, "I'm so sorry to interrupt. Sam, you'd really better get some rest before dinner. Make sure you've got enough energy to do Allison's chicken justice."

He pushes his chair back. "You're right. Thanks for stopping by. Don't be a stranger, okay?"

She shakes her head. "No, of course not." She means it. She beams up at him as he pulls himself up the stairs. When he's out of sight, she turns to me and touches her chest. "He's a good one, that Sam. I can't tell you how much my husband looks up to him."

I paste a smile on my face. I want to tell her there's no need to eulogize him yet, that he's still here in the flesh, with all his flaws and goodness both. It would only make her gasp and run out the door to tell her friends it's too bad that poor man married such a shrew. So instead, I just swallow it down and shift in my seat while her eyes travel around the room.

She frowns when she looks out the window at the fields. For the first time in days, I study them, too. A crop can deteriorate just as quickly as a body, it seems. Without Sam's ministrations, the cornstalks have begun to sag, and the soybean plants are wilting. Dark clusters of crows rise from certain corners.

"Who's going to manage the fields while Sam is sick?" she asks, like it's a temporary inconvenience.

"Nessa will when she returns," I say, though in truth, I hadn't thought about it at all. "She should be back in a few days." It sounds like an apology.

"Hmm" is all she says, squaring up the pages of her notepad. The disapproval in her voice is unmistakable.

CHAPTER THIRTY: DANIEL

Nessa does her best. She laughs a little when I point at the waffle iron, which churns out waffles in the shape of the state of Nevada. She loads up her plate with stale English muffins and Hostess donuts. But in the end, she only picks at her food. I open my mouth a couple of times to ask what Charlie said, then think better of it.

Finally, when I throw our plates away, she comes back long enough to say, "I need to get back home."

"Sure," I say, "of course. If you want me to drive the car back, you can go ahead and buy a plane ticket —"

"No," she says, more forcefully than I think she means to. The woman eating next to us stops feeding her toddler and glances over her shoulder. "I need to drive," she says, more softly.

On our way out the hotel door, the wobbly wheel on Nessa's suitcase catches on a pebble, and the whole thing thuds to the ground. She swears under her breath and blushes when a bellhop scurries over to help her. My phone buzzes while I'm bending over to pick up the luggage tag that freed itself from the suitcase's handle. I forget to check the caller ID before answering.

"Can you believe this bullshit?"

I stop short. "Ray?"

"They're calling me a schizo, a fucking psycho. It's all over the internet. Just for telling the truth? And it all gets pinned on me?"

"How did you get this number?" Stupid question — everyone gets a full contact list when they become an official member, in case of emergencies.

He ignores me. "I get it, you guys value your privacy. Sure. Maybe I was a little drunk during that radio call-in. A little bitter because you guys didn't let me do shit. But this? I'm getting pulled into court left and right, paying for damages I didn't make."

A kid shoves past me in the doorway, his scowling face focused on his phone. His parents follow behind, arguing in whispers. And Nessa stands by the valet stand and stares into space. "Look," I say, "I know it sucks, but what do you —"

"You have to talk to Lionel. He listens to you. Get him to come out with the truth, take back the story. I know he must've been the one to start it, right? Right? There must be something, anything you could do, he could do." His voice is high and panicked. He takes a breath, and it lowers. "I got fired last night. Again. My wife, she laughed at me at first, but now she thinks I've been hiding all these bullshit secrets from her. She's talking about moving out." The valet pulls up in Nessa's car. "Please," Ray whispers.

"I'm sorry," I say. And I really am as I watch Nessa drop into the driver's seat, her face blank. It could just as easily be me, thrown out into the cold with humiliation to keep me company. "But there's nothing I can do."

"I could still list the names, you know," he murmurs.

"Who would believe you now, Ray?" I say, trying to make it sound gentle without inviting an actual response.

He sounds resigned now, tired. "You can't hide forever, you know," he says.

A headache starts to form behind my eyes. "Wanna bet?"

"I sure do. Look what happened to your girlfriend."

My fists clench, along with my stomach.

"This work drove her crazy," he continues. "You're in too deep, buddy. You're next. Get yourself out, and tell everyone I was right. Give me a hand."

"She wasn't crazy," I say. "She was an addict." And I hang up and walk toward the car.

It takes us a fraction of the time to cross the country back east that it did on the way out. Nessa is barely talking again, and when she drives, the road whips by so fast, I'm afraid to close my eyes. It's no better when I'm behind the wheel, Nessa curled up on the passenger's seat, tapping her fingernails on the window. She's like a cattle prod, burning red, keeping my foot pressed on the accelerator. Migraine pills rattle into her palm over and over again.

Lionel calls when we reach Kentucky. We haven't spoken since I called him at Charlie's. I don't want to ask Nessa how far gone Sam is or what we'll do about the circle if it's . . . too far. It's time for Lionel to know there's a delay. Maybe an indefinite one. I keep my voice jolly on the phone, glancing at Nessa, but she just picks at a hole in the knee of her jeans, pulling away at the thread.

"I was beginning to think we'd never

speak," he says. "I know you're close to your milestone circle here, but I'm not sure you're taking this seriously enough, my friend."

"No, I do. I am," I say. "You did a great job on that Ray story, by the way."

"It's time to talk about you," he says impatiently. "Should I be congratulating you?" Two other pairs of circlers had been close to fifteen at our last meeting, the one with Ray's outburst. I sat there staring at the stains on my shoes while the four of them laughed around me after the meeting ended, talking over themselves about their plans for the big one. Lionel stood in front of us, smiling as he sorted his papers.

"Um, no," I say. "There's been a family — something came up. With the farmer." Nessa plucks at her seat belt, and it thumps against her collarbone. "This might not be the one after all."

"I see." He pauses. "And you're still there, in Munsen?" He must be paging through his ledger, written in his own oddball code.

"Not exactly. We're — I'm on an errand. I'll be back soon, and I'll know more then."

"And you'll call me. We'll determine if it's best for you to stay."

Somehow, by the time I hang up, Nessa's fallen asleep, a tight ball wedged up against the car door. Which is the only reason I'm able to pull off the highway onto the Mammoth Cave exit.

When I've parked, I reach over and shake her awake. Gently at first, but then more urgent.

Her eyes finally spring open. "Where are we?"

"We're back at the caves," I say. She looks confused, and I start to feel like an idiot. "I know when you said this place makes all your problems seem smaller, this wasn't what you meant. It's not like I think they're going to fix anything about your dad or with Charlie. But I thought maybe you could use a break, and reality shows don't really seem to be cutting it, so." I motion toward the windshield, voilà, like I was somehow responsible for this.

She stares out the window, not smiling. She doesn't look angry, either. "We don't really have time for this," she says as I jump out of the car and open her door for her.

I hold my breath until she steps out. I have this weird sense that she'd just stop in the middle of the parking lot if she could, so I keep one hand under her elbow and guide her to the visitor's center.

Something catches my eye as we pass the benches. It's my bracelet — Claire's bracelet. Not so green anymore. More dull and brown, half buried in the mud. I haven't even reached for it since we last left the caves. It feels kind of like betrayal, leaving it there in the dirt.

But it's just a bracelet. So I keep walking.

Inside, I turn to Nessa. "I'm going to buy us some tickets. We'll be back on the road in an hour. I promise."

She nods, not meeting my eyes. "I've gotta go to the bathroom." I watch her walk across the room, and the door to the women's room swings shut behind her.

CHAPTER THIRTY-ONE:
NESSA

After ten minutes or so, I come out of the bathroom stall. The pit in my stomach is all that I am now, a black hole that's pulling me deeper and deeper into myself. There's no way out, not really.

The bathroom is empty. I slide the lock on the outer door, solid.

He's dying. He'll be gone soon. It's all your fault.

I look up in the mirror, but I don't see anything. I turn the faucet on, as hot as it will go. Let the water flow clean through my hands.

onetwothreefourfivesixseveneightnineten

CHAPTER THIRTY-TWO: DANIEL

As I finish paying for the tickets, I think back to what Ray said about Claire. Even now that she's gone, I'm still defending her. Anger and grief still flare up at the mention of her name. I still want to save her.

When the man behind the counter hands me our tickets, there's no sign of Nessa. She must need some time alone to gather herself up. Being on the road can be tough like that, your only spare minutes spent in motel room beds, staring at nothing.

But I can't stop picturing her glazed green eyes. Or Claire, her silences growing thicker after each meeting. Those damn orange bottles. I should've pulled one from Nessa's purse, read the label.

Maybe she slipped out of the bathroom while I was paying. I hurry to the building's exhibit hall, trying not to run. There's a series of posters about bats and some disease that's threatening to kill them.

Blown up to more than life size, their faces are gruesome, their eyes black and gleaming, nostrils gaping. There are two girls standing in front of one, maybe ten years old, pointing at the photos. No Nessa.

I pull back the heavy red curtain along one wall. Behind it, there's a small room with a big screen showing a movie about the caves. A woman is breastfeeding alone on one of the benches. She looks up at me, annoyed. I duck my head, sorry, sorry. Back out into the room.

The two girls are staring at me now, their mouths open slightly. I walk slowly, so slowly, over to the bathroom. There's no one in sight except for the man behind the ticket counter. He's watching a soccer game on his phone, the cheers rising tinny from the speakers. I lean in toward the bathroom door. All I can hear is a faucet running.

"Nessa?" I tap on the door three times. Then, louder, "Nessa, are you in there?"

No response. The man at the counter looks up from his game, dares me with a bored glance to do anything weird. I step back from the door.

I'll check outside. She probably decided this was a bad idea and went back to the car. She's not sitting on the bench. The bracelet tugs weakly at the corner of my eye, but I walk by, breaking into a jog as I reach the parking lot.

The car is empty. Just a scattering of crumbs and Nessa's mashed-up pillow in the passenger's seat.

I run back to the building. A metallic taste spreads through my mouth. I turn my back to the ticket counter and knock on the bathroom door until my knuckles sting. "Nessa, are you okay?"

Just the faucet, running and running.

"I'm coming in, all right?" I call and lean on the door before she can respond.

It goes nowhere. Locked.

My heartbeat rattles. I run to the ticket counter.

"Excuse me. Hello? Hi." The man finally puts his phone down. "I think my friend locked herself in the bathroom. Can you unlock the door?"

"I'm not authorized to let you into the ladies' room, sir," he drawls, slow as taffy stretching.

"Look, I know it's a little weird, but" — I lean in, lower my voice — "she found out the other day her dad's dying, and she's in a real bad place. I just want to make sure she's okay, you know?"

He sighs, long and heavy. Glances at his phone one last time. Opens a drawer and pulls out a ring the size of a bracelet, bristling with keys. I smile gratefully at him as he ambles over to the bathroom door and unlocks it, steps back with his hands raised like he wants no part of this.

Nessa is standing at the sink. The air rushes back into my lungs.

"Jesus, you scared me half to death. Did you know that door was locked? Didn't you hear me calling?" It sounds like I'm scolding her.

But when she turns to me, her face is wet, her eyes red and empty. And then I see the steam rising and billowing from the sink.

"What are you doing?"

I step closer, turn the faucet off. Her hands are shaking. The skin is red. Blisters rise angrily between her fingers, across her palms.

CHAPTER THIRTY-THREE: NESSA

It's like this:

Everyone has bad thoughts once in a while.

Did I remember to turn the oven off, or is the house going to burn down?

Was that a rock my car just ran over or an animal?

Has my husband's plane landed yet, or is it going to crash?

For most people, those thoughts are just pebbles in their shoe. They pause, shake them out, and keep walking — *yes, it's off, I always turn it off; it was probably just a rock; no, it's just running a little late.*

With obsessive-compulsive disorder, though, no matter how hard you dig, you can't take the pebble out. You keep walking anyway, because you have to. And the whole time, the pebble is there, digging into your flesh. Sometimes, the pebble is sharp, and it makes you bleed. You limp through the gash, or you fall. Sometimes, it leaves a blister, red and raw and beating with your pulse, and it's all you can think about.

But the worst part is that the whole time, you know it's just a pebble. You know you should be able to slip your shoe off and toss it back to the side of the road it came from. You see other people doing it all the time. And you can't.

And then the pebble starts to talk to you, and you feel even more miserable, even crazier. Pebbles do not talk. They don't.

These ones do. They whisper, sending hissing messages up your spine. Count every stair you walk up, and the house will not burn down. Turn the car around, and check that it was a rock, then check again to be sure your eyes were right the first time. Keep your hands clean, and your husband will stay safe.

There's no connection. You know there isn't. There's no cosmic balance that will safely bubble your house, your car, your family. But the more you follow the pebble's whispers, the louder and louder they become, until they are screaming, and the pain is almost worse than that in your foot. Because while they're getting stronger, their voices are learning to say other things, too.

You really are crazy, aren't you?

You are a bad person, for letting us pebbles in in the first place.

What is wrong with you?

OCD is not eating the brown M&Ms first because, you shrug, you just like it better that way. It is not preferring your books organized by color, even if it makes it harder to find what you're looking for. It is not neat handwriting, it is not a particular brand of notebook, it is not foods that don't touch, it is not counting the stairs as you walk up and down.

It is any and all of those things, if the pebbles tell you to. It is blisters on your feet and on your hands.

CHAPTER THIRTY-FOUR: DANIEL

I grasp Nessa by her wrist, avoiding the skin on her hand, and pull her out of the bathroom. The man is still standing outside the door, leaning against the wall and swinging his keys from one finger. His eyes widen when he sees the burns.

"Whoa."

She stares at her feet. Her hair falls across her face.

"She'll be fine," I say, like I have any clue. "And thanks," I add over my shoulder as we leave.

I wait until she's buckled into the car to take out my phone.

"What are you doing?" she says.

"Trying to find the nearest hospital," I say while I scroll. "At the very least, we need to get those burns checked out." I chuck my chin toward her hands, limp in her lap. "And I also think you should talk —"

"No." She turns to face me. Whatever had

been clouding her eyes is gone now, hardness in its place. "We don't have time, not now. They'll want to keep me overnight for observation, and — no. Find a drugstore, I'll tell you what to buy. I'll pay you back, whatever."

I want to refuse. I should, I know, already be driving. But somehow, it feels like I'm the one drowning, grasping at nothing, clawing at cold, dark water. Nessa has clearly been here before. So I find a pharmacy and go.

We spend the night at the Kentucky border, at a motel the same as all the rest. We sit side by side on one of the beds, rolls of gauze and tubes of ointment laid out between us. I start to wrap her hands into thick white clubs. She doesn't even wince.

"I was diagnosed with OCD when I was in college," she says.

I can feel her watching me. I keep my face blank, focus on weaving a strip of bandage between her fingers.

She fidgets, and the movement shifts her hands in my grip a little. "The hot water thing didn't come until later. Same with my fear of planes. But I've had OCD for as long as I can remember. Once, when I was in fifth grade, my parents went away for the weekend and left us with our neighbor." She blows out, and her breath shuffles across my face. "I was convinced something terrible was going to happen to them, that I'd never see them again. I spent an hour in the bathroom that Saturday, flossing my teeth. I know," she laughs, though my eyes are still trained on her hands, "it sounds so dumb. I told myself that if I did all the right things, all the things my parents wanted me to do, they'd come back, safe and sound."

I finish wrapping her hands, and she holds them up, stares at them. The fuzz rimming the bandages glows against the bedside lamps.

"Eventually, my gums started to bleed a lot," she says, matter-of-fact. "It dripped down into the neighbor's nice white sink. She finally heard me crying and opened the door. And the look on her face." Her head droops. "I knew I was crazy."

"I'm sure she was worried," I say, but I'm not sure, not really. After the rush of relief I felt when she wasn't on the floor with a bottle in her hand. When I realized what was actually happening, that I had no idea what was happening. Did I fall back? Did I wish, for a second, that this was something I recognized? Did I wonder all over again who exactly this person was?

She lies back on the bed, her wrapped hands suspended above her chest. "She was scared. And you know what? I don't blame her. Or you." She glances at me, and I make myself meet her eyes. "People have a hard enough time understanding all the weird things that go on inside their own, normal brains. Throw in a mental illness, and they really freak."

I shift away. My eyes travel the room, looking for something else, anything solid. They land on the pill bottles she's lined up on the nightstand. There are three of them. "These are your medications, then."

"Yep. These are how I manage to stay charming." She rolls to her side, her legs brushing up against mine, and taps the bottles one by one. "Luvox for daily maintenance. Xanax if the panic's getting really bad. Ambien if I'm having trouble sleeping. Unfortunately," she says as she rolls back to the center of the bed, "I have to pay for them out of pocket. That's, like, three bucks a day, a lot more if I need the Ambien.

"The drugs are so helpful. Not for everyone," she adds quickly, and I know she's thinking of Claire. Everybody does. "I was a mess while we were trying to find the right dose. Totally out of it, gaining weight, the works. Now, though." She draws her hands across her face, pulling the corners of her mouth into a clown-like smile.

In the silence that follows, I realize how much I'd missed this, her voice, over the past few days. The way it sweeps you under and along, brushing across your skin.

So I keep going.

"Do you have a therapist?"

She sighs up toward the ceiling. "Not really. It's just hard, moving so much. I have one in Vermont I still see once a year or so. He writes me my prescriptions, and that's that."

"Must've been hard, going in to get diagnosed." All those new patients of my mom's in her home office, standing in our bathroom a little too long.

Her eyes move toward the sunset collecting between the curtains. "I had to, for my mom."

I wait, but she doesn't say anything else.

"I know it's scary to find out something like that." I picture Claire, beside me in the car, twisting and retwisting her hair into a tight bun, slamming the door behind her, arms across her chest as she walked up to the community center.

"Maybe at first," she says. "But no. Somebody took what I thought was the worst part of me, the ugliest part. And they held it up to the light, and they shrugged and said, 'Eh, we've seen worse.' "

"It's brave of you," I say, because I can't help it. She glances up at me, and I clear my throat. "I mean, to go out and live in the world, have all those crazy adventures, not stay tied down to one place with a — an illness like that."

She rolls her eyes. "I carry this thing with me wherever I go. Doesn't matter if I'm in Vermont or Timbuktu. I'll always have to deal with the same shit." She pats her hands against her stomach and sits up. "When I was in Georgia, one of the farmhands fell off a ladder and broke his leg. It was a bad break, a compound fracture. I'd used the ladder the night before, just to change a lightbulb in the barn. He fell because he hadn't opened the ladder properly. It had nothing to do with the fact that I'd been the last to use it. Still." Her voice grows quiet. "I was convinced his fall was my fault. Every time I saw him in his cast, the guilt was overwhelming. It was all I could think about. So I packed up and moved as far away as I could. But it's not any better when I'm at home or when I was in college. Half the time, when I'm in Vermont, I'm certain the drinking water is contaminated with chemicals, and I can barely make myself

301

drink it."

One of her curls springs free of her ponytail, and she reaches up to tug it, but her bandaged fingers can't bend. She winces a little as her burned skin flexes. She turns to me and crosses one ankle over her knee. "This disorder, it's part of me. It's a thing about me. It's not the only thing."

Before I realize what I'm doing, my hands are framing her face, cupped against either cheek. Her eyes widen, but she doesn't pull away. "I believe you," I say. She's so close, I can breathe her breath. So close, I remember how desperate I was when I couldn't find her. I was afraid of losing her.

She smiles small, lips closed. "I know you do."

Embarrassed by the memory, I take my hands away. Why would I be so worried about losing someone I barely know?

She takes an Ambien that night, throwing her head back to drink her water. And then it's just me, lying in the dark once again, my hands laced across my chest. Wondering what the hell we're going to do next.

CHAPTER THIRTY-FIVE: MOLLY

The doorbell rings, a long, elaborate nursery rhyme that Sam installed as a joke years ago and then never got around to taking down. We stare at each other from across the living room, our eyes wide with panic. Having given it a couple of days in the fridge for show, I'd just finished scraping Allison's chicken into the kitchen trash, and there was no disguising the sharp scent of hot sauce and blue cheese dressing.

"That can't be the next car on the meal train already," Sam says, pulling off his reading glasses and folding his newspaper.

I shoot him a look as I stand up, because of course it is. Who else would it be? I hurry a story together on the way to the door explaining why we threw away all that time and effort — something to do with fentanyl, Sam's stomach, and spicy foods.

When I finally open the door, the woman standing there is tall and willowy, with thin hips and a silk watercolor scarf tied sideways across her throat. "You really do need to change that doorbell, love," she says, wheeling her suitcase into the house.

"What — what are you doing here?" I say, my hand still on the doorknob.

"You didn't really think I was going to let you alone, did you? I booked the next flight out I could get."

"Hey, Maggie," Sam calls from the living room.

"See? He's not surprised to see me. He knows better." She walks over to the living room, and as she reaches the doorway and Sam comes into view, I hold my breath. She smiles and says, "There he is. Hi, Sam."

It was Sam and Maggie before it was Sam and me. The two of them went to every party and mixer together our freshman year, where they held court on the couch or the lawn chairs, men and women alike flocking to them. I was there, too, sipping punch in a corner and trying to look politely uninterested as one sophomore or another droned on at me about classes and football games.

Then, one night, when Maggie was deep in conversation with one of her admirers, Sam walked me home. I didn't want him to, and I swore that I could find my own way back to our dorm. He insisted, though.

I caught Maggie's eye to make sure she'd be all right, and she cocked her head to the side a little, looking between me and Sam like she was making some sort of calculation.

After that, it wasn't Sam and Maggie anymore. It was Sam and me, or Sam and me and Maggie. I resisted at first — it was wrong, I knew, stealing your best friend's boyfriend, or whatever he was to her. It was unfeminist at the very least, cruel at the worst. "It's not stealing," she insisted, waving me out the door. To my surprise, I didn't particularly want to argue with her about this one.

She walks into the living room and sits on the arm of Sam's chair, tossing her arm over his back. "Let me guess," she says. "This was where you sat when you interviewed Nessa's boyfriends."

He shakes his head vigorously, but his eyes are fool's gold, luring in the unwary. "Only the ones who deserved it."

She cackles at that, wiping a tear from her eye when they've stopped laughing. "It's good to see you, Sammy."

"You too, Mags." He pats her on the knee. "Well, I'll let you two ladies catch up." He smiles at me. "It's time for my nap."

"I'll help you," she says, springing to her

feet and brushing aside his protests just like she once did with mine. She circles his waist with her arm as if she's leaning in to tell him a secret, but he's the one who leans, and I have to look away.

While they shuffle and murmur in our bedroom, I carry her suitcase up to Charlie's. It's heavy, although she always over-packs, so that's not an indication of how long she's planning to stay. I heave it onto the bed, the bones and muscles in my back popping and groaning, and smooth my hand over the blanket.

When everything's settled, Maggie's standing outside our bedroom, her arms crossed as she chews her lip. She sees me before I have a chance to back into Charlie's room. "Molly," she says, and her voice is not whole.

I step over to her and link with her elbow, tugging her gently back into Charlie's room. I don't want Sam to hear.

She does not fall into my arms or cry on my shoulder. She runs her hands over her face and presses on her eyes. She is wearing a string of colorful beads beneath her scarf, little wooden planets, and she twists the strand between her fingertips. They clack together, one by one.

"What will you do about him?" she says.

"Keep him here as long as we can, I suppose. The doctor says the fentanyl should do for another week or two, and then he'll need more care than I can give him. He said insurance almost certainly wouldn't cover in-home care." It's a speech I've prepared in case anyone asked.

"Let me cover it," she says, and I know from how quickly she does that this is the first time she's thought of it.

"It's sweet of you to offer, but you know we can't accept that."

She's already shaking her head. "You listen to me. You gave me the greatest gift I could dream of — kids that I only have to visit when I want to. I fly out every once in a while, and they treat me like God's gift while you do all the cooking and cleaning. And in return," she continues over my laughter, "I'm going to give Sammy the best damn death he could ask for."

This time, I don't bother saying no.

"So, how's Charlie?" she asks as I sit down on the creaking rocking chair next to hers on the porch. A cigarette dangles from her lips, and she holds the carton out to me, her face flat. I hesitate for only a moment before taking it and tapping one out for myself. Without missing a beat, she leans toward me with the same silver lighter we used in college. As far as I know, she hasn't smoked since then. As far as she knows, I haven't, either.

"He's the same, you know. Out in San Francisco." We exhale in unison, and the cloud hides my face.

She's still staring at me when the smoke clears. "When was the last time you spoke to him?"

I sigh and kick out my legs, swinging my feet back and forth a little. They're still in my house sandals, cheap plastic things that once had drawings of the Eiffel Tower printed on the foot beds. Charlie brought them back for me after his semester abroad. "See? We'll always have Paris," he said, kissing me swiftly on the cheek as I took them out of their crisp plastic wrapper.

"It's been six months since my last trip." She's well aware of this, since she sends Sam bland, cheerful text updates when I go, furthering the story that I'm visiting her instead. "I was supposed to go out again this month, but I can't leave Sam now."

"Does he know about —" She flicks her eyes upward.

I consider saying I'm not sure if Charlie knows about God, no, but I know she wouldn't laugh.

"I expect Nessa told him. She went out there a couple weeks ago to get him to come back." I don't have to look at her to know what she's thinking, so I add, "He doesn't want to hear it from us, anyway."

Maggie's eyes are wet again as she takes another drag — not that Charlie's ever shown his walls to her, not really. When he was small and Maggie came to visit, he would climb all over her, as if he could live in her limbs like a tree house.

She opens her mouth, but before she can say anything, there are two men in front of the porch. I hadn't even heard them drive up. It's Allison's husband and his former farmhand, their combined shoulders as broad as the porch steps. Their eyes are fixed low on the ground. I shove my cigarette toward Maggie, who takes it, bewildered, before they look up.

"Ben and Eli! What can I help you with?" I hope it sounds airy and gracious.

A car horn beeps twice behind them, an encouraging *toot-toot.* Craning my neck to peer past them, I see Allison in the driver's seat of their old pickup. She wiggles her fingers at me and backs the truck up the driveway, and now they're stranded here.

Ben clears his throat and lifts his eyes to somewhere in the general vicinity of my neck. "Allie mentioned you guys could use some help with the fields."

I am ready to shoo them off and tell them not to be silly, that we can manage fine on our own, but in all honesty, I'm not sure I can. More importantly, they have no way of getting home until Allison decides we've been given our due and comes back to pick them up.

I open the front door for them. Their heavy canvas jackets whisk against each other as they climb the stairs. "That's so thoughtful of you two." Maggie throws both cigarettes over the porch railing, where I'll have to retrieve them later, and follows us in. "I'll admit we're a bit at loose ends at the moment, as Allison — Allie — probably told you. Luckily, Sam takes very careful notes, so it should be easy enough to figure out what his plans were. I really have no memory for these things. Let me see." I should stop talking, I know, but the three sets of eyes on me are too much. I shuffle through the stack of clipped coupons and delivery menus on the counter by the phone until I find Sam's notebook and wave it over my head like a flag.

Ben and Eli bend their heads over the book, their nail-bitten fingers traveling over his handwriting. I've hardly ever heard Ben speak, but now the words flow smooth as water between the two of them. The loss of their farm, their laundry flapping like wings on lines outside their trailer, is a fist in my gut once again.

"This all looks straightforward enough," Ben says, his eyes moving toward the door. "Shouldn't take us too long."

"Well, go on ahead. Don't let me keep you. I'll have some coffee ready for you when you want to take a break."

Eli smiles gratefully at me, whether for the dismissal or the coffee, I can't say. They shuffle on out the door.

There's a lumpy smile on my face when I turn back to Maggie, and I'm scrambling for something to say, maybe something that recalls our days in high school giggling at the big 4-H boys in our class.

Her head is tilted, studying me, and she says, "That was really kind of them."

"Yes," I say, easing into a chair at the table. "It was. This town would do anything for Sam."

"I guess so," she says, still staring at me as she sits down next to me.

CHAPTER THIRTY-SIX: NESSA

That night, I lay in bed feeling something like relief. It was as if I'd let the air out of a balloon, and now the tautness was gone, only slack rubber left. I tumbled easily into sleep on my Ambien wave.

When I wake, the sun mottled red behind my eyelids pulls me back into myself. My hands pulse with pain in all the old places. My insides feel more raw than empty.

I open my eyes, and Daniel is still there, his back turned to me, his side rising and falling. I should have told him to leave, to get as far away as he can, but then how would he get back to his car and his life? We're stuck here together, in this place where the earth beneath our feet is riddled with caves.

Growing up, it was always my mom who bore the brunt of me. It was a slow, steady slide from kissing my skinned knees and checking under my bed to fielding my daily what-ifs: What if I have cancer? What if you get bitten by a bat? What if Dad falls off his tractor and hits his head?

The pebbles changed depending on what I'd seen on the news or heard at school that day. Eventually, my parents started turning off the TV and radio when I came home, though I hardly noticed at the time. It was only in high school, when Charlie started yelling at my parents about needing to watch the nightly news for his civics class, that I saw what had happened. "Can't you see she's crazy?" he hissed. "We can't all live in her world, by her rules."

And still, every morning, while my dad made coffee downstairs and before I went down to join him, I crept into bed with my mom. I would catalog what was wrong, what had been rubbing up blisters the day before and all through the night. When I grew older, the fears grew harder to grasp. It was less about death and decay, more about the dark, mysterious folds of my brain.

Every time, she would smooth her cupped hand over my head and kiss my temple, her breath warm and stale. She would promise me that everything would be all right, that I would be just fine. She would wrap her arms around me tight and squeeze. And no matter how old I was or how much I knew better, that was when I could finally loosen. It was like her words plucked the pebbles out of my shoes and threw them far, far away.

There were always more pebbles, though. Every day, new pebbles.

It took me a long time to figure out what it was doing to her. I was nineteen and home from college. I opened my eyes that morning to my dad's wandering whistle and wiggled my toes under the blanket, back in this place where the pebbles went away.

I padded down the hall to my parents' room. Their door creaked open. Mom was asleep still, her mouth softly open, pushing dust motes in and out with her breath.

"Mom," I whispered. I shook her shoulder. My list that morning was long and backlogged. I wasn't being friendly enough to my quiet roommate. I was starting to think the boy I was dating wanted true love, when all I wanted was to skitter away. I might be failing my American lit class, and every time I reached for Frederick Douglass, my throat closed up with the thought of all I was throwing away. And did she remember if the toaster oven she'd bought me had an auto-off feature? Because I was pretty sure I'd forgotten to unplug it before I left, so our dorm might be burning down as we speak.

My mom finally opened her eyes, and it took a moment for her to see me. In those seconds, I saw, for the first time, how tired she was: purply shadows under her eyes, smile weak and brave. And I wondered where exactly she'd been putting those pebbles. Maybe, instead of throwing them away, she'd been tucking them in her own shoes to keep them from rolling back to me.

"There's my girl," she said, drawing her covers back to make room for me. I crawled into the pocket she'd made and curled into her side. Her hand smoothed her usual rhythm over my hair. "Tell me everything," she said.

I wanted to; I did. Every single morning, I want to. Instead, I swallowed, clenched my hands together, and said, "There's not much to tell. How are you and Dad doing with your empty nest?"

Her hand stilled. "We're fine," she said faintly. "We're just fine."

I found myself at the college counseling center for lack of a better place to go. I'd tried to manage the pebbles myself, reciting them quietly to myself at night, but it only kept me awake, the sound of them rattling around in my skull, and my roommate had started to give me weird looks in the morning. I wasn't expecting anything to work, but at least I hoped I wouldn't be the craziest person the counselors had ever seen.

I repeated this over and over in my head as I sat in the waiting room, peeling the soles of my shoes back from something sticky on the floor and flipping through a parenting magazine someone had left behind. I was just getting into an article about how many hours of TV a child should watch when somebody called my name.

I'm not sure who I was expecting to be standing there — some combination of Freud and Mr. Rogers, maybe — but it wasn't Ricky. Ricky, with her pleasant plumpness, her jewel-toned chenille sweaters, and her glasses on a beaded chain around her neck.

"Hi," she said, shaking my hand. "My name's Dr. Marsh, but you can call me Ricky."

She led me back to her office, which was just another office like all the other ones I'd seen at the school. A computer hummed through its screen saver, a bulletin board was papered over with old Christmas cards, and stacks of unlabeled binders covered the desk. There was an extra box of tissues next to the chair she motioned toward, but that was about the only difference.

She settled into her own chair, scooting it away from the desk and toward mine. She peered down at her clipboard. "So, Vanessa, what can I help you with today?"

"It's Nessa, actually. And yeah, it's stupid really, no big deal." I stopped just short of saying I'm a waste of time. I could picture her marking me down on her worksheet. Self-esteem: low. Her eyes moved to my hands in my lap. I unlaced them and flexed my fingers.

"It's just," I tried again. "I get these worries, these ridiculous worries. About diseases, or about what people think of me, or about, I don't know, fires. I used to tell my mom about them all the time, and I'd feel better for a little bit, but I think she's getting tired of it, so I thought maybe I could come in and talk to you instead."

It sounded profoundly unappealing when I said it out loud, even for someone who's paid to listen to college kids complain all day. Ricky had uncrossed her legs and leaned closer, placing her elbows on her knees with her fingers steepled near her lips.

"Tell me, Nessa, how long have you been talking to your mom like that?"

Though her face was blank and empty, it

felt like she was asking how long I'd been sleeping with that security blanket. I coughed. "I don't know. Ten years? Twelve?"

She nodded but didn't write anything down. "And have you ever been fixated on cleanliness — washing your hands, wiping the counters? Or have you ever needed to count things, to calm your mind down?"

I winced. "Yeah, a little. I was an odd kid." I looked down at her green suede clogs. She asked a few more questions like this, ferreting out all the habits that made me cringe.

Finally, she cleared her throat. "Well, we have a couple of options here. You're welcome to come in any time you'd like and chat about what's on your mind. But I suspect you may have an underlying disorder, and if we work on targeting that, it may serve you better in the long run." She turned back to her desk, and I heard the word *disorder* over and over as a drawer squealed open.

"I have a diagnostic test in here that you can take, just to be sure," she was saying. She pulled out a packet and held it out to me. "If you're willing, of course."

The words on the page jumped one at a time: *worry, excessive, unwanted, urges, impulses*. And the title: "Diagnostic Criteria for Obsessive-Compulsive Disorder."

■ ■ ■ ■

I called my mom as soon as I left the counseling center, cold air biting my nose. In the end, it had been no different than a vocabulary quiz. Quick with your pencil, yes/no/maybe, sometimes/always/never. Don't think too hard about what your answers say about you — although they say a lot; they say almost everything. Then Ricky took the packet back and compared it to an actual, literal score sheet, her gray head moving back and forth between the two stacks on her desk. And finally, she looked up at me, smiled encouragingly, and said, "Let's discuss your treatment plan."

"Hi, Mom," I said when she picked up. "I don't have much time. I'm on my way to class" — a lie, I wasn't sure why — "but I wanted to tell you, I went to the counseling center today, and they told me I have obsessive-compulsive disorder, so . . ." So you don't have to worry about me anymore. I'll let you sleep in from now on. You are finally free.

"Oh." She paused. "Well. Are you going to seek treatment?"

"I made a weekly appointment, and we're going to try something called cognitive behavioral therapy. And we might try some medication, too, depending on how that goes." I stopped.

"That's good. That's great."

If I didn't know any better, I could swear there was disappointment in the spaces between her words.

"I'm glad you're okay, honey. Good luck in your class."

"Thanks," I said. I stood there with the phone pressed against my ear and my fingers going numb, my feet balanced on the edge of a sidewalk. Students moved around me, a stream of puffy jackets and ducked heads.

When Daniel wakes up, the pit has already opened again, sucking me down and down and in. It's almost like the walls are whispering, though I know it's not the walls; it's just the pebbles. *He's dying, he's dying. You're losing him, and it's all your fault.* For a second, I'm not even sure who they're talking about.

He turns to me, smiling sweet. "Let's change those bandages, hmm?" he says.

I hold my hands out, wrists together like he's handcuffing me. The fabric has stiffened with greasy stains from the ointment. He leans in close to unwind them. I study his scalp beneath his hair, pink and fresh, and steady my hands so he won't notice.

CHAPTER THIRTY-SEVEN: DANIEL

I thought for a second that the old Nessa was back, talking and talking. But I can tell before I even look up from the new bandages that she's gone again. She basically drew me a map to herself last night, and I still don't know how to get there. So she spends the day staring out the passenger's window and picking at the edges of the medical tape.

We make it to the northern border of West Virginia by late afternoon and stop at a sketchy pay-by-the-hour motel to take a quick nap. She says she wants to call her mom for updates. I step into the bathroom and turn the fan on so I don't have to pretend I'm not listening.

When I come back out, she's sitting on the edge of the bed, her hands dangling between her knees. Her face is pale. She stares at me.

"What is it?" I say. I stumble over to her.

"Is it your dad? Is he worse?"

"No, it's not that." She turns her face to the floor. "Did you leave your circle plans behind at the Shannons'?"

"No way. They're right here in my pocket." I reach for them reflexively. The crinkle is reassuring, but only for a second. "Oh shit." I drop down onto the second bed. "The draft plans. I stashed them away so I could find a dumpster somewhere safe. They found them, didn't they?"

"Yeah. My mom explained them away. Don't worry."

I gulp for air. This is it. I've blown it. Word will get out. Not only will Sam not get his magic, but Lionel will find out, and I'll be the local eccentric, too. Everything I've made, nothing but a punch line. Something black appears at the edge of my vision. I want to grab at the edge of the bed. My fingertips are too numb.

Nessa is trying to talk to me, but I can't understand. It's like she's calling at me from miles away. She holds a paper bag to my mouth and nose, the one that held our sandwiches from lunch. "Breathe," she commands, and this one word, I get. So I do. It smells like pickles and bread. "And again."

She does it over and over, ten or twelve times until my heartbeat slows. She lowers the bag. "Panic attacks," she says. "Yet another fun side effect of OCD." She tells me about when she started getting them. She was thirteen. She was too embarrassed to tell her doctor about these things that felt like heart attacks but weren't really. So Sam made an appointment for himself and listed off the symptoms as his own. He came home with a package of brown paper bags for her to try.

Thirty minutes later, the fog's gone, and I can actually respond, talk back.

"Do you want to talk about it?" she asks quietly.

"No." I'll have to trust Molly's excuse. Try not to picture Connie showing the plans around town. She wouldn't do that, I don't think. The draft plans are different enough from my final version that she shouldn't be able to make the connection once the circle's done. I hope.

"In that case, I need to shower." She stands and holds out her hands. "Wrap these up for me?"

I use the plastic grocery bags and roll of duct tape we salvaged from the back seat of her car. I smile up at her, but she looks away. I need to find some way to help her. Anything.

When I hear the water running, I rummage through her duffel bag, my heart pounding. The phone's wallpaper is a picture of their barn, the sky so blue, it could be a stock photo. I push aside my second thoughts and I dial.

"Has he deteriorated already?"

I was expecting his voicemail, maybe hoping for it.

"Hi, Charlie. It's Daniel, actually. I didn't have your number, so I had to use Nessa's phone."

"What's wrong? Where is she?" His voice is harsh.

"She's . . . um. She's okay, I guess. She had an . . . incident. With her OCD? Her hands are burned pretty bad. I'm not sure what to do."

He sighs. "Where are you now?"

"On our way out of West Virginia. We should be back in Vermont in a couple of days."

There's a rustling on the other end of the line. "Okay. I'll be there. Thanks." He hangs up.

I drop the phone back in her bag and sit for a minute, watching a spider march its way across the ceiling. I need to make the next call from my own phone.

"Daniel! Twice in one week? We must've won the lottery. Let me go get your mother so we can put you on speaker."

"Actually, Dad," I say, "I was hoping to talk to her alone for a minute. I need her professional opinion on something."

"Oh." I hope he's not as let down as he sounds. "Of course. Just a minute."

The spider makes it all the way to the corner of the room, where it has stretched its web. Its legs move together, up and down. It must have caught something.

"Dad says you need some advice?" my mom says, a little breathless.

"Um, right. So this friend I'm traveling with. She has OCD. And her dad's really sick, and I think it's messing with her. I'm just not sure what to do."

A little pause of surprise passes down the line. "Is she medicated?"

"Yeah." I lean over to where Nessa has lined up her bottles on the bed and recite their names, carefully turning each one so it's exactly as she left it. "We could probably be in New Jersey by tonight." I feel like a kid again, pointing out a shiny new toy we just happened to pass in the store, not daring to ask for it.

"Well. She's not my patient, Daniel. It would be highly unethical for me to treat her, and anyway, there's not much I can do in one visit. OCD is not my specialty. You know that," she says primly.

"Yeah, okay, fine," I say, half angry and half embarrassed. I should have known. "Thanks anyway."

"If you can drop by this evening, I don't have any patients scheduled. I can have a quick conversation with her and see if I can't get her back on track with her therapist."

The air rushes back into my lungs. "Great!"

Nessa steps out of the bathroom, wrapped in a towel. I hadn't heard the shower turn off.

I clear my throat, lower my voice. "That would be great. Talk soon, then." I hang up before my mom can reply, close my eyes so Nessa can fumble on her clothes. She doesn't ask who I was talking to.

After I finally freed myself from Lionel at Claire's funeral service, I stumbled over to my car. Though I could barely see the door handle in front of me, I managed to climb into the front seat. I rested my head on the steering wheel, refusing to watch as people in black filed out of the church. I remembered my dad's hand on my shoulder that night before I left home, steadying and calm.

The phone was ringing in my ear before I

knew what I was doing. My dad's voice hit me like a bus. "What's wrong?" he said, and it all came out, all the things I didn't want to tell them on our monthly phone calls.

"My girlfriend, Claire, you remember her. She was an addict. Alcohol and I don't know what else. I thought she was doing fine. I was helping her. She was doing great. But then one day, she disappeared, and now — I'm at her funeral." I picked at my thumbnail and watched through the windshield as Lionel and Leslie scurried to the parking lot.

I'm not sure what I expected my dad to say. I wanted to be crouched beside him in the woods, the sun warm on my back as he pointed at a beetle. Maybe he would tell me something about their life cycle that sounded vaguely profound and then point at their tiny beetle genitalia.

Instead, he just swore softly. "Shit. I don't really know what to say."

"Don't worry about it." I closed my eyes.

"Do you want me to go get your mother?"

"No." I shook my head, even though he couldn't see it. "Please don't tell her."

"Oh. Okay." He sounded uncertain. It was hard to tell how long he'd be able to keep the secret. I wasn't sure why I bothered. They worked in tandem, the two of them.

There was a rapping on my window. I opened my eyes, annoyed, but instead of Lionel, Claire's parents were standing there. Their faces were broken. Her mom clutched something in her hands. I didn't have to look twice to know what it was — a picture of me, printed on cheap paper. Claire kept it tucked in her wallet, between her credit cards.

"I've got to go."

He only made it a couple of days. The phone's buzzing was like a drill to my head when I saw her number come up.

"Oh, honey." Her voice made me wince. "I'm so sorry."

"Yeah, well." I traced my finger along the edge of the motel room's side table before muting the talk show playing on the TV.

"Where are you?" she asked.

"I'm working. At a farm in Omaha," I lied without thinking.

"I wish you would come home. You were always —"

Always so quiet, wanted to save people, such a sweet boy.

My fist curled up, and I couldn't undo it.

"— was very sick," she was saying. "You need to know that it wasn't your fault. You know that, right?"

"Yeah, whatever." I knew even as I said it how annoying it was, teenaged.

She fell silent.

A few beats passed before she said, "Well. You call us if there's anything we can do."

After we hung up, I hurled the phone against the wall. It chipped the cheap drywall, and a rain of plaster fell down around it. I turned the talk show volume back up.

She wants what's best for me. She wants me to be happy. I know that. Of course I do. But I'll be damned if her voice didn't uptick with excitement when I told her I needed her.

CHAPTER THIRTY-EIGHT: MOLLY

I knew we'd made a terrible mistake as soon as we drove up to the land, the truck bucking beneath us. We'd bought the acreage sight unseen, using up all our savings. And now we would suffer the consequences.

Sam stepped up to the edge of the weeds. Mosquitoes nipped at my arms as I joined him. He kicked at a particularly large rock and rolled it over with one boot.

"Well, this is . . ." he began.

"A disaster," I said. A slate shingle slid off the roof, shattering into nothing when it hit the rotting porch.

He hugged me to his side. "Our disaster," he said.

Sweat equity would only go so far until we had to buy things, so many things. Lumber, nails, seed, pesticide — on and on it went. That's what I told Sam the morning I gathered up my pocketbook and asked him to drive me into town to find a job. In reality, I found that Thomas had followed me east, staring mournfully over my shoulder while I scrubbed grime out of the tub and painted over chipped doorjambs. I feared if I didn't get out of the house, I would scream.

There was no bank in town, not back then, but I'd seen a *Now Hiring* sign scrawled in the window of the general store. I asked Sam to wait outside for me, and he kept the engine running, listening to the weather report with the window down. As if we had anything in the ground to worry about.

The bell over the door tinkled when I opened it, and I winced. Nobody looked up, though — not even the girl behind the single cash register.

She looked like she was sixteen, maybe seventeen, with her bleached hair piled up into a ponytail. She wore heavy eyeliner and a denim jacket even though the air in the store was soupy. A small fan sat on the counter, wheezing on her face.

"I don't know, Becky," she sighed into the phone, leaning into the counter as she ran a long, pink file over her long, pink nails. "I just can't wait to get out of this dumb town, you know?"

As I drew closer, I read the name tag

pinned to her jacket: Allison. I cleared my throat, and she rolled her eyes, nice and slow. "Anyway, I've gotta go," she said into the phone. "Customers." The word was like a slur somehow. She giggled at Becky's response before hanging up.

"Can I help you?" she said, her eyes traveling from my last clean blouse to my discount-store slacks.

"I'd like to fill out a job application, please," I said, keeping my chin up high.

She smirked. "You're a little older than what we normally hire."

I planted one hand on my hip. "I've got news for you. I'm probably only about seven years older than you. It goes by faster than you could ever imagine."

To this day, I'm not sure where the words came from. Allison stopped chewing her gum and stared at me for a moment. Then she tossed her ponytail over one shoulder and laughed and laughed.

"Fair enough," she said. She blew a small peach bubble and drew it whole into her mouth while she pulled an application out from behind the counter.

Allison's parents still owned the general store then, and somehow, they trusted her with all the hiring decisions, so we'd only been back home an hour before she called to offer me the job.

"So, like, can you start tomorrow? I've got homework and stuff," she said. I could hear her gum cracking.

"Of course," I said, twisting the phone cord around my finger.

Sam looked up from the living room floor, where he was tearing up carpet, and flashed me a thumbs-up.

"Rad. I mean, good. See you then!"

My shift started at nine. Every day, I would have Sam drop me off at the store fifteen minutes early. I spent most of the day selling cigarette packs to men who wouldn't quite meet my eye and canisters of baby formula to women who looked like they were pleading for something. After school, clusters of children would come in, crowing over comic books and magazines they would never buy. At lunch, one or two older women would come in for a cellophane-wrapped sandwich. They laid their hands on my arm, their eyes sympathetic, when I told them where we lived. I would move my arm out from under them to get them their change, saying we were making progress, little by little, defending Sam while he bent and knelt and hammered.

Sometimes, Allison would stand behind

the counter with me and whisper loudly about boys. And sometimes, her father would come out from the back office, staring off at something while he stood in front of the soda fridge.

One morning, early on, I slipped around the counter and walked up to him. "Thank you so much for the opportunity, Mr. Peabody," I said, voice and eyes both lowered. At the bank, my boss had smiled smugly when I'd done this, stopping just short of patting me on the head.

Mr. Peabody looked almost alarmed, glancing around the store to be sure no one had heard. "That's all right, Molly," he said. "Don't mention it. Just keep on working hard, and you'll do fine, like the rest of us."

So that's what I did, for two whole years, until I found I couldn't open the cash register around Charlie, growing in my belly. By that time, Sam had cleared out the fields and was bringing in his first harvest, so we didn't need the money quite so much anymore. Though Thomas's face still watched me in the middle of certain nights, I mostly found myself picturing Charlie's features instead, his fingers and toes, his eyes shut tight against the world.

Allison started dating Ben just before I left the store. He was from the next town over, and I could tell from the hush in her voice that she felt this was her ticket out. She stopped bleaching her hair and let the red creep back. When Ben came by the store, she would tilt her chin up to him and stare and stare.

The Peabodys sold the store shortly after I left. The next time I saw Mr. Peabody was at Allison and Ben's wedding. He was standing in the corner of the church basement, smiling a little with those same distant eyes.

These are the things I didn't tell Maggie at the time. When she called, I brushed over updates on the kitchen, the house, and Sam. She had bundled me off into this new life, and I was too ashamed to complain about what I found there. I asked instead about her law school applications and who she was dating out west.

Last night, as I lay awake in bed, all I could think of was how foolish I'd been not to tell her. She would've understood, no matter how different our lives turned out to be. And so, today, after Allison drops Ben and Eli off for their second day of work, I tell Maggie all of it, bracing my hands on the edge of the kitchen table. I spill these truths, hoping she will understand the tangled weave of this town and how I'd found myself caught in it, held by old acquaintances who believed themselves to be friends. By those who love Sam. She watches me, her eyes not quite narrowed, her chin in her palm. When I've finished, the ticking of the old clock on the wall is the only sound.

She clasps her hands and says, "It seems like Allison isn't just sending her husband over for Sam's sake." She studies me, and I rock back and forth on my chair a little, knowing what she means: she'd sent him over for my sake, too. I don't know how that could be true. "These people really care about you. You know that, right?"

I hitch my shoulders up a touch, not quite a shrug, but not quite assent.

"Have you looked into those loans for your bakery yet?"

"No," I say, turning away.

She sighs. "Are you going to stay here when Sam is gone?"

The question pinches. "I don't really know where else I would go. I never thought I'd have to start all over."

This is where the Maggie I know would tell me to buck up. She would start imagining a future for me so vivid that I'd find myself dreaming along: that bakery, its pine floors, the warm scent of bread. She would almost make me forget the weight of Sam's absence that I would carry with me, forever at my center.

Instead, she presses her lips together and stares down at her hands. I prod her under the table with my toe. She says, "I'm getting a divorce."

At first, I want to say no.

By the time Maggie met her husband, she had given up on marriage entirely. "I just can't find anyone who can keep up with me," she would say, and I let her, even though her smile faded further at every friend's wedding. Then she met him — a journalist, a traveler — and I knew they were happy. I knew, at last, that it didn't matter that I was the one who ended up with Sam.

"What happened?" I say, not much louder than breathing.

She traces her fingertip along the lip of the mug. "I can't remember the last time we just sat on the couch together, reading the newspaper, and it didn't end in an argument." She smiles ruefully, then her chin starts to wobble.

I hesitate only for a moment before coming around the table and gathering her up. She clings to my arms.

"I wasn't going to tell you. I really wasn't."

"It's okay," I say into her vanilla-scented hair. Of course it is, of course, though a small part of me wonders how on earth I can help her while my life fades. Everything happens all at once, in one big snarled mess, and sometimes it's beautiful, and sometimes it's not.

That damn doorbell rings again. I let her go and walk to the door, still rubbing at my face as I open it.

Ben is standing there, his eyes moving every which way, a snapped-off cornstalk top lying like a small body in his hands.

"Eli and I noticed out there that some of the cornstalks looked like they were spray-painted or something."

With a creeping horror, I realize that the stalk is, in fact, striped with a slightly unnatural shade of green. Somehow, I had completely forgotten about Daniel.

"We saw them yesterday and didn't want to bug you about it," Ben continues, "but we don't want to mess with one of Sam's systems if that's what this is, is all. So we were wondering if you knew what it meant?"

CHAPTER THIRTY-NINE:
DANIEL

"I know we need to get back to Vermont as soon as possible and everything," I say, glancing at Nessa in the passenger's seat, "but maybe we could make a quick stop at my parents' in New Jersey?" I'm not sure how much the sink incident had to do with the unexpected cave detour, but I'm not taking any chances with another surprise stop. Through the corner of my eye, I see her turn to face me, the seat belt straining.

"Are you kidding? Now? When my dad's . . ."

I rush to fill the gap. "They're five minutes off the highway, and it's been a while since I've seen them. Plus, I'd need one more stopover before we make it up to Vermont anyway. My legs are about to fall off. Not that I'd make you sleep there or anything. We could leave after dinner and then find a place to stay farther north or something."

When I finally look at Nessa again, she's

frowning a little. "You said your mom was a therapist, right?" she says.

"Yeah, but —"

"I don't have time to be psychoanalyzed right now. Come on."

I reach over and pat her shoulder a little, fumbling with my eyes on the road. "Please? It might help, and it'll only take a few minutes. You need to take care of yourself before you can take care of your dad, right?"

She freezes until I take my hand away again. She turns back toward the window, but then says, "Okay."

A few minutes pass, and my muscles loosen a bit before she says, "Tell me a little about this place where you grew up." She looks at me sideways. "Since you're feeling so talkative today."

The place I grew up. College town, run by the professors, in theory. But really, it's run by the students, swarms of teenagers who changed every year and always looked the same. When I was younger, they all seemed so wise. My parents always hired my dad's students to babysit for me. One of them had long, shiny hair and would sit next to me on the couch, flipping through the channels and listing off all the things I should and shouldn't do when I was old enough to date. I stared at her and nodded when I thought I was supposed to. I couldn't really imagine her in my dad's class, labelling thoraxes and antennae.

Nessa rolls her eyes. "Yeah, okay. Older woman on your couch, what a thrill. What about, like, friends, pets?" She lifts one foot onto the dashboard, picks at her shoelace. "Girlfriends?"

"I had a grand total of one girlfriend, mostly because I thought I should. Jess. We kind of fell out of touch."

Nessa drops her foot back down, leaving a dusty print behind, like she'd been climbing up walls. Maybe she was expecting another Claire, thinks all the women I'm attracted to are screwed up. And maybe they are.

I shift lanes to pass a truck that's weaving lazily back and forth. "I had a group of friends, you know, same as anyone else. Really only one close one, Ken, but we don't have anything in common anymore, so. And one cat named Mocha. My parents got her when I was a baby because one of their professor friends told them it would keep me from developing allergies. But turns out, my dad was allergic, so my mom chased her around every night so she could shut her away in the basement while we slept."

I laugh at the memory, my mom reaching

warily under the family room couch where Mocha had lodged herself, the cat's green eyes flashing.

Nessa smiles dimly, watching the cars as we pass. "That sounds nice," she says.

Nessa is asleep when we get to New Jersey, so I'm alone as I pull down the street to my parents' house. Everything is neat and squared, the houses straight-shouldered, white, gray, brick. Students walking along the sidewalk, running their hands over the hedges. They look so young, I'm surprised they can stay upright under the weight of their backpacks.

There's one coming down the front walkway when I park. My parents added two entrances to the house after we moved in: one that leads directly into my dad's study, so he can host office hours from home, and one that goes to my mom's office. The third door, the front one, is for the rest of us. This setup is supposed to make people feel safe, cocooned from the rest of my parents' lives.

But the truth was, no matter where I was in the house, I could always hear the crying or the arguing, over grades or something larger. After those appointments, my parents would come find me. If it was my mom, she would place one hand on my head, saying nothing, like she was drawing something from me through my scalp. If it was my dad, he would collapse next to me on the couch, rub his face, ask what was on TV.

This time, it's a student, a freshman, looks like. He sticks a pair of headphones in his ears and bobs his head silently at me as I pass, like a bull lowing. Maybe he thinks I'm a classmate.

I pause in front of the door and rock back on my heels. I'm deciding whether to knock first or try the doorknob when it swings open, and there's my dad. He sweeps me into a hug, clapping me on the back the way guys do at football games. The skin between my shoulder blades stings a little. My mom stands behind him, touching my arm before he even lets go.

"Wow, have we missed you," my dad says as he steps back. His smile is uneven.

"You guys repainted in here," I say. The walls are stark and white. The height marks that once inched up the frame of the front hall closet are gone.

"Where's your friend?" my mom asks.

I touch the edge of the door, still open. "She's asleep in the car. I thought I'd come in and say hi before waking her up."

My dad shoots her a look, a warning.

"Well, go ahead and invite her in," she says.

I do as I'm told. But when I rap on the car window, Nessa isn't asleep after all. Her bandages sit in a white pile at her feet, and she's just finished stretching another flesh-colored Band-Aid across her palm. She looks up at me. For a second, we stare right into each other's nervousness.

She opens the door and stands, and the moment is gone. My hand hovers above her back, her shoulder, as we walk up to the door, never quite gaining purchase.

"Welcome, welcome," my dad says, ushering her through the door while my mom watches. "I'm Nick, and this is my wife, Theresa."

He holds his hand out, and Nessa raises both hers in the air apologetically. "I would shake your hand, but mine are kind of a mess," she says. "I'm sure Daniel told you about my accident."

I hadn't. My dad glances over her head at me as we walk into the living room and says nothing.

"Well, the roast's still in the oven, but Nick made his famous guacamole recipe to nibble on while we wait," my mom says, motioning toward the small bowl of green mush sitting on the coffee table.

"The secret is, we buy it by the tub at the grocery store," my dad says out of the side of his mouth, leaning toward Nessa. It's an old joke, one I used to roll my eyes at, but my mom grins at him, and Nessa laughs as we settle in, Nessa and I on the couch, my parents across from us in their armchairs.

The next twenty minutes are a blur. My parents ask Nessa question after question about Vermont, her family, the farm. She grows more and more animated with each one, more colored-in. My parents murmur in all the right places, coo sympathetically, but my mom won't stop looking between the two of us, like she's trying to puzzle us out. I'm glad we left a half cushion of space between us.

And then, Nessa leans back and says, "So, Theresa. I think Daniel wants you to fix me."

My dad coughs. My mom's eyes widen. Nessa smiles, but she crosses her arms over her chest. The silence is taut.

CHAPTER FORTY:
MOLLY

Ben shifts his feet, left to right, and I find my voice, somewhere down in my abdomen. "It's —" I say, and I turn back to Maggie, who's leaning over her chair to see. "It's —" The clock's still ticking, whispering. *It's what? It's what?*

They would never believe the story Sam fed to Lisa Zinke. They would laugh at the notion of finding every cutworm-damaged stalk and tending to it before it goes too far. Such a strategy would be another piece of evidence in the mounting case against Sam Barts's sanity. So, then, it's an art project of Nessa's — everyone thinks she's a sunflower, tall and otherworldly and beautiful, so they might believe this strangeness.

I glance up at the ceiling, toward our bedroom. Sam won't be getting up for another couple of hours, closer to lunchtime. He's no help to me right now.

I need to buy some more time, just a few

more minutes to polish up a story.

Ben is looking sorrier and sorrier to have asked me. He twirls the cornstalk between his palms, back and forth until it blurs.

"Come on. I'll drive you two home. You've done enough for the day. I'll tell you more when we get there." I edge past him toward our truck.

Maggie follows, uninvited, saying, "This I've got to see." She's smiling again, so I don't protest.

Ben mutters something to Eli as I pass them at the base of the front steps.

Ben and Maggie insist on taking the back seat, leaving the front for Eli, who looks almost put-upon by the assignment. They move the bags of birdseed and heavy tarps from the back bench to the bed of the truck. Then, they sit there like shamefaced teenagers at the back of the class.

I bend and flex my fingers around the clutch and can't imagine what I'm going to say. My mind is empty, drained by panic. I have to come up with something. Sam will be crushed if they find out. I picture Daniel's face, what it might look like rumpled with anger or disappointment at me. And Nessa will surely be unhappy, too, attached as she now seems to be to that boy.

I don't know whether I'm relieved or not

when I see Allison's truck in front of their house. It's a brand-new double-wide they have, and it looks almost the same as any other house in town, low-slung, with vinyl siding. The wooden frame it sits on is still greenish, with numbers from the lumber yard scribbled along the edges.

When I knock on the door, Allison opens it. She stands there with her legs spread wide and her hands in fists on her hips. It occurs to me that I should have called her before we came over.

"Benjamin Remy, I told you to call me when you were ready. You're supposed to be helping Molly, not making her drive you all over town," she says.

He touches her elbow, the gentlest thing. Her eyes drop to his other hand, which is still holding that stalk, pinched between his fingertips.

"It's all right," I say. "There's actually something I needed to speak with you all about. I hope it's okay we just stopped by unannounced like this."

She pauses, just for a moment. "Of course," she says and steps aside.

"This is my friend from childhood, Maggie. I'm sure you've met before." The apology in Maggie's eyes is quick but impossible to miss, and suddenly, I'm sure they haven't met. I feel myself shrink by a couple of inches. Not only have I invited myself over to her new house, but I've brought a stranger as well.

Allison smiles wide and opens the door even wider. "Absolutely."

The door leads right into their kitchen. It's smaller than the one in their old house, to be sure, but the cabinets gleam, and a small pot of mums is the only clutter on the laminate countertops. One of their daughters, Nadia, is spreading peanut butter on a piece of toast, and when she hears the door close behind us, she nods before ambling back to her room with her plate.

"We tell her she should stay on campus and enjoy herself on the weekends, but she keeps wanting to come home," Allison says. I can tell she's trying to make it sound like a complaint. "She's a shy one, just like her dad.

"Go on. Have a seat. We don't have a living room set anymore" — she looks away and combs her fingers through her ponytail — "but there's plenty of room at the kitchen table."

Ben and Eli straddle the bench running down one wall of the kitchen. Maggie picks a stool that sits a little bit too high, and the two wooden chairs are left for Allison and me. She pulls a container of store-bought muffins out of a cabinet and places it on the table, twittering about how she wishes she had more to offer.

Then they're all waiting for me — Maggie and Allison staring at my face, Ben staring at the table, and Eli staring over my shoulder. I tap my fingers lightly on my lap, and I know exactly what to say. They'll keep it a secret, even from Sam. If I don't tell them the truth, they'll put it together themselves once the circle is revealed, and then all hell would break loose, hurt feelings and rumors flying. I know now that I can't pretend it's a project of Nessa's. It's my husband's, and his alone.

"As you all know, Sam is sick. For good this time." I can't see their faces as I speak. "He got this idea in his head during his last remission, and for the life of me, I couldn't get him to let it go. When we came home from his last scan, the one where they found the tumor" — I waver just a little — "he decided he had to act on it."

I look around at them all. Maggie is smiling with her lips closed, no doubt remembering all his far-fetched college plans: to hitchhike across the country, and to marry me. Allison and Ben wear matching expectant expressions, and for a moment, I feel

351

like one of their daughters, about to tell them something they won't like. If I didn't know any better, I would say something dawns on Eli's face.

"You see, there's this community. All over the U.S., apparently. These people, they make crop circles."

Allison laughs, one big bark. "Well, that's the strangest thing!"

I flinch a little. When nobody joins her, she falls silent.

"I thought so, too. You know Sam, once he's got one of his ideas . . ." I trail off, and she sets her elbows on her table, her fingers kneading the flesh of her upper arms. Of course she knows. There's not a person in this town who doesn't know.

They all stay silent, so I swim on. "He contacted this boy. Daniel."

Allison gasps. Ben grunts. Eli and Maggie watch my face.

"He's still helping the Shannons with their harvest," I say hurriedly. "That much is true. On certain nights, though, he comes out to our field. He's marking the corn off before he bends it over to make the crop circle." I nod toward the stalk laid across the table next to the muffins, a sprinkling of dusty dirt collecting under its tassel that Allison will sweep away as soon as we leave.

"Or he was, anyway, before he and Nessa left."

I stop just short of telling them the truth about where Daniel and Nessa went. Somehow, between crop circles and my son, Charlie seems to be the bigger secret, the one I need to protect.

Maggie bows her head the way she does when she's smothering a laugh. Ben runs his finger along the stalk and says, "Is it just some big joke?"

"He wanted to make a message and try to get more young people to come start farms here." The words feel clumsy in my mouth. Allison tenses up next to me. I keep talking in spite of myself. "At first, he wanted Daniel to literally write words in the corn, but I believe Daniel convinced him to do something a little simpler."

Ben shakes his head. "I'm sorry," he says, "I don't understand —"

"It's true," Eli says. Out of all of us, Ben's the only one who doesn't look surprised to hear his voice, low and deep. "I found this video interview one night when I was up late, looking for jobs. A cousin of mine told me to check out this link, see if they were hiring. He meant it as a joke, I think."

Ben looks down into his lap, the tops of his ears turning red. I tell myself not to watch him.

"It was one of those interviews where they put the guy's face in shadow so you can't tell who it is. One of the things he talked about was why. You'd think at least some of them would be a-holes about it — excuse me," Eli says to Allison, Maggie, and me, "but really, the way he talked about it, it seemed like their hearts were in the right place. Enthusiastic about the art and all, I mean."

Ben hmphs and leans back in his chair.

"It's just so strange," Allison says again. She starts biting on one of her chipped nails.

"And Sam wants this done before he . . . gets much worse," Maggie says to the center of the table.

"Yes," I whisper.

"Do you think Daniel can do it? I mean, do you think there's enough time?" Maggie looks at me then, her eyes shrewd.

I find I can't say anything. The room is silent save for a thin thread of music escaping from Nadia's room.

"You know," Allison says, "I always thought we had you to thank for our marriage. If it weren't for you encouraging me to give Ben here a chance, I might've been up and out of the state before he even got up the courage to ask me out."

I look up at her, bewildered. I have no memory of this. I felt so much older than her at the time, so lost, in no position to give her advice. Nor am I sure what this has to do with crop circles. She and Ben are staring at each other, a little smile curving between them from across the table.

"You say Daniel's doing it alone," she says, "but I bet it would go faster if he had other people with him."

I look from her to Maggie to Eli, and now, all of them are smiling. I want to say no, that other people knowing about it would spoil the surprise, that Sam would be disappointed. Really, I'm not sure that it would, that he would. This small pocket of people helping with his vision might make him happy. Daniel will almost certainly be upset — furious, even. He'll be gone soon enough, though, a passing breeze forgotten.

"We want to help," Allison says, placing her hand over mine. There's no room for a response.

Chapter Forty-One:
Nessa

I want to swallow the words back down as soon as I say them.

Theresa clears her throat once. "Well. I think you and I both know I can't fix you, not really." She leans forward, and her voice warms. "I'm certainly happy to chat, though."

I smile and hope she sees it as sincere. "That would be great." Daniel was right: it's been a while since I talked to a therapist, and I do need one now, before I face my dad. Part of me wishes it weren't Daniel's mother, but beggars can't be choosers.

Nick excuses himself to take the roast out of the oven, and by the time we're passing tiny new potatoes and browned brussels sprouts at their long dining room table, their conversation has revved back up again.

Not Daniel, though. He's as quiet as ever, quieter than usual. He leans in so close to his plate, his nose almost touches it, and he shovels food into his mouth. Theresa keeps glancing over at him while she tells me about their recent vacation to Mexico.

"I'm telling you guys, they've got fauna like you wouldn't believe," Nick says as he cuts big wedges of cake (the dessert is also store-bought, he told me). It's like he's describing a woman's body, and Daniel grins.

"Daniel, remember when we went to Costa Rica and your dad was so distracted by those beetles, he didn't notice the monkeys had stolen his lunch?" Theresa asks.

I bite my lip, but the sullen spell over Daniel has somehow broken, just like that. "It took him ten minutes to even look up," he says, and she shines.

"So," she says as I'm cleaning the last of the cake crumbs off my plate with the back of my fork, "Nessa. Should we head back to my office and have a little talk?"

Nick draws my plate out from under me.

I stand up, though my stomach grips tight around every bite I've just eaten. Daniel watches me uneasily from across the table, and it's not clear if his eyes are saying he's sorry or giving me a silent pep talk.

Her office is pretty much how I imagined it, a Zenned-out version of Ricky's. The walls are a soft gray, and photos of Daniel are scattered across her desk. She moves one of them a centimeter to the left before she sits down, a silver-framed print of a very small Daniel curled up under a tree, frowning down at a book. An orange-and-white cat gets up from the armchair facing the desk, flexing its back. It weaves between my legs twice before sipping daintily from the rock fountain burbling in the corner.

"That's Luna," she says.

"Right," I say, though Daniel hadn't mentioned her.

Before I get a chance to ask how long Luna's been around, Theresa says, "Please, have a seat."

I perch on the edge of the armchair, its springs pressing against my tailbone.

"You have OCD." She folds her hands together and drapes one leg over the other.

Onward. "I was diagnosed almost ten years ago. My compulsions are mostly hand washing, in really hot water." I hold my hands up, and the adhesive on my bandages tugs sharply at my palms, at the many layers of scars underneath. "It used to be confessing to my mom, so at least this one only hurts me and not anyone else." I pause and smile lamely. "I'm on Luvox every day, Xanax on bad days, Ambien on really bad days," I continue into the silence, ticking them off on my fingers.

Theresa's a little stunned by the flood of information, but she does an admirable job of covering it up. When I stop talking, she tucks a stray hair behind her ear and reaches for a pen. Finally, she says, "And have you tried any other medications?"

"Yes." I stare down at my hands, bend and flex. There were the pills that seemed to sever the connection between my neck and my skull. The ones that anchored me to my bed, as if the sheets and blankets were stiffening concrete, the sun through the windows painful. And there was the time in the shower, with the razor in my hand, when it cut cleanly through my skin and I wanted it to. When the blood beaded up like a stoplight, I threw the razor away, into the corner of the tub, and let the water rush over my shin, running pink to clear.

I look back up at her. She's dropped her pen on the desk, and it rolls over to the edge and falls to the floor. Luna jumps and hisses, offended. Theresa startles at the sound and clears her throat, touches her hair, waiting for me.

I start again. "This is the only combination that works. Most of the time. I mean, I know there's no such thing as cured, but my obsessions are mostly in the back seat now, not driving. It only gets bad during stressful times, like . . . like now."

At this, she says something soothing, like I knew she would. I run my hands up and down my arms for something to do. She straightens in her chair. Luna takes this as an opportunity to leap into her lap.

"Daniel may have told you I'm a family and couples therapist." It sounds like a question, but he didn't, so I don't answer. She waves a little — *it's all right* — cat hair floating between her fingers, and continues. "So I'm not too familiar with the treatment plans for individual illnesses, and I would highly recommend you schedule a visit with your therapist," she says, tucking her chin down and peering up at me, like she's wearing glasses.

I nod away the lecture I know I'll get if I refuse.

"That being said, I have used cognitive behavioral therapy in the past, and I read a bit about its applications in OCD. Would you like to do a little now?"

As the sun sets outside the window behind her, she walks me through an exercise, one that I first did with Ricky. I know the rules already, but her voice is so soothing, like the stars in the sky hovering over you from the passenger's seat. On my twelfth time through the exercise, I decide it's been enough and tell her my levels are down, though panic still tightens its hands around my throat. She studies my face, as if she can see the truth in the color of my cheeks. I keep my gaze level. The truth is, it still helps, lobbing my pebbles into the pool of another person and watching her rippled surface fall back into stillness.

She sighs and turns back to her computer. Without lifting her eyes from the screen, she says, "You and Daniel are close friends?"

I start to speak, then pause. "I guess so," is what I come up with. "We didn't meet until a few weeks ago, but we've spent a lot of time together on the road and everything."

She picks at something in the palm of her hand and says quietly, "Is he happy, do you think?" She glances up at my face, which is, unfortunately, a little bit stricken, and says, "I know I should know. I spend my entire career reading people, but there's something different about figuring out your own son."

I find my voice. "Yeah, I think he's happy. Yes. He loves what he . . . does."

"I should have been more supportive of him when he said he wanted to become a farmer, like my dad." She runs her hand over Luna's back, and the cat purrs, impassive. It occurs to me that Theresa has no idea, that Daniel's never told her about the crop circles. "I didn't understand it, why he would want to do that to himself, and all of the sudden, I felt I didn't understand him, either. And now I'm afraid he'll never tell me anything at all."

Her eyes meet mine. I shift in the chair. She removes Luna from her lap, shaking the stray hairs off her hands.

"Well," she says, "should we get back?" She stands, and I follow her out of the office.

CHAPTER FORTY-TWO:
MOLLY

For a moment, I catch myself growing giddy at Allison's table, as if we're planning a surprise party. I let the excitement sweep me away from the worries, from the small voice asking if Sam will find out. We decide that when Daniel and Nessa get back and I hear them whispering on the front porch, I will call Allison. I will let the phone ring twice and hang up, and that will be her signal to wake Ben and call Eli. It's not clear why we need a signal and why I can't simply tell her on the phone, but Allison seems convinced that if I speak, I'll wake Sam. Maggie and I glance at each other at that, and she bows her head quickly while I bite back my lip. We both know that Sam is all too used to sleeping through our late-night conversations. I'm afraid of pricking a hole in Allison's joy, though, so I say nothing.

When Maggie and I stand up to leave, Allison hugs me like always, and to my surprise, Ben follows suit, folding his long arms around me.

"We'll come by tomorrow to keep working on those fields, okay?" he says.

I nod into his chest, tears stinging the backs of my eyes.

Sam is sitting at the kitchen table when we get home, huddled close over the newspaper. Maggie and I had been laughing over the ridiculous signal system, and she pauses when she sees him, but I just smile.

"Been painting the town?" he says.

I go as close to the truth as I can. "We were just over at Allison Remy's."

He chuckles, expecting something about her buffalo chicken.

"Ben and Eli have very nicely offered to help us out with the fields while you recover," I say. There's no need to tell him they already spent a full day doing so yesterday while he slept. I can feel Maggie watching me.

He frowns, but then his face relaxes when he decides what this is really about. "That will keep them busy while they look for another lot to buy." He nods firmly into his paper, case closed.

Maggie and I look at each other and grin.

That afternoon, we order pizza from the place the kids used to like. Maggie dabs fruitlessly at the pools of grease in the cheese, and Sam brags that mine was better, that one night ages ago when we turned my bread dough into a crust and set the smoke alarm screeching several times trying to get the right char on the bottom.

Afterward, on the couch, Maggie says, "So, Molly." She reaches into her jacket pocket, and something crinkles. When she pulls out the paper, its battered envelope, the flap I'd left sealed finally torn sloppily open, I lose everything. "I found this in the back seat of your truck this morning."

Sam's face lights up, expecting news, a joke, excitement. He doesn't remember throwing it away, dismissing it as junk mail.

"Oh?" I say and clear my throat. I attempt to sound neutral and bland. "What is it?" I'm begging her to notice, to understand. He doesn't know.

"It's the letter from that small business nonprofit. About the loan? God, it's a few weeks old by now. I don't know how you missed it."

At last, she sees Sam. He's staring at me, mouth open. And then she looks at me, too, and the disapproval is sharp in her eyes.

My fingers twitch, and I pack them into fists.

"You know," she says slowly, sandpaper

across my skin. "The loan. For the bakery you wanted to open."

"A bakery?" Sam repeats.

"It's nothing," I tell him. "A silly dream. I knew we couldn't afford it, so I didn't bother telling you. I only wrote that organization because Maggie wouldn't let me alone." I don't look at her. I refuse.

"I see," he says.

I stare at my lap and wait for more, but nothing comes.

Finally, he says, "Well." He plants his hands on the arms of his chair. "I'm tired. Think I'll go take a nap."

Neither of us moves to help him. Together, we watch him move up the stairs, one step at a time.

"How could you?" I hiss when he is gone. "You knew I hadn't told him. You think that's what he needs right now? His feelings hurt by some pointless secret?"

"Which secret?" She turns to me, and she doesn't look ashamed or sorry. "The one about your visits with Charlie? Your damned cigarettes? The fact that you have ambition, and somehow you're stupid enough to think he doesn't know that?"

We stare at each other, frozen in something close to hatred. Then she drops the letter on the couch next to her and rubs her eyes. "You're right," she says. "I'm sorry. It's not my place. But I'd kill for what you have." She stands and walks toward the stairs. "And you keep fucking it up."

When she's gone, I sit alone, shaking. How dare she? Now, of all times? Wasn't she my friend? Didn't she encourage me?

In a few breaths, I am still. She is my friend, yes. She was Sam's friend first, though. It was unfair of me — probably unbearably so — to forget that.

I consider napping on the couch to avoid them both and slip away into sleep for an hour or two, but I'd rather not wake to them above me. Upstairs, in our bed, Sam is already asleep, curled up on one side. I watch him as I smooth lotion over my arms, papery skin catching and skidding under my hands. His breath is shallow and painful, no more full, strong snores. I pick up my knitting from beside the bed and walk back down the stairs, as carefully as I can.

I decide to make pancakes — breakfast for dinner, Sam's favorite. I watch the puddles of batter bubble and set in the pan while Maggie teases Sam about his painkiller lollipops. They have barely spoken a word to me.

A knock comes at the door, three sharp

taps, with the screen a rattling aftershock. I put down the spatula and scrape a stray dab of batter from my hand. "That must be Ben confirming things about tomorrow," I say to nobody in particular.

When I open the door, my breath escapes.

"Hi, Mom," Charlie says. His hand is propped against the doorway as though he's already preparing to push off. And his face, his face. It's still the same one that told me stories about his day at nursery school, but it's pasted over with that same defensive frown he's worn since high school.

"Charlie," I say, and it's strange, finally giving a voice to the word in my head. Then, before I can stop myself or wonder if Sam can hear me, I say, "I thought Nessa said you couldn't come."

"Yeah, well," he says, "our plans changed." And then he shifts to one side, and I see the man standing behind him, tall, dark, and bracingly handsome. He waves a small wave.

It takes a moment to place him. When I do, I say, "You must be Zach! Please, come in. So rude of me to leave you waiting." I hold out my hand to shake his as they pass, but instead, he puts his arms around me, my hands caught close to my chest like a prayer. He smells like citrus and my son, and I wish I could stay there.

Though Charlie has never introduced us, I know about Zach, of course. For some reason, Nessa doesn't think I do, and every time I ask her about Charlie, her mouth purses, and her eyes shift. I busy myself with something else while she recovers.

It was a little more than a month ago, in the height of summer — wedding season. Sam was out in the fields, and I'd just slid my third loaf of bread for the church bake sale into the oven. My face was still flushed from the heat of it when the phone rang. When I heard it was Charlie, my heart raced with fear and joy. I brushed my hand over my head, dismayed at the bits of hair that had broken free of my bun.

"Is everything okay? I mean, how are you?"

"Yeah, it's fine."

I mined his voice and found it eager, excited even, but there was a shaking edge there, too.

"Listen." He took a gulp of air. "I got married."

I dropped into the closest kitchen chair. "To Zach?"

"Yes, of course to Zach," he said, the armor back up.

"That's wonderful, honey. I'm so happy for you," I said, and I wanted to mean it.

"Yeah, well. I just thought you should know, I guess. You can tell Dad if you want to."

When he hung up, I couldn't move, couldn't even turn off the receiver, so the dial tone wove its way through me. He had told me about Zach on our occasional phone calls, feeding me details like crumbs that I pressed together into something resembling a meal. I knew, for instance, that Zach wasn't a doctor, that they met in a record store, probably, I imagined, near the punk albums that Charlie loved so much. I knew that they liked to go to the movies together, that Zach liked cooking and golf. I had to stifle a laugh every time Charlie mentioned they'd been watching the Masters, imagining him clapping politely when the ball dropped into a hole.

I fed these meals to Sam and refused to notice his grunts and his throat clearings or the way he wouldn't quite respond when I wondered aloud if Zach was taller or shorter than Charlie, what his parents were like, where he was from. I would not, could not have a husband who was uncomfortable with our son finding love.

And now he was married. And we weren't there. I should have expected this. From the very first time he told us about his sexuality, I knew I was making a mistake, that I was supposed to do more than say "Oh" while Sam gaped and Charlie shrank into the couch. Then he was gone, just a few weeks later, and I could do nothing. As soon as he hung up, I moved to the computer and looked up small business loans.

Now he's here, with his husband, standing in the middle of our kitchen. Maggie stares at him, then at Sam. My breath burns hotter and hotter in my chest until finally, Sam stands. He walks over to Charlie and claps him into a hug, his eyes shut, fentanyl stick clenched between his teeth. Charlie's arms are stuck down at his sides, but he taps lightly at Sam's back. Sam says something, and it sounds like "Welcome home."

Zach looks a little stunned, his eyebrows high, and I wonder what Charlie has told him. I touch his shoulder, and he startles, then turns away from his husband and father-in-law. "Can I get you anything?" I ask. "Glass of water, maybe?"

I can't seem to remember anything else in the refrigerator, but Zach's mouth quirks into a smile, and he says, "Water would be great."

By the time I've filled a glass, Sam has released Charlie, and they're sitting in the living room with Maggie. She's leaning toward Charlie, gesturing wildly while he picks at a loose thread on the arm of the sofa. Sam is leaning back in his armchair, hands clasped over his stomach and eyes closed as he shifts the fentanyl from side to side in his mouth.

I set the glass down in front of Zach, sitting at the kitchen table with his feet neat and sturdy on the floor, his legs perfect right angles, as if he were built for that exact space. "You didn't have to wait in here," I say, and I hope it sounds welcoming. I sit down next to him. "We can go to the living room with everyone else if you like."

He studies my face for a moment, his eyes traveling from my hair to my chin. My fingers twitch in my lap, but I don't straighten anything.

He reaches into his pocket and pulls out his phone. He hits the flat of his palm on the table, once, twice. The simple silver band around his ring finger taps cleanly against the wood. "I've got some photos from our elopement on here. Would you like to see them?"

"Oh," I say, "yes." My vision blurs.

CHAPTER FORTY-THREE:
DANIEL

So many times over the years, there have been things I wish I could tell my parents about. The grasshopper that landed on my shoulder in a dairy barn one afternoon, the periodical cicadas that emerged from their seventeen years of hiding and screamed. The farmer who spent the whole day listening to Rage Against the Machine on his headphones, the one who planted a field of tulips for his wife.

Somehow, when I step into their house — our house — all I've got is the carapaces of every fight we've ever had.

After my mom and Nessa leave, I wait for the "your mother" that comes every time my dad and I are alone. Instead, he sits down next to me on the couch and starts telling me about some scandal in his department, a professor who started sleeping in his office after his wife kicked him out. "And of course, we're all wondering," he says, "what did he do to make her so mad at him? Everyone else thinks it's an affair, but I just can't see him doing that. Can you?"

I haven't really been listening, too busy straining to hear crying coming from the office. But there isn't any, and when I turn back to my dad, he looks kind of desperate, and I know it probably has nothing to do with the story he's telling.

"Sorry," I say and shake my head a little. "Which professor is this?"

"Professor Herman," he says patiently. "You remember. William?"

And I do remember, vaguely. He used to come to my parents' Christmas parties in one of those tuxedo T-shirts. He'd hand my mom a bottle of wine, which she'd wrinkle her nose at after he'd turned his back. He always laughed the loudest and would thump my dad on his back on his way out the door. When I was younger, I thought he was the coolest nerd I'd ever met. But when I got to high school, I wondered if he'd taken a wrong turn on the way to the locker room, found himself in a lab, and started calling himself William instead of Billy or Willy.

"Um, no," I say, "it definitely wasn't an affair," even though it definitely was.

My dad smiles, satisfied. Then he settles

his hands on his lap, and I know it's coming, the thing he really wants to talk about.

"I know it was a while ago now, but it's been on my mind ever since." He touches my arm, keeps his eyes on his fingertips as they fall back to the couch. "I hope — I hope it was okay I told your mom about your late girlfriend. I know you didn't want me to, but I just, I didn't know what else to do."

Part of me wants to tell him then about all the times I've wished Mom could tell me what to do, where to place the bandage and be on my way. When he looks up at me, though, his eyes are teary, so I look away and shrug, wondering if he can tell how much I hate myself for doing so. "I kind of knew you were going to."

He's still staring at me, but his face is more solid now. "You know," he says carefully, "I can't imagine what it must've been like, losing her like that." For a second, I think he means my mom, but no. It's Claire. "If anything happened to your mother — well. You and I both know I wouldn't make it very far." He laughs faintly, and I join him a little, to stop it from echoing lonely through the room.

"What I mean is," he says, "I wouldn't want to underestimate what you've been through. But, well, you're still so young, Danny. You might come across someone else one of these days. I don't want you to force yourself to be alone. As much as alone sometimes seems like the easy way out, the truth is, it's not."

I turn to face him head-on. For the first time, I imagine him at my age, holed up in a library somewhere, doing research. He and my mom met pretty late in life, or late for their time, anyway. They used to tell me I was their miracle baby, something the doctors advised them against, my mom past her prime for things like that.

They never talk about their life before each other, though. Just as I open my mouth to ask, my dad stands, groaning with one hand to his back, and walks to the kitchen. I hear the crack and sigh of his 8:00 p.m. beer. "That's enough of that. How's the farming going?" he says when he returns, two brown bottles in his hands.

He holds one out for me, and I take it. The condensation clams up my palm. So I tell him what I haven't been able to before, about the feel of a cow's flank under your hand and the way a tomato tastes when it's fresh off the vine, warmed by the sun. He leans toward me, nodding as he sips, like I'm telling him something new, important.

I'm about to describe the Shannons' milking system when he looks away. He studies the mouth of his bottle before he says, "Your grandpa would've been proud of you."

"I know," I say.

"And so are we," he says. The words almost hurt.

It seems like forever until the office door opens again.

"Ah, here they are!" my dad says, like he, too, has been listening for clues. "Everything okay?"

My mom's face is a little tense, and Nessa shoots me a wide-eyed look from behind her back like she's trying to tell me something. I have no idea what it could be. Nessa sits down across from us while my mom hovers somewhere behind me.

My dad hops up from the couch and retrieves another beer, then pauses before handing it to Nessa. "Can you — I mean, are you taking — with the SSRIs . . . ?"

She smiles up at him, uncomplicated. "In limited amounts." She takes the bottle from him, and he sits back down. He glances at my mom, still standing, and it seems weird that he didn't get her a drink, too. Last I knew, that was their routine, one bottle of beer each and falling asleep in front of the nightly news.

She lays her hand on my shoulder, and then it's obvious, not so weird anymore. It's my turn.

"Could we maybe —"

"Yup." It's more abrupt than I mean, and I avoid Nessa's eyes while I follow my mom back into her office.

"Christ," I say when I've shut the door behind me. "Could you be any more obvious that we're talking about her?"

She rests her head in her hands at her desk, so I stop and drop into the old armchair. Luna rubs up against my legs, and I scratch the base of her tail to make up for the fact that I completely forgot she existed.

My mom's face when she lowers her hands is pink and blotchy, the way it used to get when she thought she'd lost me somewhere.

"You need to tell me the truth," she says. "Are you involved with Nessa?"

"No," I say immediately, but for some reason, I squirm. "Why?"

"Well." She spreads her hands out on the desk in front of her. My toes curl under. "She's a very nice girl, and her disorder is by no means debilitating. But with what happened to your last girlfriend —"

Claire, I think to myself. *Her name was Claire.*

"— I worry that you're finding these people, these girls, who you want to save. And addiction, mental illness, these are things you cannot fix." She levels her gaze at me, staring through me.

"I know that," I say. "Obviously, I know that." There was a time when I didn't. I thought all I needed was to find the right group, the right meeting, the right thing to say to wipe Claire's face clean. Even after she was gone, I was convinced the contest would fix it all. Like somewhere, she'd be happy if I hit fifteen.

My mom shakes her head, not believing me, and I want to ask her if she pulls that move on her patients and, if so, how that's working out for her. Instead, I say, "That doesn't mean I'm going to sit around and do nothing while someone I — that I care about is in pain."

"No, I know. But, honey" — her face softens like butter — "we want you to find someone who will look out for you, too. Who will help you while you're in pain. That's what a healthy relationship is."

I am about to raise my hackles again when I think of Nessa, in the parking lot of Mammoth Cave the first time, eyeing me worriedly when she thought I wasn't looking. I think of her hand in mine in the darkness of the cave, thick-skinned with calluses — and, I know now, a few scars. I think of the smell of pickles in the paper bag.

I rub my hand through my hair, hoping that she didn't notice the shift on my face. "So, between you and Dad, I guess tonight is Find Daniel a Life Partner Night?" I mean it as a joke, and I grin until she takes it as one, smiling wide.

"We want you to be happy, that's all," she says, and luckily, her eyes stay dry.

"I know you do," I say, even though all I feel is overexposed.

"Okay," she says, brushing her hands over her desk. "That's really all I needed to talk to you about. Shall we?" She walks over and smooths down my hair.

I hold myself steady until she walks away. "Sure," I say and follow her back into the living room.

Nessa is sitting on the couch next to my dad now, her legs coiled under her like a spring, nodding eagerly as he describes his most recent research. My mom settles into her chair across from them, folds her hands in her lap, moving her eyes between the two of them.

When I don't sit down, Nessa swivels

toward me.

"We should get going," I say, looking only at her face, not my parents'.

"Oh," my mom says, and the disappointment in it makes me wince. "We can fix up the guest room for Nessa, and your room's always ready for you. You guys don't have to leave."

"Thanks, but we need to be back in Vermont by tomorrow," I say.

Nessa unfurls herself and stands.

They come with us out to the front hall. My dad rests his hand on the shiny brass doorknob.

"I'll call you guys next week," I say, even though it's still nowhere near our monthly check-in.

My mom's smile is too bright to look at. My dad hugs me. "We'll look forward to it," he says.

CHAPTER FORTY-FOUR: NESSA

As we walk into the motel, the lobby smelling of cigarette smoke and disinfectant, I try not to picture Theresa and Nick's guest room. It probably has a fluffy down comforter worn soft and big, wide windows to let in planks of sunshine. Maybe she even arranges little soaps next to the sink, their shapes so perfect, you know you're not supposed to use them.

I can see the tension melting away from Daniel's shoulders as he pays for the room, so I say nothing until he slides the key card into the lock.

"They didn't seem so bad," I say.

He waits for the door to slam shut behind us, as if they might have followed us. "They worry too much about me. Old habits and everything."

I can't argue with that. After he and Theresa left, Nick spent five minutes fiddling with his beer bottle and tearing off the label before he gathered up the courage to ask how we met.

I swallowed a smile as he brushed bits of label paper and adhesive off his pants. It was less direct than his wife, but I knew he wanted the same reassurance. So I said, "Oh, you know. He was working at a farm in my hometown, and the people he was working for kept talking about how he was the best farmhand they'd ever had, so I decided I had to meet him." I was laying it on thick, but he tapped his fingers on the cushion beside him in invitation.

I make the same motion on the stiff two-seater couch now, but Daniel starts digging around in his bag, coming up with his half-empty bottle of generic shampoo.

"You never told your parents about what you really do? About the crop circles?" I say.

"No." He turns to me and says sharply, "Why? Did you?"

"Definitely not." I look him in the eye so he knows I'm telling the truth. "But why haven't you? Who are they going to tell?"

"Probably no one." He sighs. "But the rules are clear that only the absolutely necessary people can know about our work."

He looks pointedly at me, and I know that, strictly speaking, I'm not a necessary person. I send a quick prayer up to whoever that he never finds out I told Charlie.

"Besides," he says, like an afterthought, "it's weird enough for them to have a son who didn't go to college and works on a bunch of farms. Like a step backward for the family almost. I guess they're proud of me now, but I think if they knew what I actually do, their heads might explode." He tips the bottle over in his hands, and the fluorescent blue shampoo glugs from end to end.

"Maybe they'd find it interesting," I say, but he snorts and shakes his head on his way to the bathroom. I wonder who I would talk to if I didn't have my parents, or Charlie or Shawn. How long would it take before I filled entirely with pebbles, a bucket too heavy to lift?

I turn on the TV to *Jeopardy* reruns. As Daniel emerges from the bathroom in his pajamas, tousling a towel through his hair, Alex Trebek asks, "According to Nathaniel Hawthorne, this was Hester Prynne's punishment."

"What is a scarlet letter?" Daniel replies as he folds the towel in half and drapes it over the back of the fake-wood desk chair. "What?" he says when he turns and sees me staring. He grins. "I read a lot when I was a kid."

"Just not any *Anne of Green Gables*," I tease.

He flops down next to me. He spreads his arm across the back of the couch, the residual heat from the shower rising from his skin against the back of my neck. He smells faintly of mint and soap.

"Not yet," he says, and my stomach flutters, not unpleasantly.

"Quick question," I say, pretending it's nothing, though the words have been pressing against my throat since we left his parents'. "Did your mom warn you to stay away from me?"

The smile drops from his face. I can almost see the cover-up forming behind his eyes, but then he changes his mind. "I told you they worry too much."

I nod once and manage to keep myself from wobbling as I turn back to the TV. The contestants are working on Final Jeopardy, all of them bent protectively over their answers.

"It's okay," I say. "I don't blame her."

There's a pause while the contestants announce their wagers, chests puffed out. Then Daniel says quietly, "She doesn't know as much as she thinks she does."

I turn toward him, but he's staring at the TV. Not thinking twice, not thinking at all, I rest my head against his chest. He curves his arm to fit neatly around my shoulders, and I fall asleep with his heartbeat filling my ear like the ocean in a shell.

Every relationship I've ever been in has started out with me plotting its end. From the second I feel their eyes on me, over the farmhand meal or from across the cafeteria, I can picture it, my gradual slip back out of their lives, the half-sincere apologetic letters I will leave behind, placing a soothing and chaste hand on their shoulders. And from there, I move backward, over what I will be calling my meds this time — thyroid treatment or migraine pills, usually. Once, only once, I told the truth on a whim. The guy's eyes had widened, then darted side to side, looking for the hidden cameras or for an escape. I didn't even need an exit strategy that time. One benefit of farm work was that it clouded over my burn scars with calluses, but I came up with excuses for those, too, just in case. I could see it all, every beat, every measure, how I would keep them from learning too much. So that by the time they'd made their slick or stumbling way over to me, before they even opened their mouth, I'd worked out whether to make my smile engaging or distant, if it was worth it to meet their eyes or if I should look over their shoulder, pretending to wait for someone else.

Which is why I'm so surprised when Daniel shakes me awake, just inches from my face, a puddle of drool sticky beneath my cheek on the scratchy couch pillow.

When he whispers "Do you want to move to the bed?" and though I know he means nothing by it, his eyes are close, so close, and I can see every muscle in his face.

When I loop my fingers around the back of his neck, feeling the soft bristle of his hair, realizing in that moment that I've assumed it was coarser than it is.

When, instead of standing up, I pull him closer, and it feels like it's supposed to, his eyes not even widening, not one bit.

Our lips meet like they've done it before, a thousand times. My mouth opens, and his follows, my tongue running between his lips. I rise to meet him, pressing myself against him, and his fingertips hold me in, pushing me further, in and in. I steer us blindly toward the closer of the two beds, laughing breathlessly against his teeth when my shin bumps against the coffee table, sending a dull pain up my leg. I can feel his smile against my own, and I know he wants to check, see if I'm okay, if I'm bruised or my head's in one piece, but we are falling onto the bed, and the springs are squeaking, and I'm pulling, pulling at his T-shirt, and his lips are on my neck, and there is no time for excuses, no time for escapes, no time for thought.

Chapter Forty-Five: Molly

I wipe my eyes dry and hand the phone back to Zach, the screen frozen on an image of Charlie beaming up at him, just outside the frame. Nessa is off to the other side, her head bent back, and I can tell which laugh she's laughing based on the angle of her throat. Even the justice of the peace, frown lines dug deep into his face, is tipping slightly into a smile.

"Thank you," I say, though it comes out a whisper.

"You're welcome," Zach whispers back. He glances down at the phone, and his face glows with a smile not meant for me.

I glance around the kitchen. My eyes land on their luggage, matching suitcases, the ones I'd sent them as a wedding gift after Charlie'd told me the news.

"I'll move your bags upstairs," I say.

It's not until I reach the base of the stairs that I remember. "Oh," I say, and all four of them stop and turn to look at me. I picture Maggie's suitcase, the explosion of colorful silk and skirts strewn across the floor. Maggie's makeup bag is open on his dresser, his framed awards and family photos obscured by perfume bottles and nail polish. Charlie will take this personally, his childhood room misused. "Charlie, Maggie's in your —"

"I'll sleep in Nessa's room, just like old times," Maggie says smoothly.

I want to apologize for our house, for the row of three bedrooms upstairs and no guest room, but she squeezes past me on the staircase. Her hand touches my shoulder, and I can't tell if it's intentional.

Once all the luggage has been redistributed, the corners of Charlie's bedsheets tucked in, and Maggie's suitcase deposited under Nessa's desk, I wipe my hands across my jeans and say, "What would everybody like for dinner?" I'll dump the pancake batter in the trash when no one is looking, I decide. It's been sitting out too long by now.

"Let me handle the cooking," Zach says, standing up from the couch.

"No, I couldn't." My hands flutter up near my chest.

"Yes, you can," Charlie says, to my surprise. He smiles up at Zach. "You can trust him in your kitchen." Zach grins back at him, and I soak it in, how loved Charlie is.

"Well," I say, avoiding Sam and Maggie's eyes. "At least let me cut up one of my loaves of bread."

"Now, that I will accept," Zach says as he passes me.

"Make sure you make something with red meat! Molly's letting me cut loose now she's decided health food won't shrink my tumors."

They're the first words Sam has said directly to Zach. He pauses in the doorway, then says, "Red meat. Got it." The tension slips just slightly off Charlie's face.

I spend the rest of the evening busying myself with straightening and scrubbing, flitting back and forth between Charlie's pull and Sam's chilly eyes. Finally, when Zach finishes, we all sit in the living room, plates of beef stir-fry balanced on our laps. The slices of meat and chunks of broccoli are silky with sauce, poured carefully over mounds of rice. The hunks of bread seem incongruous next to it all, hefty and earthen, but when I mentioned that the loaf might be better for breakfast the next morning, Zach picked up the knife from the counter and held it out to me, saying, "Not at all. Cut." So I did.

Maggie takes a bite and lets out a guttural groan. "Where did you learn to cook like that?"

Zach smiles, bending toward his plate to hide it. "My dad. He's the chef in my family, and he lived in constant fear of me succumbing to the LA takeout culture."

She folds another bite into her mouth, then chews and swallows it. "Well, if I weren't already divorcing my husband and if you weren't gay, I would leave him for you in a heartbeat."

It so perfectly encompasses all the things we haven't said out loud that I am helpless, laughing in surprise with everyone else. When the room has died down again, I say, "That's where you're from, then? LA?"

Zach nods. "Just east of there, born and bred. What about you guys?" To our blank stares, he says, "Are you and Sam from Vermont originally? Where did you live before here? What brought you here?"

Maggie stops eating. Sam clears his throat. I start to tell the usual story — that we came out here for cheap land and a change of scenery — but it gets snagged in my chest.

"Mom and Dad used to live in Nebraska," Charlie says. Then he gestures at Maggie. "All three of them did, actually. But they never talk about it." He's almost winking at Zach.

Into the silence, Maggie says, "Who needs to remember those boring days before you kids came along?"

Charlie rolls his eyes, but his cheeks flush a little, and Zach chuckles.

The dull ache stays lodged beneath my breastbone all night, pulling me down while the others talk about farming and lawyering and doctoring and, once, golf. Eventually, I gather up all the plates and forks. I stand at the sink with my back to the living room and let the conversation wash over me, but I cannot get clean.

It's only when Sam and I are alone in our room that the question breaks free. I can hear Zach and Charlie murmuring to each other through the thin walls, clear as anything, so I huddle close to Sam under the covers and whisper, "Do you forgive me?"

Sam grunts and turns over. "I can't believe you didn't tell me about the loan. After everything we've been through, not to tell me what you really want. How could you?"

"No, no, not that." My stomach curdles again at the memory of all I kept from him, but I tell myself he'll get over that soon enough, forget it entirely. I throw the covers back, get out of bed, and start pacing the floor, the pine boards cool and slick beneath my feet. "For what I did to you back in Nebraska."

I know even as I say it that it's an unfair thing to ask. I should just know the answer from the clusters of wildflowers he sometimes leaves for me on the kitchen table, propped up next to his newspaper in his empty coffee cup.

I don't know it, though. Not for sure.

"Oh. That." He sighs.

"It was unforgivable, I know that. I shouldn't ask you to forgive me." Zach and Charlie's voices still, but I can't whisper anymore. "There's not a day that goes by I don't regret it, and I know that's mine to live with. But —"

"You're right," he says, and there's a thorn in his voice that makes me stop pacing. "It was unforgivable." He raises himself up on his elbows, wincing. "But if I want Tommy to give you business advice after I'm gone, I guess I'll have to get over it."

I stare at him. "Tom— Tommy?"

He smiles, but it looks painful, and I count back the hours to his last fentanyl. "I know you called him Thomas, but did you know most of his friends call him Tommy?"

"No, I didn't," I say faintly. My hands begin to shake.

"That's all right," he says. "Took you years to agree that Vanessa was Nessa and Charles was Charlie. Come here."

I walk over to the bed and sit on the edge of it. His eyes move back up to the ceiling.

"That day, when you told me, I was so mad at you, I couldn't see straight. I went down to the pay phone by the post office, speeding the whole way. I called information and asked for a Thomas Grossman. There was only one in our hometown."

He glances at me, and I loosen my hands, clutched together at my stomach. I want to reach out, but I'm afraid his anger will be hot on him again, like it was all those years ago. I don't move.

"I was going to give him a piece of my mind. And I did. I yelled at him, how dare he, does he realize what he's done, on and on. I only stopped when the postmaster came out and grabbed my shoulders and told me to get a grip before I started scaring the customers away."

There was a period of time back then, a few years, when every time I had to mail a letter or buy a roll of stamps, the man behind the counter would look at me like I was diseased. I always studied my face in the rearview mirror afterward, figuring out what was wrong in my reflection.

"When I finished ranting, he said exactly two things to me. Tommy. He said how sorry he was. Every day, he was sorry. And he asked me if you were happy. And I hung up the phone on him. I didn't know how to answer."

He shifts back onto his side to face me, and I know he wishes he could bring himself upright, fully seated without my help.

"This farm was always my dream, not yours. I know that, and a part of me knew it back then, too, but I couldn't face it until he asked. I was never really sure if this was the life you would've picked for yourself, if it weren't for me."

I start to protest, but he raises one hand to stop me. It's an old man's hand, the pads of his fingers puckered and pale, the skin between his knuckles wrinkled. I don't know when or how it got that way.

"One day, a few months later, I walked in from lunch, and instead of making sandwiches, you were sitting on the living room floor, holding Nessa in one arm and building a castle out of blocks for Charlie with the other. He was asking if we could live in the castle instead of this house, and you were laughing."

Hard as I try, I can't recall the day he's talking about, but his eyes are dancing.

"I called him back that afternoon, and he'd barely picked up the phone when I said yes, you were happy. I wanted to rub it in his face, that you were happy with me and not with him. All he said was, 'Good. Keep it that way.' It rankled me, him giving me orders like that. I started calling him every year or so, to tell him you were still happy, even in those times when I wasn't sure."

He moves onto his back. My mouth opens, but he keeps going.

"Eventually, we became a weird sort of friends, and we started talking about other things. He got married, you know, and has three kids, a few years younger than Nessa and Charlie. When I told him I was sick, he sounded sad, and not just for your sake."

He turns his head and looks at me.

"What I mean is, he's somebody you could reach out to, after all this." He motions down at his body, almost flat under the blankets. "You remember, he worked for the SBA. Maybe he could help you through the whole loan thing."

I don't remember. I don't.

I love you like a sickness, I think. *I love you in my bones.* I don't say a word. Instead, I stretch my body out next to him and place my arm over his chest, my leg over his own. As if I could be a frame to house him, the beams and studs and foundation protecting him from everything.

Hours later, I pull the letter out of my nightstand drawer and walk to the window. Even holding the paper close to my nose, I can barely see the words in the dark, but the message is clear enough. "Unfortunately," it says, "we don't believe the market can support another bakery. Please consider attending one of our small entrepreneur seminars."

Out the window, below me, there's movement on the porch steps. It must be a raccoon. I throw up the sash to shoo it away, but my eyes adjust, and it's Maggie, slumped against the railing. The cloud of her cigarette smoke beckons me through the screen, fanning the flames in my throat. She knew. All along, she knew. There was no need to tell Sam if the bakery was going nowhere.

She leans over, down, and props her head between her knees, cigarette dangling from her fingers. Even from this distance, I can hear her sigh shuddering. She wants a marriage clean and open, shiny and perfect, improbable. Secrets, no matter how trivial, cut straight through her.

I close the window and walk down to join her.

"I'm sorry," she says as soon as I open the screen door.

"No, you're not." I sit down beside her on the step.

She laughs and wipes at her face with one fist. "You're right, I'm not. You should've told him."

"I know." I take the cigarette from her fingers and inhale. "They rejected my application," I say with an unwelcome crack in the middle of the sentence. And that's what it feels like: a sentence. I will stay here. There will be no bakery.

"Did they?" she says, feigning surprise with raised eyebrows.

"I know you read it, Maggie."

"Fine." She sighs. "We'll figure something out. You don't need them." She leans into me, shoulder to shoulder, wrist to wrist. "You were born to bake. Do you remember the look on your face when I first gave you that cookbook? It was like I'd gifted you a box full of grannie panties."

The laugh bursts out of me, feeling fresh and forbidden in the night air. When it ends, my heart is straining in my chest. "I was born to be here, with Sam," I say quietly.

"That might be true," she says, "but a person can be born to do more than one thing, you know."

I stare out at the fields, deciding whether to believe her or not. The corn is silent, unrelenting, unforgiving. In the end, it doesn't matter if Maggie's right or not, because she promises, "I'll help you sort this out. You don't need that nonprofit for you to find your feet. You always manage on your own. So fuck 'em."

The cigarette is nearly gone now. I grind it out into the bannister, for once not caring if it leaves a cindered mark behind. "I suppose you're right," I tell her, and myself as well.

CHAPTER FORTY-SIX:
DANIEL

Afterward, Nessa falls asleep with her head on my chest. Her hair in my nose makes it hard for me to breathe, and so does her bare leg over mine, her toes pushing up against my shin.

In the quiet, all I can think about is Claire.

It's not cheating, I know that. I know my uneasiness is stupid, crazy even. My dad is right — there's no need for me to live in mourning forever, alone. It felt good. Of course it did. But I also can't honestly say it's what Claire would've wanted.

I can still hear her whisper, "You're mine, you're mine," and it was true. Even as I sat in the church parking lot after the funeral and explained to her parents who I was. Even as I watched the car windows cloud up with my breath, waiting for her meetings to end. Even as I grew warier, watching her move around a field. Even finding her passed out next to her car when we were supposed to be finishing a project, sour-smelling vomit under her mouth.

Nessa's arm feels like a weight. I peel myself apart from her, skin stuck to skin. She mumbles something to herself and burrows her head into her pillow as I flip off the lights and crawl into the other bed.

When I wake up, Nessa is fully dressed and sitting on her bed, back straight up against the headboard.

"Good morning, sunshine," she says, but she doesn't really look like it is.

"Morning," I say. I rub some of the life back into my face. "Sorry for moving beds last night and everything. I couldn't sleep and didn't want to —"

"It's okay," she says and looks out the window. "I think you know a little too much about me to get into this." She waves her hand across her body. "Like I said last night, I totally get it if you don't want to go there."

"No," I say. She moves back against the headboard a bit. "That's not it." I wish I could just leave it at that. I feel her eyes on my skin as I dig clothes out of my bag, but when my head emerges from the collar of my shirt, she's only staring at my face.

I sit back down on the edge of my bed. "Last night was not a mistake," I say. "It wasn't exactly what I had in mind," I continue, and she smirks a little, "but I was happy when it happened. It's just —" Now it's my turn to look away and out the window, at the late-summer trees slowly changing color against the sky. "It's Claire."

"Ah," she says. She looks like she understands, but then she says, "You don't want to jump from one head case to another."

If only my mom could hear this. I shake my head. "No, you're two totally different people, regardless of what you're . . . dealing with. And maybe that's the problem." I force myself to meet her eyes. Her head is tilted a little, out of ideas. "It's weird, I know," I say apologetically. "She's been gone for almost two years now. But I don't know. I guess I still miss her for some reason. I'm not really over her."

"Oh," she says. She hugs her knees tight into her chest for a moment. "Okay." She springs off the bed and hoists her bag off the floor, already packed. She smiles big, too big, and says, "Should we hit the road? I really want to get home before dark."

She's making this easy on me; I know she is. Still, when I stand up to follow her, my stomach drops down around my knees.

CHAPTER FORTY-SEVEN: NESSA

Throughout the five-hour drive up to Vermont, I ask innocent and generic questions about his family and point out rest stops where we can switch drivers. Daniel barely looks at me, though, and I think maybe it's because he can see the anger roiling beneath my skin. His answers are minimal, and after each one, I think, *Claire is gone, and he'll still never leave her.*

When we finally pull up to my parents' driveway, I get out of the car without a word, without even stopping to get my bag, and march unseeing up to the house. From behind me, from far away, I hear him shut the car door and walk away, the driveway crunching under his feet.

I throw the door open, and there is Charlie. Pouring coffee into a "#1 Dad" mug. He smiles almost shyly when he sees me.

"What —" I swallow, then start again. "I thought you weren't coming." It feels like saying it will erase him right back out of the kitchen.

He shrugs and looks away. "I changed my mind. Where's your . . . um . . . friend? Daniel?"

He's only teasing, but my throat still closes up, and I shove the door with my hip. "He's nowhere. Gone."

He looks surprised, but before he can say anything, I realize why he must be here. "Is Dad — is he —"

"He's upstairs, sleeping," he says.

All the air in my lungs unravels.

"Mom went with Zach and Maggie to buy stuff for dinner. If you can believe that." He keeps his eyes on me as he takes a sip of coffee, but I always knew Mom would love Zach.

"Aunt Maggie's here?" I say, glancing out the window. Sure enough, there's a beige sedan with Arizona plates parked next to my parents' truck, a rental car. I was so distracted on my way in, I hadn't even seen it.

"Yeah. I think she's got issues with her husband or something, so she came."

"That's good," I say, barely hearing him. "That's great. She'll help Mom."

"Mm," Charlie says and falls silent.

"I'm gonna go say hi to Dad," I say,

brushing past him.

"You should know," he says, spinning to face me and setting his mug on the counter without looking. "He's not well."

I stare at him. "Yeah. I know."

"No, I mean —" He tugs at his hair, leaving it crazy and clumped. "He's very frail. Mom hasn't said, but I have to imagine he's only got a couple weeks left."

His words will not seep in. It's like I've been shrink-wrapped, packaged into another life where my family has an expiration date that's always just out of reach, and I wasted weeks chasing down my stubborn brother, who now stands in front of me like it's nothing. It all finally bubbles up and out of me. "Don't worry," I say, "I've seen it before. I was here every time the cancer came back, remember? Or you would, if you'd ever come home."

I don't have time to watch him react. I take the stairs two at a time, my hand skimming across the wall, the family photos hung in the stairwell passing in a blur. I only slow down when I reach the door of my parents' room. I pause and shake out my shoulders, like a shiver.

It's true what I told Charlie. I've seen it all before, the wreckage of chemo. The graying skin, the loose clothes, the bald head naked and vulnerable. That doesn't make it easy, not ever. Bit by bit, I open the door.

And there he is. He's lying on his back on the bed, three or four quilts layered over him. His mouth is open a little, and his breath whistles out between his teeth. His cheeks are hollowed out. His hands look bony and frail where they lie on top of the blankets, no longer the strong hands that fixed combines and showed me how to work the tractor gearshift. I squint, struggling to reconcile this man, dull and flat, with what Charlie'd heard him say. All of my dad's confusion and unwillingness cracking us all apart. For a reeling minute, I want to grab his shoulders and shake him, hard.

He lets out a painful-sounding wheeze, and the moment passes. I wait for a second before bending over to kiss his head, the skin stretched taut across his skull. I half hope he'll stay asleep.

His eyes open, blurry before they find my face. "Nessa," he croaks.

Before I start to panic, he clears his throat, and he sounds like himself again. "Don't worry," he says, propping himself up on his elbows. "I've still got my voice. And hey, I get to keep my hair this time." He raises one hand, shaking a little, and runs it over the few wisps covering the top of his head.

A laugh pops out of my mouth. It's like the laugh opens the gates, and I hide my face in my hands. Yes, it's the same as every other time, except his jaw is no longer set to fight, and there's something in his eyes that I can't bring myself to understand.

"Come on now," he says.

I hear the covers shuffle as he tries to get out of bed.

"Listen to me," he says sternly. "I may look like hell, but I'm still your dad, and I still tell you when you get to cry. Is that clear?"

I laugh again in one shuddering gust. I draw my hands away from my face and wipe them down the front of my shirt, then give him one sharp salute.

He nods. "Good. Now, how was Georgia?"

My mouth open and closes, empty, as I scramble back to the excuses we gave him. Before I can say anything, he smiles slyly, and I know he knows. "The same," I say, smiling back.

"Great," he says. "Glad the crisis was averted. Now, go away and make sure they're making me a nice, meaty lasagna for dinner," he says, waving me out the door.

"Will do," I say, but he's already leaning his head back against the pillows and closing his eyes.

I take the stairs down an inch at a time. I can tell nobody's back from the grocery store yet, and I don't have it in me to apologize to Charlie. He's at the kitchen table, staring down at his coffee, the mug almost full. I sit down across from him. He looks up at me, scowling.

"I think Mom had an affair," he says. "Or maybe cheated just once or something. I don't know."

My hands come up to grip the edge of the table, looking for something, anything to hold onto. "What?"

"It was a long time ago, I think. That's what it sounded like anyway."

"How did you —"

"They were talking about it in their room last night." One corner of his mouth lifts, and in a flash, I'm fourteen again, huddled in my bed, listening to the precise cadence of the music Charlie blasted at the end of a bad day, every drumbeat and word, like it was playing in my own room.

"Holy hell," I say, resting my head between my hands on the table. Its edge digs into my forehead. "Poor Dad."

"He seemed okay. I think he made his peace with it a while ago."

"Should we be mad at Mom?" I ask, because, I don't know, it seems like maybe we should. I look at him, my temple pressed to the coolness of the table.

He swallows. "I think she's probably mad enough at herself," he says.

I lift my head up and sit back in the chair. "You're right," I say.

He takes a sip from his mug, then makes a face when he realizes it's not hot anymore. He pushes it away and places his hands on the place mat. "What actually happened with Daniel? Did he decide to ditch the crop circle, or . . . ?"

"No, he'll be back. Or maybe not. Who knows?" I look away. "We hooked up." The words feel cheap in my mouth, amateurish, but they're the ones we used in high school, and it's a force of habit with Charlie. The surprise touches his face just a second too late, and I roll my eyes. "I know, I know. You guys thought we were together all along. I'm pretty sure this entire town does, too. We spread a lie about where we were going and why so Dad wouldn't find out we were trying to get you," I explain, and he smiles.

"Anyway, we were just friends, until last night, at least." I pick at my place mat, peeling the lamination away from its face. "It turns out he's still hung up on someone else."

"What an idiot." His mouth is set and straight when I look up, but then he says, "I knew I never liked him." He winks, and it's so like Dad, I can't speak. He takes both my wrists and draws them toward him. Most of the Band-Aids are falling off, the adhesive blackened and weak. I know how it looks. The skin is shiny and raw as meat, blotchy and ugly. I know he wants to tell me about proper wound care or ask me about my Luvox doses. He looks up at me, working his mouth around the words. The door opens.

CHAPTER FORTY-EIGHT: MOLLY

For a moment, I am lost when I see Nessa and Charlie at the table, sharing a cup of coffee. I knew she was coming, of course, that she would be here any day. Still, in all the times I had imagined them here together, I'd pictured them as teenagers, huddled over their homework or laughing at something we said when they thought we weren't looking. Now, finally, they're here, and they're full-grown adults.

"Hey, Mom," Nessa says with a wooden smile. She hides her hands under the table, but not before I see the bandages and pink skin crisscrossing her palms.

"Oh, sweets," I say weakly. At that moment, the screen door smacks open, and Zach and Maggie come bustling in behind me with the rest of the groceries.

"Aunt Maggie!" Nessa squeals.

Maggie drops her bags on the counter with a thunk and flings her arms around my daughter, so easily. "Hey, kiddo," Maggie says into her hair.

"Charlie was just telling me about your husband," Nessa says, backing up. "How awful."

Trust Nessa to cut right to the bone of the matter. Charlie stares out the window, studying something. Maggie lays her hand on Nessa's cheek like she's a child. Instead of squirming away, Nessa smiles right back.

Zach clears his throat, still standing behind me, and says, "Charlie, want to help me put away these groceries?"

Charlie stands, not meeting my eye, and the two of them move around me in a well-practiced dance, opening cupboards and passing boxes. I feel abruptly out of place, obsolete.

I slip up the stairs and to our room. Sam lies on his side, staring at the door, or rather through it, and he is so motionless, my heart gallops. At last, he opens his arms wide, and I lie down next to him, my back pressed up against his chest, nestled and safe. I cup one hand around his elbow and whisper, "Our kids are home."

"I know," he says, his words muffled in my neck. "Things must be getting really bad." There is laughter in his voice, but also not.

I stare at a line of pink flowers running up the wallpaper we glued all those years ago, tracing my eyes from floor to ceiling, over and over again until it blurs.

Dinner tonight is a sloppy square of lasagna that drips red sauce on its way to our mouths. Maggie insisted on making it herself, and although the pasta is a little crunchy around the edges, Sam makes appreciative sounds at the back of his throat while he chews.

When we are done eating, I collect the dishes once again, plates clacking against each other in the quiet.

Maggie watches me and says, "I think I'm going to take a little night drive."

"I'll come with you," Zach says quickly, and the escape is so obvious that none of the four of us bother to reply. Nessa's eyes dart between Charlie and Sam, but Charlie just stares at Zach, and I turn my back to the pleading in Charlie's eyes.

Maggie and Zach hustle out the door while I stack the dishes in the sink. I wipe my hands on a kitchen towel, drying each individual finger and rubbing the sheen back into my wedding ring. In the living room, Charlie and Sam sit on opposite ends of the couch.

"Where's Nessa?" I ask, dread rising in my stomach.

"She's taking a shower," Sam says. He motions toward the couch.

I take my spot between my husband and my son. "It's so good to have the two of you home. The three of you, really. Zach seems lovely." I pat his hand carefully, and I'm rewarded with an equally careful smile.

"We just wish we'd had a chance to meet him sooner," Sam says.

I close my eyes but can still see Charlie stiffen.

"Or seen more of you, really. But the eleventh hour is just fine, too." Sam's voice is airy and leavened, but I wince all the same. He never could quite tell when his jokes were a touch too bitter.

Upstairs, there's a heave and a clank as the hot water moves sluggishly through the pipes. All three of us glance warily at the ceiling, our worst-case Nessa scenario binding us.

Charlie turns to face Sam. "Just so we're clear," he says evenly, "I'm here for her." He jabs one finger upward. "I know you all disapprove of me. I know my husband and my job don't fit into your perfect vision for this family. Soon enough, I'll be gone again, and you'll be free to imagine whatever you like about my life." He stands, shaking my hand off his arm, and escapes up the stairs.

I turn to Sam, ready to berate him for pushing our son away again. Before I can say anything, I see it: Sam is even smaller than usual, deflated. His eyes are wide and lost. His hands are clenched like mine, gripped tight around a family we can't seem to keep.

Not now. Not this time. I am standing, taking the stairs two at a time in a way I haven't in years. Charlie is about to close the door to his room, and he recoils when I slip in after him.

"Listen to me," I say, my hands cuffing his forearms. His face hardens, but I press on. "Of course we want you close to us. Of course we do. But Zach seems truly wonderful. I'm so proud of you, Charlie. We both are."

He refuses to look at me. His neck has folded, his chin tucked into his chest, and his hair falls exactly how I used to comb it every morning. He doesn't believe me. I realize with a sinking shame that I haven't given him any reason to.

"Come," I say on an impulse and tug him down the hall to our bedroom. I kneel beside Sam's side of the bed, wrinkling my nose at the musty smell of our sheets and peering past the clods of dust. Charlie inches back toward the door, his arms crossed in front of him.

"Look," I say and reach out with the top book in the stack I'm holding.

He extends one hand to take it, an involuntary motion, and I pile the books one by one in his arms. *What Coming Out Means. Beyond Sexual Orientation. Helping Your Child.* Some of them have cracked spines and softened corners, dog-eared pages and penciled underlining, and some are still crisp and new.

Charlie stares down at them. He turns one over, his eyes moving across the back.

"They're all his," I say quietly, just a bit more than a whisper, and he nods. "We're trying," I say, struggling to keep my voice steady. "I know it's not enough. But he's dying. Your father is dying. No matter what I do, no matter what we try, he is tired, and he is drifting away. I'm sorry for how much we failed you, but I cannot let you drift away, too. I will not." I repeat myself to cover the traces of my fear.

He bends down and places the stack at his feet, then splays it out with one hand, a fan with all the titles showing. "You're right," he says, looking up at me with eyes so angry, I shy away. "It's not enough." His

417

shoulders begin to shake.

I kneel down to meet him, and he turns his face away, and it is red and clenched and wet. I realize with a start that I haven't seen him cry since elementary school, but my instinct is the same.

I reach out and carefully, gingerly hold his shoulders. They hiccup away from me a little, but he does not get up, so I lean in closer, tipping onto my toes, and draw my arms around him. He moves in toward me, a counterweight, and lays his face against my shoulder. "I'm sorry," I whisper, tucking him further into my arms. "It'll be okay." When he was younger, he used to ask me how I knew that, begging me to map out his exact path to okay.

I am glad he doesn't ask me now.

CHAPTER FORTY-NINE:
DANIEL

On the next clear night, with the moon a big, white plate in the sky, I stand at the mouth of Nessa's driveway and stare down at the house. When we got back a couple of days ago, she didn't say a word to me, just closed the car door and then the front door, two walls to keep me out. There was a car parked next to their truck with out-of-state plates, and I figured it was Charlie's. Maybe she was right now discovering that I'd told him, finding new reasons to hate me.

I thought about not coming back. Just for a second. The Shannons were so pleased when I walked in the door, Connie smiling conspiratorially at me, and I thought it might be easy, finishing up their harvest and then moving on, finding another number fifteen. And whatever excuse Molly gave Connie for the draft plans, she must've accepted it, because she never said a word about it. Nobody gave me a second glance around town. The secret was safe. I could start fresh somewhere else.

But I couldn't sleep. And the other circlers kept calling me — first one Mason twin, then the other, then Becca — leaving no messages when I sent them straight to voice-mail. I couldn't be responsible for them and the infighting in their group, not now. Still, their names on my phone reminded me of what I was neglecting. I'd lie awake in the Shannons' guest bed, staring at the ceiling and running my hands over the blanket's ruffled edge. And when I tried to eat, there was a sour taste in my mouth, and the cereal and sandwiches felt like sludge going down. The Shannons stared at me, chewing slowly.

I'm here because of Sam. I've never left a project unfinished, not once. I tell myself it's Claire's face I see when the shame creeps up on me. Nessa probably won't be outside anyway.

I walk down the driveway, the gravel shifting under my feet. I keep my eyes on the field and turn my back to the house, so I jump a little when I hear her voice.

"Took you long enough."

She is sitting on the porch in that same rocking chair, her finger in her book.

Of all the words in my head, all that comes out is, "I didn't think you'd be here."

She lays her book on the chair, stands up. "And miss out on the fun?"

As she comes down the stairs toward me, the curtains flick open and closed in a window on the second floor. My face burns when I imagine what she's told them, what they think of me now, and I'm glad I'm standing outside the circle of the porch light.

"So," she says, stopping a few paces away from me and shoving her hands in her pockets, "what are we doing tonight?"

I clear my throat and try to be professional. "We should be able to finish up the marking. Then we can do all the bending on the next night and be done with this whole thing." I motion outward so it's clear I'm talking about the field. Luckily, the paint held on while we were gone, so there's not much left to mark now.

For a while, I can almost pretend nothing has changed. We work in silence, taking turns spraying and walking up to the road. But then, on my second trip down the hill, instead of handing me the paint can, Nessa touches the side of my arm, so slight, I can hardly feel it.

"I feel like I need to tell you something," she says, her eyes fixed on my face. "I think you might've thought I wanted something serious out of this. And I don't. This was

421

just something fun for me. After we're done with this" — she jerks her head toward the middle of the field — "I'll go back to California, and you can go back to wherever. I know what Claire meant to you."

The moonlight shines on her face, and I can't look away. I don't want to believe her.

There's a rustling behind us. Barely hushed giggles loud as gunfire. My chest tightens, and so does Nessa's grip on my arm.

"Drop," I mouth to her. We crouch together. The dirt creaks under my feet. The whispers come closer and closer.

They will find us eventually. My mind churns, searching for explanations for what they'll see: the farmer's daughter and the stranger, huddled on the ground, surrounded by corn glowing crazy like fireflies. She is teaching me how to find the best ears for feed. We are secretly seeing each other, just like everyone thought. I blush again at this one and turn my head away, toward the street.

A woman's voice rises harsh above the others, whisper-yelling, "Nessa? Are you there?"

Nessa spins toward the group. I reach for her, but she's on her feet, and all I grab is her ankle.

"Maggie?"

A breathy cheer goes up, and the patch of shaking cornstalks comes nearer and nearer. I stand up, blood rushing to my head, vision fading out. I think about leaving, snaking through the field away from them all. But then someone pushes through the last layer of corn and stands in front of us, shorts and a T-shirt, hair flying loose, face full of excitement like she didn't think she'd find us.

Nessa takes one step toward her, then stops. "What are you doing here?" she says.

And then I see the rest of them, easing out through the rows of corn like something from a horror movie. The redheaded woman I've seen a couple of times at the grocery store, squinting at the prices in the canned soup aisle. The man I'd walked past outside the bank one morning, muttering into his phone about a job listing. And another man, so tall, it feels like I'm peering up his nose instead of in his face.

"We want to help," the first woman says.

My entire body burns. This is not right — no. Word has gotten out after all, spread around town. They are talking about it in their living rooms, and they will miss the point. There will be no magic, no bright, clean smile on Claire's face, not this time. I will lose, miss it all. It'll be ruined.

Nessa turns to me, and I realize I haven't said anything yet. "I — no. You can't," I sputter. Though it's too dark to see, I can picture their disappointment, know it from the way their shoulders fall all at once.

"Come on," Nessa says, reaching for my arm.

"I just — give me a minute," I say, not quite an apology, and I walk back up to the road, stumbling over ruts in the dirt. I can feel my fingers tingling again, that panic attack. I slow my breathing so no one will see it happening.

I don't hear her following me until my feet reach the cracked pavement. The shuffling of the stalks trails behind me, and then she stands there, panting.

"You told them," I say, and I can't turn around.

"No," she says loudly, then softer, "Absolutely not. I told Charlie, but there's no way he would've told anyone else."

I turn then and say, "But how?" Even though I know it doesn't really matter, there's no undoing now. I'll have to leave. That's the only way to protect the circlers and me both at once. If there's never any circle, then it was always just a rumor. I was just an odd smudge of nothing passing through. I'll cut ties with the group entirely, never talk to Lionel again. Nothing can get traced back to them. And he can't find out what I've done, pin it all on me.

She looks back over the field. "I don't know. Maggie's my mom's best friend, so she must've cracked and told her, but the others — I don't know."

I don't say anything, start walking away, back toward the Shannons'. She makes a strangled little sound, and her sneakers thump against the asphalt as she runs past, then in front of me.

She stops with both hands up. "I know you're mad," she says, "and I know this probably breaks every rule in the crop circle code. Please, please don't leave. I —" She pulls her bottom lip through her teeth, and I can picture exactly how it reddens a shade.

"My dad needs you to finish this," she continues. "And maybe this is a good thing. All these people, they love my family, and they won't tell anyone else. Maybe it'll help us move faster, help us make sure we can finish this before — while he can still see it."

It's not true. It's not a good thing, no. She moves closer, her face pale, and my heart stops hammering in my chest. All of a

sudden, I realize her eyes on me are everything I need in that moment.

CHAPTER FIFTY:
NESSA

His hands twitch by his sides, and he looks over my shoulder, but he's loosened, and I know he'll stay for now. I want so badly to ease up into him, bury my face in the hollow of his clavicle, and hold on.

I stay where I am. While I sat on the porch for the second night in a row, staring up at the road, I lectured myself in my head. He *was* an idiot, obviously, and I was not to touch him under almost any circumstance. When his shadow appeared on the horizon, my hands began to wobble.

"Okay," he says.

I keep my smile to a reasonable width. "Let's get to it," I say. I reach for his hand but then think better of it. There's a tiny breath of silence before his footsteps follow mine.

The four of them stand together behind the first row of corn, far enough so they can pretend to be discreet. Maggie stares at me, but I shake my head. Allison's husband stands a few paces away, staring at the ground with his hands in his pockets. I motion him over, and when Daniel comes crashing through after me, we are all in a line and at attention.

He stumbles for a moment and gapes at us like he'd forgotten.

"We're ready," I say.

He closes his mouth. "Right. So. Here's what we're going to do."

He puts Maggie and me on watch up at the road and assigns Allison and Ben to be runners between us and Daniel and Eli, who take turns spray-painting. When he pulls out the plans to show everyone, his face clears in an instant, and he smiles. "Now that there's more of us," he says, "we can make this a little more complex."

He pulls a pencil out of his pocket and bends over double, pressing the paper to his thigh and scribbling on it. The pencil pokes and snags the paper in a few places, but he doesn't seem to notice. He finishes and holds the picture out for us to see. We lean in close like it's a fire.

It's beautiful, really — even more so than before — a spiraling maze of interlocking circles. I feel the warmth of his arm against mine and lean back before I ignite.

Up on the road, Maggie's fixed in place, staring at the flecks of paint schooling together into something like art. The circle is too far from the house to see anything from the windows, so this is all new for her. It's strange, but I can barely remember the first time I saw it.

"Pretty amazing, right?" I say to burst the silence.

"The circle or Daniel?" she says, her elbow jabbing my side. "No, you're right. It's not like anything I've ever seen before."

I relax. We stand in silence for a few minutes, watching the paint wink when the wind sifts through the stalks.

"How's it looking?" Allison says, laboring up the hill.

"It's amazing," Maggie says. She grins at me.

Allison reaches the road, one hand on her belly. At Maggie's nod, she turns toward the field. It takes her a few seconds to see it. "Oh." She touches her mouth. "Oh wow."

"Yeah," Maggie says. She lays a hand on Allison's shoulder.

"Well." Allison brushes her hands against each other, businesslike. "That's good, then. I'll tell the boys they're doing a good job." A river of pebbles loosens in her wake and clatters down after her, down the hill.

The breeze smooths over the back of my neck, picking up and twirling the hairs that lie there. Maggie makes a sound like a horse, blowing her bangs out of her face.

It's been a long time since we were alone together. When I was younger, she would sweep into our house a couple times a year. The three of them would be up well past midnight, leaning into each other and laughing. Charlie and I would sit cross-legged on the floor next to them, hardly daring to move, amazed that we hadn't been sent to bed yet. Since she slept on my floor, it was always my job to wake her up the next morning after the rest of us had eaten breakfast. Her face would be crammed into her pillow, which made me giggle, and she groaned when I poked her in the side. After a few moments, she would sit up in her nest of blankets and ask me what I'd dreamed about the night before. For weeks afterward, I would beg my mom to let me sleep on the floor, just like Aunt Maggie.

There's an odd texture to the space between us now, a stiff and formal kind of nostalgia.

"Thank you for coming and staying with my parents," I say. "I know it really means a lot to my mom."

"Nowhere else I'd rather be," she says,

easy and rehearsed. She glances at me and sighs. "The truth is, I feel kind of bad for dumping all my shit on your mom at a time like this."

"Oh yeah, I'm so sorry again about your husband — ex-husband, I guess." I should have started with this. My insides twist with embarrassment.

She just shrugs. "Marriages fall apart every day."

The cornstalks part, and Ben steps out. He stands silently with his arms folded and whistles low through his teeth at the sight. "Damn," he murmurs.

"We doing good so far?" Daniel climbs up toward us, and my heart stops beating for a second, suspended. He stands next to me and studies the field.

I inch away from him. Somewhere in the distance, an owl calls, too loud in the night.

"Not bad," he says, nodding. "I think we're almost done. Finally."

Even I can tell my smile is weak. He motions to Ben, and the two of them teeter back down the hill and into the field.

Maggie pivots at her waist to face me, her arms crossed.

I glance at her sideways. "What?" I say, though I'm not sure I want to know.

She looks away, over the fields, toward the

431

black and toothy mountains in the distance. "Don't be too much like me, kiddo."

Now I do look at her, honest, loyal Maggie, who never shies away from a fight but always leaves you laughing. One of her visits fell right after Charlie's disastrous birthday, and I woke before sunrise to see her mattress empty. I crept down the stairs to the kitchen, and there she was, sitting at the table with Charlie, coffee mugs pushed aside. Charlie's back was to me, and his voice was low, but I saw his pain in her face, bent forward and close to his.

"What do you mean?" I say.

She keeps her eyes fixed on the horizon, and I wonder if she's heard me, but then she says, "Don't give up on the person you love because you think it's the right thing to do."

I want to ask what she means again, to pretend I don't understand and to shrink away from acknowledging this particular truth. Her words settle on me, and I wonder why she's really leaving her husband. Who has she given up? Who does she think of when she can't fall asleep?

An image rises in front of me, the three of them sitting on the couch together, my dad and my mom and then Maggie. Dad is telling a story about someone in town, with

Mom making gentle course corrections. Maggie leans forward, elbows on knees, her eyes bright on his face, waiting for the punch line.

And just like that, I don't know if Maggie is here for my mom or for him.

"Okay" is all I think to say.

CHAPTER FIFTY-ONE: MOLLY

I wake up to the smell of burned toast and the sound of bacon hissing on the stove, groggy from a night of tossing and turning. After I'd called Allison, I couldn't sleep for hours, wondering if Daniel would turn tail and run when he found out the others knew, if we'd be blacklisted on some forum somewhere, if Sam's dream would never be realized. A consequence I hadn't considered: Daniel's fear outweighing his pride.

Sam has kicked free of the covers, a sheet of sweat glistening on his forehead. I tuck one blanket back up around his shoulders and touch my lips to his cheek.

In the kitchen, Maggie is muttering a steady stream of swears and grabbing at the blackened slices of bread in the toaster with two fingers. Charlie sits at the table with one ankle resting on the other knee. He raises his hands, innocent, and says, "I offered to help, but she wouldn't let me."

She spins around at the sound of his voice, the ties to her robe flapping. "Oh, hi. I think I've managed to ruin your bread." She glares at the plate and the charred remains that lie there.

"There's plenty more where that came from," I say as I step around her to slide the now-smoking skillet of bacon off the burner. "You're up early."

"I thought I'd make you guys some breakfast, but I can't even get bacon and toast right." She slumps into a chair.

Charlie grins over her head at me, and the glow spreads down my shoulders, all the way to my fingertips.

I hide my face in the fridge, letting the cool, dry air mist over me. I surface with a clutch of eggs clacking softly in my hands.

"How did it go last night?" I say, keeping my voice casual and cracking the eggs swiftly into a bowl.

"It was fantastic, so much fun," she says. "Nessa and I stood up on the road to make sure they were getting the markings right, and it was just like the most beautiful painting you've ever seen, with the moon and the stars and the patterns and the field." She drops back into her chair and cranes her neck to face me. "You really should come out and see it with us."

435

"I expect I'll see it when all that's done," I say, whipping a glug of milk into the eggs. Every time I've driven past the field, I've turned away. I know it's glow-in-the-dark paint that looks like nothing in the sun. Still, somehow, I don't want to see.

"You and Nessa are helping with the crop circle?" Charlie sounds casual, but beneath it, I can hear a snip of hurt.

"Oh yeah," she says, "and a couple people from town, too. Allison and Ben and their farmhand, I think." She rushes to add, "No one else knows, though."

Charlie plants one finger on his place mat and spins it around in a pirouette. "I think I'd like to join you guys next time," he says. He looks up at Maggie. "If that's okay."

Maggie leans over to shimmy his shoulder back and forth. "Of course it's fine," she says, though I'm not sure she knows that it is. "We'd love your help."

He takes his hands off the place mat and relaxes. "Great, and I'll bet Zach will want to help, too."

"Help with what?" Zach comes down the stairs, bending below the edge of the ceiling to smile at Maggie. "What are you two signing me up for?"

"Hey, Mom?" The cry comes through Nessa's door. "Can you come here for a minute?"

Sam is still in our bed, so it can't be about him. I look at Charlie, who peers up the stairwell, his brow knit. Zach eases the bowl of eggs out of my grip, and I run up the stairs, shouting, "Coming!"

My mind races over what I might find, tears on her face or new burns on her hands or —

When I whip the door open, she's sitting on the edge of her bed, eyes slightly widened at the urgent thunder of my feet. She touches the space next to her.

I close the door behind me, step over the tangled mess of Maggie's makeshift bed, and sit down. She folds in closer, her head on my shoulder, and my hand makes its path over her hair, the curls.

After she called me with her diagnosis, I sat on the couch with the phone in my hand, staring out the window. It had been named, the monster in her closet, the one none of us could see that poked its scaly claw into her skin while we weren't looking. It had been named, and maybe she could fight it.

It didn't occur to me what that meant until her next visit home. Sam rolled out of bed that first morning, and I stayed put. I couldn't fall back asleep, and the minutes ticked by as I studied the frost rimming the windowpanes, then turned toward the door. I heard her feet coming down the hallway, and I drew back the corner of the covers and readied my smile. Her steps paused for the briefest moment outside our room. And then they faded away, down the stairs, and Sam stopped his aimless singing in surprise.

I knew then that someone else would be holding her secrets, some doctor in an office far away who I would never meet. Nessa's words would tumble out only for this doctor now, twirling her hair around her finger like she'd done since kindergarten. He'd nod solemnly, writing one or two of her words down on his clipboard, but probably not the important ones. When she left the room, he would slip her words into a drawer in his desk with all the others, filed and done.

"What's wrong, sweets?" I whisper now.

She shakes her head a little. "Are you okay?" she says in a small voice.

My hand stills, cupped over her ear. "You don't have to worry about me."

Her hands fidget in her lap, knotting together. "What will you do?" she whispers.

I look away, at her bedside table, crowded with tubes of lip balm and thick legal thrillers — Maggie's. I have not allowed myself to imagine the future, not really, when the fields are spent and mowed to brittle stumps, the corn trucked away to feed the neighbor's cows, their hides standing stark against the slushy snow. Perhaps I will call Thomas and ask him about interest rates and about that scar on his back, make a new friend again. Perhaps I won't. Perhaps I'll stay here, alone in this town, learn to settle into Allison's hugs and see if the general store is hiring, if I can make the cashier laugh when I ask for an application. Perhaps I'll move out west with Maggie to a less "saturated marketplace," scandalize the neighbors, two almost-elderly women living together for no apparent reason. Perhaps her neighbors won't find that scandalous at all.

Nessa is still waiting, winding herself tighter.

I sigh. "I can't say for sure, but I'll find something." I hesitate. "Mostly, I expect, I will miss your father."

It's not a comfort, not really. In another time, I would have worried for hours, days, wondering what my words would grow into in Nessa's mind. Her hands come apart, slowly, controlled, and she puts her arm around me and hugs me close.

CHAPTER FIFTY-TWO: NESSA

Dad can't come down for lunch today. We all heard him shooing Charlie away from his room, his voice hacked to bits by coughs. Charlie's face was drawn when he came down the stairs, and he didn't speak a word to any of us.

The four of us sit crammed around the table, dragging our spoons through bowls of soup while my mom scurries around the kitchen. Zach and Maggie make a couple of attempts at conversation, but their words drift, unanswered, to the floor.

A sharp knock comes. "I'll get it," I say, jumping to my feet, even though my seat is tucked into the corner farthest from the door. I squeeze past Charlie's chair, stumble over its back legs, and bang my shin. I am wincing when I open the door, balancing on one leg, and Shawn bursts out laughing when he sees me.

"You all right?" he says. He reaches out to

support me with one arm. In his other, he holds a huge foil pan wrapped in plastic wrap.

"I'll make a quick recovery, I think," I say, pulling a frown for effect.

Zach chuckles, and Charlie shakes his head, smiling.

I point at the pan. "Is that for us?"

"Yup. Melissa made you guys some baked ziti." He hoists the pan a little higher.

"How nice of her," my mom says, taking the food and slotting it neatly into the fridge, angling the door so he can't see the stacks of disposable dishes and glass casseroles marked with masking tape.

"Yeah. She always thinks of these things," he says, his smile warm and shyly proud.

"Come sit with us," Maggie says, motioning toward my seat. "Nessa can pull up another chair from somewhere."

"Oh, that's okay," he says, swinging his arms back and forth. "I should get back to my kid and all." He looks down at his feet, probably feeling out of place.

I feel a sudden urge to cling to his arm and beg him not to leave me in here, alone in this snow globe of grief. "Let's go for a quick drive first," I say. I hustle him out the door, waving to everyone over my shoulder without turning back.

I slam his truck door behind me and lean my head back against the passenger's seat. I inhale the plastic scent of his air freshener deep into my lungs. He turns his key in the ignition and waits.

"How about the lake?" I say, though we haven't gone in daylight in years and its shores are always crammed with families on days like this.

"You got it" is all he says.

Sure enough, the parking lot we pass is full of cars, and I can see people lounging on plastic chairs, their kids shrieking and splashing in brightly colored bathing suits and their dogs swimming after sticks like their lives depend on it. Shawn pulls down the dirt road we found years ago, tree branches scraping and thwacking against the sides of the truck. He parks in the small clearing at its end. From here, the others' yelling and conversations are distant and muffled sound effects.

I half expected the lake to be changed somehow, a shade darker or lighter in the face of everything from the past few weeks. It's just the same, though, framed by trees and wide as the sky. Over the ticking of the engine, I can hear a squirrel tittering in the trees above us. An osprey dives down into the water, its legs stretched out like landing gear. "My dad always thought they were the most amazing animals," I say, pointing at the bird, which rises from the surface with a fish glinting in its talons. "Still does, I mean. Think that."

Shawn says nothing, studies my face.

"He hired this guy to make a crop circle in their field," I admit.

He laughs and settles back in his seat, dropping his hands from the steering wheel to his lap. "That doesn't surprise me at all." He rocks his head back and forth, stretching out his neck. "He loves those big, weird gestures. Remember when we graduated high school?"

He built a billboard out of plywood and painted it with letters three feet high that read, "Congrats, Nessa and Shawn, class of 2009!" He had a poster printed at Staples that he carried to the ceremony. It had my face on it in glossy full-color. I begged my mom to limit his signage for my college graduation.

"You got Charlie back," he says.

"Sort of, I guess. I don't know how much of it was really thanks to me." And it all comes out, the whole story, the whole trip, or most of it anyway. I don't tell him how Daniel's hands felt against my back or how smooth his skin was. Shawn watches the dashboard as I talk, occasionally reaching over to pick off a crumb of lint.

When I finish, I exhale, one deep breath that shivers over the ends of his hair.

"Let me see your hands," he says, holding out his own.

I cover them with mine, and he bends close to them, rotating them gently back and forth. The afternoon sun cuts harsh shadows across them, dark lines and patches like bruises, but the skin is healing now. It's not the first time he's seen them like this. Not by a long shot. Sometimes, I wonder if that awful date would've gone differently had I known that what I had was not a defect, not some unchangeable flaw, but an illness. Maybe I would've been able to accept a partner who knew everything, who knew it all.

Not that it matters now. He has Melissa, and I — well, I'm not sure what or who I have.

Shawn places my hands in my lap, snugly between my knees. He looks up at me, his eyes so close, and says, "You're going to be all right."

"Yeah," I say, though I know the relief is short-lived, I know he can only toss the pebble so far.

■ ■ ■ ■

In my parents' driveway, I reach for the door handle to get out of the truck, then change my mind. "Daniel said he thinks we can finish the circle tomorrow night. Would you maybe want to come and help?"

He hesitates, the engine grumbling in the pause. He turns his head toward the house, and there's my dad in the upstairs window, leaning one hand against the pane. Through the glass, his palm is white and fleshy, like the belly of a fish. I can almost see the stick from his painkillers poking out of his mouth. He raises his other hand in a motionless wave.

Shawn lifts one hand from the steering wheel in reply. "Sure. I'll be there."

He needs help walking to the bathroom. This morning, after I talked to Mom, I heard Charlie checking on him in bed. "How are you feeling?" he said. "How's your pain?"

"Same old, same old," my dad said. And then he lowered his voice so much, I had to strain to hear it. "Son, I'm sorry. I was so —" His voice broke.

Charlie sighed. "I know."

445

There was a pause. I hoped they were hugging, but I knew they probably weren't.

"Come on," Charlie finally said. "Let's get you up and at 'em."

After breakfast, when Dad was back in bed, Charlie said he shouldn't be going anywhere unattended anymore, even three feet down the hall. He's too weak; he could fall. His words slit right into my stomach, a paring knife, and my mom looked slapped.

Charlie and I worked out a system of shifts that he and I would take, guiding him down the hall to the bathroom and back a few times a day. My mom clamped her hands together in protest and kept saying there was no need until Maggie said, "You do not need to be there for him every time he takes a leak." My mom dropped her hands to her sides, took out her big metal bowl, and started dumping bread dough ingredients into it. A loaf already sat on the counter, burnished and freshly browned.

This afternoon is Charlie's shift, not mine, but the guilt from leaving them all at lunch is creeping its long fingers through my abdomen and hooking into my gut. When Charlie lays his medical journal flat across the arm of the couch and checks his watch, I stand. "I'll do it," I say, my book tumbling out of my lap.

"But it's —" he says, but I'm already halfway up the stairs, too far away to hear about the protocol.

My dad's awake on his back with his head sunk into a crater in his pillows, staring at my mom. She's pulled the old rocking chair over from the corner of their room so it butts right up against the bed. She's fallen asleep in it, her head lolling back and her mouth open. Her knitting is draped across her lap, the needles loose in her hands; she is making something small and brown that looks vaguely like a hat.

Dad starts when he sees me.

"Ready for your pee break?" I whisper.

He rolls his eyes. "You kids are so paranoid. I'm a grown man. I don't need an escort." He pushes himself up and swings his legs out of bed, tapping one foot against the chair as he goes.

Mom bolts awake and clutches her knitting needles. When she sees my dad, she lays her needles on the bed and wedges herself under his armpit in one motion, lifting him to his feet.

She checks her watch as I take his other arm. "Oh dear, it's getting late," she says. "I should start dinner."

"Maggie's got it covered." Her eyes widen in alarm, and I stifle a laugh. "Zach is

447

supervising. Heavily."

"Well. Okay." She sits back down with a thump and reaches absently for her knitting, looking for all the world like she's lost.

I want to tell her to relax and go back to sleep, but Dad's already pulling me forward, shuffling toward the door.

His breathing gets louder the farther we walk, and he's almost gasping by the time we reach the bathroom. I reach for the door and turn to him warily.

He laughs, a wheeze, and says, "You can wait out here. Nobody wants to see this part, I know."

I close the door after him, then start humming tunelessly to myself so I don't have to listen to my father using the toilet. I stop when I hear the flush, but he's grinning when he opens the door, and I know he heard me anyway.

Mom is gone from the room when we get back, the rocking chair still moving back and forth a little. I can hear the ringing of pots and pans against each other, chatter and laughter as I ease Dad back into the bed, but before I can join them, he motions for me to sit down in the chair. I eye the bundle of yarn nested there and perch on the edge of the bed instead, one leg folded under me.

His hand on my arm is fragile and cool. "Did I ever tell you" — he pauses for air — "how proud I am of you?"

I think again of the billboard and the poster, and I smile. "Yes. Repeatedly." I lay my hand over his. "Don't worry, Dad. We're good."

"No, no," he says, waving me away. "I mean —" He sighs and turns his head toward the window, like he's talking to the sky or the trees or the wind. "This is hard work, what we do. I always thought it would be Charlie. He's the boy, you know. But it turns out it was you all along."

I've lost the thread of him. I'm not ready for him to slip away like this, far away. "What do you mean?" I say, a tremor.

His eyes are clear when he turns back to me. "I'm giving you the farm."

It's like he's taken my head by the ears and shaken, scrambling my thoughts. "I — what?" trickles out.

He nods, serene.

"What about Mom?" I say, remembering his eyes on her when I walked in, soaking her in.

"She can stay here as long as she likes, of course. But listen," he says, both his hands on my arm now. "Don't let her wallow here forever."

I can't even imagine what wallowing would look like on her. "This is her home," I say meekly.

"It's her home because I made it one. Once I'm gone, there's nothing for her here."

I flinch. How easy it is for him to imagine being gone.

"She's got dreams somewhere else she'd never tell you about," he says.

My stomach lurches, remembering what Charlie told me. The affair.

"She and Charlie both, they were never made for this. She's just a little better at grinning and bearing it," he says. He smiles wistfully, and for a second, I wonder what would've happened if he'd said this to himself before Charlie left for good. "You and me, though. This is who we are."

I turn away and stare at the floor. This morning, I'd watched Ben and Eli move through the fields, and my muscles almost ached to join them.

His eyes are still on me, and I know he sees it all. He squeezes my arm once and lets his hands fall back to his sides. "Think it over," he says, then yawns. "That long voyage over to the john really has me beat." His eyelids drift close, and he settles back

into his pillow. When I draw the blankets up
over him, he doesn't move.

CHAPTER FIFTY-THREE: DANIEL

I call Lionel from my car, parked in the Shannons' driveway.

"So you've seen it?" he says as soon as he picks up.

"Um, seen what?" I asked.

"Ray. He went ahead and posted everyone's names on an alien conspiracy forum."

The calls from the other circlers. That's what they must've been about. "Shit."

He sighs. "Yes."

A pause blooms. "How's the response been?" I say. "On the forum, I mean?"

"Luckily, it seems most aren't taking it seriously. There's a lot of teasing, and some are outright furious with him for implying the circles aren't real. I highly doubt it'll make it out to the general public, but we've contacted the forum administrator to ask that the post be removed. We'll threaten a lawsuit, if we must."

"That's a relief." In the silence that follows, I brush dust off my dashboard. *It sucks, what's happening to them,* I find myself thinking. To them, not me. My hand pauses, mid-brush, as the thought sinks in. A few weeks ago, maybe even yesterday, this news would have been devastating. But now, I realize, I feel like I'm not a part of this.

"Have you finished your fifteenth?" Lionel says.

"Well, no."

"So you'll be wanting another assignment, then," he decides.

"Actually, I'm leaving the circlers." It comes to me all at once, and I say it without thinking.

The right thing to do, the safe thing, would be to quit Sam's circle. Too many people in Munsen know about it now. There's too much risk of it getting out, especially now that there's Ray's post. Lionel would be furious with me, continuing on with that many townspeople involved.

But I can't protect the circlers anymore. They don't need me to protect them. This is no longer my life, shifting around from place to place. This isn't what I want, and the circlers aren't my family, not now. With Nessa's eyes on me last night, I realized this particular place — and the people in it — have come to matter more to me than the circlers did. It's too important now to give it up, even with Ray's leak.

Quitting will cut Lionel off at the chase. There's nothing he can do to me once I'm out. Maybe he'll pin some circles on me, but I don't think so. Ray was right — he probably respects me too much. The other circlers can fend for themselves now. Lionel will handle it.

I have to finish this circle. This town needs this circle. They need it for Sam.

"I see," he says. There's a dragonfly carcass wedged under one windshield wiper. It's probably been there for weeks. "You understand what this means."

"Yup. Yes." It means no number fifteen, an almost-was. It means no one will remember me during any of those future meetings. It means I'm no longer welcome at the place I met Claire. It means no more circles.

But tonight, they're all waiting for me, the five of them sitting on the porch steps, Charlie and Zach leaning against the railing behind them. I've brought all four of my pressers with me. Eli helps me lean them against the side of the porch.

Charlie nods a greeting. Zach says, "If it's all right with you, we'd love to help."

My eyes are caught on Nessa, who's got a smile spread across her face.

"You came!" she cries and flings herself past me.

I turn in time to see her grinning up at a big, blocky man around our age. My hands shove themselves into my pockets. A very small woman in a droopy T-shirt steps out from behind him.

"Melissa wanted to help, too," he says.

Nessa shrinks back a step, like this new woman is a wolf. Melissa closes the gap and wraps Nessa in a hug.

"I am so, so sorry for what's happening to your family," Melissa says.

Nessa's eyes are wide, startled, as she looks up at the man, but he doesn't notice. He's smiling down at his wife, one hand at the small of her back.

Melissa lets go, and Nessa backs away.

"I'm Shawn," the man says, holding his hand out. "Old friend of Nessa's. She's told me all about you." He smiles slowly, and I try not to hate him.

"I hope it's okay I came." Melissa pokes her head around him. "We all just love these guys, and we're desperate to chip in."

The spotlights of her eyes leave me no choice. "Um, sure," I say. She squeals and claps her hands while I sigh. I turn to the rest of the group, watching me. "Let's grab those boards and head out into the field, then."

They scramble to their feet and move toward the markings.

Nessa trails behind them, and I slow down to join her. Her face is tipped back toward the sky, but she walks in a perfect straight line, one exact arm's length away from me. "Beautiful night," she says.

I peel my eyes off her and look at the stars. "Yeah, a full moon is perfect. It really helps to see the paint." She turns to me, a funny smile on her face, and I know that's not what she meant.

We've reached the rest of the group. All eight of them stand at the edge of the circle.

"All right," I say. "Here's how it works." I take the longest presser from Ben's hands, find a cluster of marked stalks, and place my board against their bases, one end in the center of the cluster with the rope held taut between my hands. I step on the board slowly, and the stalks ease their heavy heads toward the ground until they snap crisply at their bases and a blanket of green lies glowing in the moonlight. Every time, it's the same, and every time, the blood rushes through my veins.

A few small gasps escape from the crowd, and I hold back a smile. I split them up into pairs: Allison and Ben, Maggie and Eli, Charlie and Zach, Shawn and Melissa, and give each one a presser. Nessa studies me as they all disperse through the field.

"I thought maybe we could keep an eye on the progress up at the road. Since you were so good at it last time and everything," I say. What I really want to tell her is that there's awe up there, watching shapes emerge in the field like a photo developing. She turns away.

Standing on the road, she is still and distant. I'm relieved when she speaks.

"It's really an amazing design," she says, "all spiraled out like that." She spreads one hand in the field's direction, her long fingers glowing and pale. They are butterflies, and I could almost catch them.

I look away and watch the groups of cornstalk tops fall. "It's a fractal," I say. "It's the form I learned at my first circlers meeting, with Claire —" I wince as I say her name, and sure enough, Nessa shifts away just a little bit more.

"I think I screwed up," I blurt.

Nessa whips around toward me. "What, you mean the design? Is it too late to fix it?" She's already looking away, trying to spot all the pairs.

"No, I mean —" I inhale deeply to stop

the shaking. It doesn't work. "I mean with this." I flap my hand uselessly between us. "With us."

She looks at me the same way she looked at Melissa. I take another gulp of air. I feel like my brain is on a string, floating away, bobbing somewhere above our heads.

"I still miss Claire," I say, and I force myself to watch her face fold when I say Claire's name. "Every day. But lately" — I feel the flush rising across my face — "lately, it's you. You're the one who's been making it hard on me."

She stares at me, looking a little confused, and I hope she doesn't say anything, because I can't seem to hear anything over the roaring sound in my head. She takes one careful step closer, then another, and another, until she's just inches away. She looks up at me and whispers, "Yeah. You did screw up." But then finally, she smiles, perfect and gleaming.

My hands unfurl and rise to her cheeks. She holds my forearms, her palms warm.

The kiss is different this time, less hungry. My mind is nowhere else but here. We're not two people, adrift and alone, clinging to each other to float. We might instead be a promise to build on.

When we break away, my heartbeat has

slowed. Nessa laughs a little and releases my arms. My hands drop to my sides. We turn back toward the field, the voices still rising and falling from the corn.

She reaches her hand out and slips it into mine. I close my fingers around it.

"My dad wants to give me the farm," she says.

"Whoa." I haven't seen him face-to-face in weeks, and there's a pang as I remember him then, full face, easy laugh.

"Yup." She tightens her grip.

"Are you . . . Do you want it?"

"I don't know." Her shoulders slump a little. "My mom will still live there, and I don't know what Charlie's going to think. Maybe. Yes."

"Charlie's happier out in California, I'm pretty sure," I say, and as if on cue, his low laughter rumbles up from somewhere to our right, just exactly like Sam's.

"I just — I can't imagine this farm without my dad." Her voice hiccups a bit.

I hold her hand tighter, because there's nothing else I can do.

"Anyway," she says after a minute or two, "either way, we're going to need a couple farmhands to help out. I'm going to ask Eli or Ben after all this is done, I think."

"Yeah," I say. It makes perfect sense, with

them already familiar with the land and everything.

"Would you —" She falters. "Do you think you'd be interested in staying and helping? I mean, I know it sounds crazy," she says, picking up steam. "I'm not the easiest person to live with, and we've only known each other a few weeks, although you could have your own room after Charlie goes back. And maybe it would make people suspicious about the crop circle, seeing us together. Obviously, I don't want to mess with that."

All I can see, one last time, is the life I pictured for myself when I first drove down their driveway. A sunny coffee shop, apron and name tag, regular customers who know my name, only speaking to ask for orders and exact change. Nights in a windowless classroom, losing all my calluses except the ones where I hold my pen, trying to cram something, anything, into my brain. Visiting Claire's grave with flowers once a week, then once a month, then once a season on birthdays and anniversaries, sometimes running into her parents, smiling sadly, not quite friendly.

I know now that all of it blew away the second Nessa surprised me on that porch that first night.

"Yes," I say, "I would."

She grins. "Good. I could've hired one of those kids who travel the country looking for farm work, but, you know, I always wonder what they're really doing here."

I laugh in spite of myself, loud before I remember to muffle it. "Oh, by the way," I say, "I got *Anne of Green Gables* out of the library."

"I knew you would," she says and pulls her hand out of mine, takes a running leap down toward the field. She looks back at me, and I follow her.

CHAPTER FIFTY-FOUR: MOLLY

Sam is asleep and the house is quiet, but I can't stop watching him. In my mind, I run my fingers over his face, gently on the thin skin there, and through his hair. A small, wistful part of me wonders if we'll ever be alone, really alone, again. Charlie will leave soon to go back to work, and Zach will go with him. Maggie will reach the point where she starts making little jokes about getting out of our hair and leaving us crazy kids alone. I imagine it won't be much longer until in-home care has to start, with nurses in sturdy shoes always bustling around Sam.

Nessa will be here, too. Sam told me quietly about their conversation while he sucked on his nighttime fentanyl, his brow wrinkling as he said he wasn't quite sure she wanted the farm. She does. She will.

A soft round of applause comes from below our window like rain. I slip out of bed to see, and there they stand before the porch, so many: Charlie and Nessa and Zach and Maggie and Ben and Eli and Allison and Shawn and Melissa, all standing around Daniel, clapping their fingertips against their palms, gently exuberant. Daniel gives an awkward little nodding bow. I wish I could wake Sam up to see it, all these people gathered only for the love of him. No. For the love of us. He needs his sleep now more than anything, though, so instead, I lean in closer, the cool glass pressing up against my forehead.

Nessa sees the motion and looks up and waves, though she can't possibly see who it is in the dark. The porch light catches her face, and she looks so happy, so simply happy, my beautiful girl. I tap my fingers against the window, once, twice, in reply, and go back to bed.

"Molly, Molls. Wake up. You have to see this." The bed is empty beside me, and panic seizes me before I register Sam's words. He stands at the window, the light framing his face, motioning for me. For one perfect moment, he is healthy, waking me up once again to watch a deer in the fields or a hawk circling the sky. His hand is planted firmly on the windowsill, his elbow trembling, and I stumble out of bed to brace him up.

Then I look, and I see what I couldn't in the dark night. There are hollows carved into the field, symmetrical circles spiraling endlessly into one another like the spine of a seashell. Small circles and big ones, spun out into an impossibly intricate pattern. On and on, and it takes my breath away. This is it exactly, what Sam has wanted. I can see in an instant how they will come — of course they will. Everyone will want to come, to see something as beautiful as this.

Sam peels his hand off the window and points. There, on the road, there's a truck, parked on the shoulder, the dust still settling around it. The door opens, and a man drops out and walks around to the edge of the shoulder. It's too far to see his face, but we can see him plant his fists on his hips.

I turn my head to look at Sam. And he smiles.

AUTHOR'S NOTE

While the people, places, and events in this book are completely made up, I did base the circlers on a real group of people called "circlemakers." In the 1970s, Doug Bower and Dave Chorley created their first crop circle in the UK, and from those efforts, a movement was born. As of 2006, an estimated fewer than fifty circlemakers were building crop circles around the world, using pressers — which they call "stalk stompers" — to make mysterious works of art in farmers' fields.

Their work is fascinating. If you're interested in learning more, I highly recommend picking up Rob Irving and John Lundberg's *The Field Guide: The Art, History, and Philosophy of Crop Circle Making* and visiting their website at Circlemakers.org.

ACKNOWLEDGMENTS

First and foremost, thank you to my family — both the one I was born into and the one I married into — for their steadfast, unwavering support. When I nervously told you all I was trying to write a book, you didn't even blink, and that made all the difference.

Thank you to Eric Smith, the most amazing and enthusiastic and genuine agent a writer could ever hope for. Your belief in this book made all my childhood dreams come true! And, of course, to #TeamRocks, the best writing support group I could ask for — especially Mike Chen, whose advice was invaluable at so many points along the way.

And Grace Menary-Winefield, a true rock-star dynamo of an editor: thank you for your excitement and support, and for many lengthy email chains on the ins and outs of fictional family dynamics! Thanks also to the entire team at Sourcebooks, who constantly overwhelmed me with their love of this book.

Thank you to Karisa Langlo and Allia Benner for reading crappy early drafts and helping me make them less crappy. And to my local writing communities, Writers' Loft (especially Dave Pasquantonio) and Grub-Street (especially Molly Howes), for holding my hand at various times throughout this surreal process.

Thank you to Lyn Des Marais of Des Marais Farm in Brandon, VT; Bill Rowell of Green Mountain Dairy; and John Lundberg, whose generosity with their expertise on Vermont farming and crop circle making, respectively, helped shape this book. And to Nora Kenny, who helped me look presentable, and to Paul Parker and Kelly Wachowicz, who were with me all the way.

Thank you to my English teachers, from my mom to Mrs. Lombardo to Mr. Potts, whose encouragement and thoughtfulness made me a writer.

And always, every day, thank you to Chris. Who saw this coming when we were seventeen. Who always checked to see if I was writing before stepping foot into our home office. Who is (maybe, possibly) even more excited than I am to see this on the shelves. Partners in crime and biggest fans forever.

ABOUT THE AUTHOR

A native New Englander, **Erica Boyce** is a graduate of Dartmouth College and Harvard Law School and an associate fiction editor at *Pangyrus*. She lives outside Boston with her husband and their dog, a corgi named Finn who has way more Instagram followers than she does. This is her first novel. She enjoys speaking to book clubs, and you can find her online at ericaboyce .com or @boycebabbles on Instagram, Twitter, and Goodreads.

The employees of Thorndike Press hope you have enjoyed this Large Print book. All our Thorndike, Wheeler, and Kennebec Large Print titles are designed for easy reading, and all our books are made to last. Other Thorndike Press Large Print books are available at your library, through selected bookstores, or directly from us.

For information about titles, please call:
(800) 223-1244

or visit our website at:
gale.com/thorndike

To share your comments, please write:
Publisher
Thorndike Press
10 Water St., Suite 310
Waterville, ME 04901